JUSTICE IS
PRONOUNCED

JUST US

Also by G.D. Flashman

Apache Dunes

2020 Colorado Independent Publishers Association EVVY Award Finalist

What readers say about *Apache Dunes*

★ ★ ★ ★ ★ "A great read. You will feel as if you are watching the action REEL time!"

★ ★ ★ ★ ★ "Best read ever!!"

★ ★ ★ ★ ★ "Couldn't put it down."

★ ★ ★ ★ ★ "Extraordinary novel!"

★ ★ ★ ★ ★ "Superb Read"

★ ★ ★ ★ ★ "Tarantino meets Walter White"

★ ★ ★ ★ ★ "Warning: you can't put this one down"

★ ★ ★ ★ ★ "Great new read!"

JUSTICE IS PRONOUNCED

JUST US

G.D. Flashman

This is a work of fiction. Names, characters, places, and incidents appearing in this work are the sole expression, opinion and product of the author's imagination only, are entirely fictitious and do not represent and are not based on any real life views of any character or event in any way whatsoever and any resemblance is strictly coincidental. Any and all references and depictions appearing in this work to real life persons, living or deceased, are based solely and entirely on the author's imagination and are in no way a representation of, or bear any resemblance to the actual views, events or opinions of such persons.

ISBN 978-0-578-74852-8 (print)
ISBN 978-0-578-74853-5 (ebook)

Cover and book design by Sue Campbell Book Design
Cover photos by Brian Knight/Unsplash.com (Chicago skyline)
AndreYuu/depositphotos.com (gunman)

Contact the author: magcltd@aol.com

For

Tommy & Anne Marie

Christopher & Lauren

Chicago 1957

Tommy

The joke was that the southeast side neighborhood between 90th and 92nd Streets and Wallace was Chicago's most integrated neighborhood in the 1950s.

True enough, it was about evenly split between Blacks and poor Irish Catholics and there was little socioeconomic difference between the groups.

The Irish Catholics had been forced from their homes by famine, onto the shores of a country that offered anything but welcoming arms. Chicago was the last stop on the journey for those fortunate enough to survive the crossing. They say what doesn't kill you makes you stronger and these people evolved into some of the toughest people in the world. They had to, just to survive.

The Black journey was a little more complex. They were freed from the odious yoke of slavery to a large extent by the political power wielded by a cabal of abolitionists in the north who, just coincidentally—I'm sure, happened to be leading industrialists on the cusp of the Industrial Revolution. Their new country had natural resources in abundance. It was a horn of plenty, lacking only a continual source of cheap labor to work in their mines, stockyards and factories.

What a mutual blessing it appeared—to the industrialists—that the slaves were now free! Free to work for slave wages under oppressive conditions, with the plantation housing replaced by projects, but they were free! Hallelujah!

The net-net, was that both groups were screwed.

The reason that integration was a joke is that railroad tracks neatly divided the neighborhood into two separate sections. We're all familiar with the fable whose moral is, "The grass is always greener on the other side." In our neighborhood, there was no green grass on either side. Rather, a mixture of dirt, sand, rocks, gravel, weeds and an occasional clump of grass. Oh—and bits of litter that would be borne on the wind as if destined to settle there.

There was no fraternity between the races born of any concept of "misery loves company". It was more of a begrudging "live and let live" with semi-frequent dustups between the respective young bucks. Nothing more and nothing less.

Few if any of the Irish kids could afford the modest tuition to Leo on 79th Street and were left with Calumet High School as their public school option. The heavy Irish Catholic concentration soon led to Calumet being referred to as either St. Calumet or Our Lady of Calumet. We may have been poor in some respects, but we never sacrificed our pride or our sense of humor. We used to say that we were so poor, that if we hadn't been born boys we wouldn't have had anything to play with!

Our Black counterparts were pretty evenly divided between Dunbar and Du Sable High Schools. Both played football against Calumet and there was a lot more on the line than just the game. It wasn't unusual to have as much violence in the stands as on the field and après game—fuggetaboutit! The Irish called it "sharing the pain" and for one or two weekends a year it was too precious an opportunity to squander.

Hopefully, that brief introduction will help you to understand a bit more of the significance of an event that occurred on a hot August night in 1957 that would be "out of sight—out of mind" until I received a phone call years later that would change my life, and the caller's life, forever. Without further ado:

The sound of pots and pans being washed and put away after dinner echoed thru the neighborhood. All of the doors and windows were open in the hope of catching even a slight breeze during the oppressive late summer heat spell.

Suddenly, a new sound erupted from the backyards—our fail-safe, home security alarms—our dogs. The average house in the hood had at least one dog in backyard enclosures that were as flimsily constructed as the houses. These weren't your cuddly Golden Retrievers or clones of Lassie. They were mutts—the proverbial junk yard dogs. I guess it's true that dogs resemble their owners. Long story short—no one was going to sneak up on us from the tracks.

The commotion brought the entire neighborhood to their back porches—particularly the men. What they saw was the silhouette of a lone man crossing the tracks and waving something in his right hand. As he cleared the tracks and stumbled down the embankment, it became clear that what he was waving was a crudely made white flag. What was also clear is that he was shaking almost uncontrollably and justifiably so. Only one of the pens had to fail for this man to be ripped to shreds.

As the intruder neared one of the pens he was greeted by our version of the Welcome Wagon: "You take one more step n****r and I let the dogs loose!"

Dynamite couldn't have moved him.

"State your business."

The man was shaking so bad he had trouble speaking. "I just - I just wanna - I just wanna talk with Mr. O'Brien, please."

Mr. O'Brien, John O'Brien, was my father and it showed that the man had some understanding of the politics of our side of the neighborhood. We didn't need to elect a leader. That mantel was assumed by my father in the tradition of the Old Sod. He looked the part, he talked the part and he acted the part. If he wasn't descended from the ancient Tara Kings, no one was.

You had to use a little imagination, however, as King John, like the other men of the neighborhood, was standing on our back porch in his work pants and "Dago" tee. But when he strode off the porch to meet the man, he exuded power and grace. I followed close behind. After all—if my Dad was King, that made me the Prince. I could deal with that.

"I'm John O'Brien, what can I do for you?"

"I know who you are Mr. O'Brien, sir. I work in the garage and I've seen you deal with your people and mine. You're a good man and a fair man, Mr. O'Brien."

My father just nodded and spread his hands as if to say, "And".

"Mr. O'Brien, we need your help tonight. We need it bad."

At this, he began to shake again and tears were streaming down his face.

"Take a deep breath—take several deep breaths. Tommy, go get a glass of water."

The man had calmed down a bit as I returned with the water.

"Sir, I can't be drinking out of your glass."

"You can and you will. I'm not asking—I'm telling you. If you don't collect yourself we'll be here all night."

He downed the water in one gulp and then took a deep breath.

"Thank you, sir. Thank you, sir."

"Now tell me why you need my help and what help you need. Start at the beginning."

"Mr. O'Brien, I got a boy just like you and my boy beat up a white boy today. He beat him up pretty good."

My father shot me a quick glance and I shrugged my shoulders. I hadn't heard anything.

"First of all, who's your son?"

"He's the one they call Fat Freddy."

My father turned to me again, but this time I nodded. I knew who Fat Freddy was.

"And who was the white boy?

"This is the problem, sir. The white boy's daddy is a policeman. His daddy is a Captain of the police."

My father and I whistled through our teeth almost in unison. That was about as bad as a situation could be for anyone, but particularly for a Black kid.

"Where'd this all happen?"

"That's the thing Mr. O'Brien. My boy and his friends weren't bothering anybody. They were at the beach on 79th Street. That's their beach. Everybody knows that."

"Isn't that the— whadda they call it?"

"We call it the 79th Street beach. The white folks call it the colored beach, sir."

"So you're saying that a group of white kids went looking for trouble to a place they didn't belong?"

"That's exactly what I'm sayin. Freddy—he doesn't go lookin for trouble."

Again my father sought my opinion and I just shook my head, No, I never knew Fat Freddy to start a fight.

"Did you try to contact the police?" My father knew that was a stupid question as soon as he asked it.

"Mr. O'Brien, there ain't any police within six blocks of here tonight. They may have closed down the streets, 'cause they're deserted."

"So what happens now?"

"That's why I'm here. We've been warned that several cars of kids from Beverly are on their way and they're lookin for trouble. My people are scared, Mr. O'Brien. They're telling the women and children to hide and they've got guns, sir. Somebody is gonna die before this night is done. Maybe lots of somebodies."

"So, you're thinking that if my son and his friends confront the cake eaters from Beverly, they might convince them to go home to Mommy and maybe nobody gets hurt?"

"Mr. O'Brien, they're ain't nobody—black, white, yellow or brown on the south side that wants to mess with your boy. That doesn't have a happy ending, and sir, I never heard anybody say your boy was a bully."

My Dad was pensive for a long while—moving around a couple of rocks with his shoe. Finally he looked up and spoke. "If I agree to let my boy help you—I need your word on two things."

"Bless you sir, bless you sir. You just tell me what I need to do."

"Number one—when my son comes over the tracks he better not see a Black face anywhere. They stay inside until everybody else is gone. Tommy, if you see one Black face outside, you turn around and come home. Number two—this ends tonight. There will be no reprisals. You hear me?"

"Yes, sir. Loud and clear."

"All right. You get on home now and tell your people to lock their doors and to stay inside until everyone else is gone."

I don't know what the world record might be for covering the distance between our backyard and the railroad tracks, but I think Fat Freddy's dad broke it.

My Father turned to me. "Tommy, they sing about the green fields back home, but I never knew a field in Ireland that wasn't also full of rocks. It wasn't the grass that made it holy—it was sacred because it was ours. Now this Godforsaken piece of earth may not look like much to others, but it's our home.

It was a blessing from God and it's our job to take care of it and to protect it. God didn't put those railroad tracks there. The people on the other side have the same hopes and dreams and fears as we do. Ireland can't be divided by a line drawn by politicians and this neighborhood can't be divided by railroad tracks. Ireland is one country, by God, and this is one neighborhood—our neighborhood. There are some rules that should be self-evident and one of them is that you don't go into another man's neighborhood looking for trouble.

I don't expect those little pukes to cause trouble. Get your lads together and send them on their way. Oh—and I mean it—if you see one Black face outside, turn around and come home and a pox on both their houses."

As we neared the top of the embankment and the tracks, the other side was eerily quiet—maybe the calm before the storm. I held my hand up as I surveyed the scene to make sure the Blacks had kept their word and were all behind closed doors.

The stillness was broken by the sound of cars approaching and Fat Freddy's dad was right—the streets were otherwise deserted. Soon the headlights pierced the darkness and the cars cleared the curb and parked side by side on the far sidewalk. There were easily more than ten, but I didn't stop to count them as we descended the hill.

The Beverly kids were now out of their cars and massed together wielding bats, clubs and pieces of chain—the weapons of choice in the fifties. I'm guessing they numbered maybe forty, which was twenty or so more than we had, but quality always trumps quantity—or, sometimes does.

As we approached them I heard one of them shout, "That's Tommy O'Brien. Those n*****s are fucked now."

I stopped about fifteen feet away, directly facing Jack Muldoon. It was clear he would be their leader. He was 6'6" and must have gone 280—half human and half ape—no offense to the gorillas. I didn't put any stock in evolution until I met Jack Muldoon. He was All Catholic League in both football and wrestling.

I had wrestled him once at Leo's Invitational. I gave him an inch and forty pounds, but could match his strength while being twice as quick. The problem was—Muldoon came in undefeated and it was foretold that he would leave as he came in. His father, like the father of the majority of the kids assembled tonight, was a Chicago Cop. The Referee, just happened to be a copper as well. Every time I had the advantage the ref would intervene, but it was taking its toll on King Kong. Finally, totally exasperated in the third period and knowing there was no way I was going to be given the victory unless I killed him—which was an option—I took him down hard and ripped his shoulder out of the socket before the Ref knew what happened. I was immediately disqualified, but I walked away from the mat virtually unscathed, while Muldoon, the still undefeated champion, had to be removed by stretcher thirty minutes later. The delay was for finding a stretcher that could hold him.

Muldoon held up his hand to his guys. "Tommy, I know you well enough to know by looking at you that you aren't here to help. Am I right?'

"Jack, I'm only amazed that you can process a thought and put it into words at the same time."

One of the Beverly boys chimed in. "Jack, you don't have to take that from him. You beat the shit out of him once didn't you?"

Muldoon looked mighty uncomfortable after that comment.

"Jack, your girlfriend there obviously wasn't at Leo, but if you want to do this by surrogate—just you and me—I'm down with that, but Jack—this time I break both of your arms."

With his guys starting to back off a bit, Muldoon spoke almost pleadingly, "Tommy, our fight ain't with you. Why are you standing up for the n*****s? They beat the shit out of Brendan Murphy."

"First of all, they didn't beat up Brenda—I mean Brendan. A boy name Fat Freddy did. How'd you like to get the shit kicked out of you by somebody named Fat Freddy? And everybody knows Brenda is an asshole always looking for trouble. Secondly, Brenda and his girl friends went to the colored beach looking for trouble. They went someplace they didn't belong looking for trouble and somebody got hurt. And tonight, you guys come to another place you don't belong -looking for trouble and you think the ending will be different. It won't.

Finally, this is my neighborhood. I live right across those tracks and those tracks don't divide this neighborhood. Anybody coming into this neighborhood looking for trouble has to deal with me first. So either get back in your daddy's cars and hurry home to mommy and forget this happened—or let's get this party started. Truth is, I wouldn't mind kicking some Beverly ass—so I hope you stay."

I was only halfway through my soliloquy when the first cars started to leave. I actually felt a little sorry for Muldoon—getting castrated in front of his adoring audience.

As we made our way back towards the tracks one of the young Black loudmouths emerged from his building and ran over to me. "You really showed them." Half of the "them" was out of his mouth when I hit him—as hard as I ever hit anybody.

I turned toward the projects and yelled. "The deal was that nobody and I mean nobody comes outside until everyone leaves and that includes us."

It's funny how fate works sometimes. Looking back on that night, I am absolutely convinced that had I not separated Muldoon's shoulder at Leo, we would have tangled and that would have been a fight I would pay to see. You can say what you want about the kids from Beverly, but the truth is—they were Irish, too, and they knew how to fight.

True to my father's admonition, there were no reprisals and the Black kids toed the line for as long as you can expect any young lads to do so. Most importantly, no more blood was shed and I'll bet you dollars to donuts that Brendan Murphy's swimming days for the rest of the summer were confined to the Beverly C.C.

Funny thing is, and it may be my imagination, it seemed like grass started to grow and flowers started to bloom where none before existed in our neighborhood. The most significant change of all, was when someone asked me where I was from—I no longer replied "St. Killian's." With head held high I would now reply, "92nd and Wallace and proud of it."

My greatest memory of all from that night was when my father, the King, greeted me on our back porch upon my return. He motioned me over to one of the chairs, reached down and brought up a bottle of Jameson and two Mason jars. He poured a generous amount in both and handed one to me—my first drink with my Dad!! He looked at me, clinked the jars and made a simple toast, "Up the Republic, Tommy. Up the fooking Republic!"

CHAPTER 1

Father's and Sons

Tommy—Chicago 1959

The summer of 1959 can be best characterized as bittersweet for multiple reasons. Sweet in that our beloved White Sox would win the American League pennant and were on their way to the World Series—imagine that! Bitter for the news that the football Cardinals would be playing their last season in Chicago.

Ditto on the home front. Sweet, because I had successfully completed my first two years of college—having figured out how to balance the studies with the jobs that I needed for the tuition, room, board and beer. Bitter, for the cold freeze that persisted between me and my dad over my decision to go to college, rather than follow his footsteps into the steel mill. I get that he had worked hard and sacrificed to finally get to be a foreman and that, in so doing, my path would be much easier and a career guaranteed. What he didn't get was that my decision to go to college and pursue my dream of a career in law enforcement wasn't a repudiation of, or somehow diminished, his accomplishments. I've come to understand later that it is a "south-side" phenomenon—a chip on the shoulder that will follow them to their grave.

Having said that, as anyone Irish understands, the real power in the Irish home is the mother and, when things became tense, her sixth sense would alert her to invite Father O'Shea to Sunday dinner. There would be no harsh words spoken with the good Father present and the price of that détente was a bottle of Jameson (two house cleaning jobs for a week) that acted as a panacea for whatever ailed either man.

Other than that—it was all good. The gang from "Our Lady of Calumet" was still together and going strong.

CHAPTER 2

Freedom's Just Another Word

Freddy—Chicago 1960

The incident in the summer of '57 was one of two events that would have a lasting influence on my life. The other, predated that incident and might have had an even great impact—the election of Richard J. Daley as Mayor of Chicago in 1955.

Daley's influence on Chicago and, in fact, politics both local and national cannot be overstated. The Irish Catholics had already put their stamp on Chicago's political system and Daley came from the same Bridgeport neighborhood and Ward as his predecessors. He was a force of nature—a master organizer with a genius facility for remembering names and faces.

He was blessed with the Irish Catholic and Jewish innate sense of fair play and compassion. That was but one of the things the two religions and ethnic groups shared in common. More on that later. A teaser—a few years up the road I would have quite a bit of spare time on my hands and access to a library.

With power that some Kings would covet, Daley never appeared to use it for personal gain or financial rewards. His aphrodisiac was power, plain and simple, and he wielded it like a benign dictator. His brilliance, or cunning—likely both, created the framework that still exists in Chicago to some degree—the principle that "everyone has to dine at the table". It was pragmatic as much as brilliant or fair. The city's population had swelled with the influx of Blacks from the South and immigrants from Europe. If the Democrats hoped to maintain power and, in fact, ensure the continuation of that power, they had to welcome the newcomers into their tent and he did.

His motive was less than egalitarian. Chicago was and remains largely segregated, but, and to his credit, each group did "dine at the table". It could have been worse.

Daley envisioned a political structure similar to a military chain of command. Each Ward and each Precinct would have their own hierarchy and the spoils would be a function of their performance at the polls. The spoils were city jobs and a city job was a clear path out of poverty. 100% participation at the polls and you were golden. 110% or more and you were platinum!

The nexus (I know what you're thinking, but be patient and you will learn why I have such a good vocabulary) between Daley's election and the incident in '57 is quite simple. He saw the divided neighborhood, separate, but equal—with Irish Catholics on one side of the tracks and Blacks on the other as being almost a political utopia. Proof that both groups could co-exist. For that grand plan to work, each side had to have a share of the pie.

Before that framework could be put into place it almost went up in smoke—or worse—with the threat of a race war precipitated by my fight with the police Captain's son, also Irish Catholic. No one was more thankful or relieved that bloodshed and the attendant publicity had been averted than "The Boss".

When he found out that it was my father who played a leading role in the resolution of that incident, Daley knew he had his Precinct Committeeman for the Black side of the tracks. My father was also rewarded with a supervisory job with Streets and Sanitation and a handful of other jobs to distribute as he saw fit. He was told that that was just a taste. Daley's macro plan was becoming reality.

While that was good for the Mayor, my father and the community—it meant that I saw less of my father at a time when I needed him most. I graduated from high school in 1959, but my junior and senior years were difficult for me in many ways. That's something I share in common with most people, I'm sure, but there were additional dynamics at play. After beating up a police Captain's son and living to tell about it, while suffering no reprisals, the kids, and some adults in the neighborhood, made me some kind of hero. I was too young and too naïve to not be seduced by the adulation. No one would dream of messing with me. Truth is, I like to think I have more of a poet's soul and that fight was the only serious fight I ever had. My groupies didn't understand why there were no reprisals. It was all about politics.

To compound matters, I let others define me. As much as I loved learning and was, still am, a voracious reader—I purposely began backsliding at school. It wasn't "cool" to be a scholar—particularly if you were a tough guy. If you were tough, you didn't need an education to get what you wanted in life—you just took it. Throw in the fairer sex and their worship of so called heroes and I didn't have a chance. I guess you could say that I could resist anything except temptation.

My Dad was too busy with work and politics to see what was happening and when we would be home together he would often see me reading so he had no reason to suspect my inner turmoil. He wanted—he expected me to go to college, but I didn't even apply. He then begged me to come to work for him, but how could the King of the neighborhood go to work for the city or any forty hour a week job? Without my father's guidance I was rudderless, yet I maintained a façade that essentially shut him out of my life.

Most Blacks left Mississippi for Chicago seeking some Holy Grail that would be constantly replenished by freedom. My father and I didn't come in quest of freedom. We came to escape the heartache associated with the loss of my mother to a congenital heart defect. As beautiful as she was—the truth is—she was never well and I miss her to this day.

And freedom—let me tell you about freedom. Freedom to me is like cocaine. It sounds cool, it gives you a rush, but you keep waiting for that ultimate high or that complete freedom and it never happens. Eric Clapton said that cocaine "don't lie". Sorry, Eric—it's a serial liar and freedom—fuggetaboutit. None of us are truly free. We're all slaves to something.

Increasingly, I spent my days aimlessly—simply playing a role and being paid tribute by the minor players who sought my protection. I say minor because the vices in our neighborhood were small in comparison with others: numbers, some weed and some small time loansharking. In each case we were essentially agents for the Italians and if you did business in my neighborhood—you did it thru me.

Daley wouldn't have been pleased to know what was going on in his Utopian precinct, but out of sight, out of mind. That all changed and life, as I knew it, was destined to change on a late spring day in 1960.

CHAPTER 3

Everybody's Got to Serve Somebody

Freddy—Chicago 1960

The only entrance I can remember being more dramatic, was Cleopatra's introduction to Rome in the movies. There were three new Cadillacs. The lead car was a fire engine red, fully tricked out Caddy convertible. The license plate read BIG and a gold dollar sign had replaced Cadillac's hood ornament.

They parked next to the curb and exited with style. Big, I assumed, stood for the obvious leader as he approached us hanging at our usual spot. He had done his homework. I can't begin to describe his outfit. Let's just call it "Super Fly": silk suit, cape, cane, fedora cocked at an angle and enough bling to make Mr. T. feel like a Puritan.

However, Big more aptly applied to his body guard who was simply the largest human being I had ever seen. At least I think he was human. Minimum of 6'9" and over 300 pounds!

The rest of the entourage were women—some mere girls and please note I did not use the word ladies. These were hos. Beautiful hos, but hos of every stripe. There were blondes, brunettes, red heads and to show his commitment to diversity—a couple of black chicks, too. My homies' dicks were harder than Chinese arithmetic.

He came directly to me. "My man, you must be the King here. Fat Freddy is it?? I been hearin good things about you."

"And who do I have the pleasure of meeting?"

"Freddy—may I call you Freddy?"

I nodded.

"Freddy, I'm Mr. Big and I'm the answer to your dreams. You see, I know what's goin down here and it's chump change compared to what a man like you should be makin. Plus—you workin for the EYEtalians and getting ripped off. What's up with that?"

I didn't reply, mainly because I had no reply. The only thing obvious was that he didn't have a clue what I dreamed about.

I nodded again for him to continue.

"Freddy—you want to keep your little rackets—that's fine with me, but you'll be workin for me now, not the fucking EYEtalians and I have a lot more product as you can see."

"Let's say I've got no problem with that. What am I gonna tell the—as you say—EYEtalians?"

"Freddy—you let me worry about them. In fact, you let me worry about everything. Let me introduce you to my man here. We call him Baby Huey."

Huey just stared at me and I did my best not to show any signs of fear—which required effort on my part.

"Huey, give these young men some walkin around money. They workin for me now."

I watched as Huey handed out twenty dollar bills to wide eyes and eager hands. "The King is dead. Long live the King."

"And Freddy, I've got somethin very special for my new junior partner. Come hear Sasha."

Sasha must have been hiding in the background, because when she emerged every tongue on that street corner was hanging out. She was a twenty-five on a scale of one to ten. Blonde hair, blue eyes and a body that might make Michelangelo cry. She was also barely sixteen and barely dressed.

"Freddy, Sasha is from Russia and she doesn't speak much English, but she is my prize and now my gift to you."

In any other situation, Sasha could have put a dog collar around my neck and I would have followed her anywhere, but this was no normal situation. I may have crossed a few lines the past couple of years, but now I was floating in outer space and reality was quickly slipping away.

I don't know where I summoned the strength from, or the good sense that had escaped me long ago, but I looked Mr. Big square in the eye and then Baby Huey and replied, "Your offer is a great one, but I'm afraid I can't accept at this time. You've given me a lot of things to think about and I'm going to need to sleep on things—alone."

Truth is—I realized instantly that that would have been the end of not just my father's career, but also any hope for the neighborhood. Everything has a price, but that was way too high a price to pay for pussy.

Mr. Big cast a wary eye at me. "You think all you want, Freddy and you have sweet dreams, but when you wake up in the morning I'm gonna be here and I'm gonna be running things. You dig?"

All I could think of to say was, "You do what you have to do."

"Oh, I'll do that for sure. Girls, why don't you let these young men show you around our new home."

I couldn't have stopped them if I tried. Then a surprising thing happened. Baby Huey walked over to me and stuck out his hand. I was taken completely off guard by his smile. It wasn't the smile of an enforcer—if enforcers smiled. There was something innocent about it.

Sure enough and true to his word, the neighborhood was transformed overnight. The hos were on the sidewalks and the streets were like a parking lot with Johns waiting in line—some honking impatiently.

The numbers, weed and loan sharking continued as before—only ramped up. I expected to get a visit from my Mob contacts, but it was like they disappeared. Hard for me to believe.

I had wanted a way out and now had one and didn't know what to do. One thing was certain—my fan club had folded. There was a new King in town.

Strange as it may seem, the person I saw most and seemed to bond with, as spring gave way to summer, was Baby Huey. We found out we had a lot in common—well a little in common. We were both from Mississippi and both wished we had never left. Like me, he also had a big heart and would rather be liked than feared, but no one else ever dared get close enough to find that out. Huey may have been blessed with the body of a superman, but he had the mind of a child. I may have been the only one to pay attention to him—to care for him as a person and he couldn't get enough of my company.

A new sound was introduced into our neighborhood—police sirens. Then one night Mr. Big's bright red Caddy was blown to smithereens while parked at the curb. My EYEtalians hadn't disappeared.

None of this was lost on my father who was responsible for the precinct. Fortunately, I was home most nights and he knew I wasn't involved in this new scourge. Like my grandmother said, "God works in strange ways." and those days actually brought us closer together.

My father had met the Mayor, but only briefly. The Mayor's business was conducted by surrogates. In the case of politics it was more often than not "The Colonel" who my father took orders from. I don't know if he was really a Colonel, but make no mistake about it—when he spoke, he was speaking for the Mayor.

The Colonel had summonsed my father to his office. He expressed the Mayor's concern over what was happening to his precinct and how it was going to be rectified.

Mr. Big might have been the new King, but Mr. Big answered to a faction of the Mob that was at odds with a rival faction for control of the South Side rackets—the crew that I had been dealing with. Everybody serves somebody.

It seemed that the friction started at the top and there was concern that Sam "Momo" Giancana had been spending way too much time in L.A. and Vegas at the expense of operations here at home. Not to mention the publicity he was attracting and publicity was something the "old mustaches" abhorred.

Friction, like gravity, trickles down and infects everyone below. So it was that my neighborhood became a battleground in one of the many mob conflicts, but not for long.

The Mayor had worked too long and too hard on his master plan and 1960 was a presidential election year with a young, charismatic Irish Catholic at the top of the ticket. It was the wrong time to fuck with the Boss regardless of who you were.

The message went out loud and clear to both the mob and the Police Department—often seeming to be co-equal branches of government. It was to be delivered in person by the Colonel the following day. This I wanted to see.

It was around noon while the King was holding court on the street corner that the black limo pulled up trailed by at least four squad cars and a paddy wagon. A policeman walked over to Mr. Big, escorted him to the limo and held the door for him.

When Mr. Big emerged approximately a half hour later, he was visibly shaken. He tersely announced that he was moving out of the neighborhood immediately and that everyone should follow him to a spot on Stony Island which would be their new base. He then quickly—and I mean quickly—departed with his harem in tow. Before he did so, he looked around desperately trying to find Baby Huey who was nowhere in sight.

What followed was likely the only time ever when you could hear a pin drop on that street corner. The King had been deposed and not a shot had been fired—at least yet. The same policeman then re-approached the crowd and said that anyone who didn't belong in the neighborhood had to leave before sundown and that there were no exceptions.

While I couldn't have been happier for the turn of events and the avoidance of bloodshed, my thoughts turned immediately to Baby Huey. Mr. Big had left without him and Baby Huey wasn't capable of independent thought.

CHAPTER 4

The Wrong Place at the Wrong Time

Freddy—Chicago 1960

I had the worst feeling in the pit of my stomach as I searched everywhere for Baby Huey. In Mississippi they called it "a bad moon rising" and it generally meant that somebody would die before the day was through.

Throughout the afternoon, it seemed I was one step behind as by the time I arrived, Baby Huey had just left. Turns out he had spent the majority of the afternoon "babysitting" a four year old whose mother was ill. The quotes are because I'm not sure who was babysitting whom. They liked to read "Curious George"—at least look at the pictures together.

Later on, I ran into some of the local punks and my worst fears were confirmed. They had told Baby Huey their version of how the police roughed up Mr. Big and forced him out of the neighborhood. The chief instigator was called Funky (Flunky would have been more appropriate). He could start a brawl in a Buddhist Temple—it was just that he was never personally involved. The proverbial shit disturber. I knew Baby Huey and knew he was packing. I had to find him before he was confronted by the police, who would show no mercy. I ran as fast as I could for our corner, but arrived just as a barrage of shots rang out. One police officer was down and Baby Huey was stone cold dead.

I rushed to his side and knelt down, aware that there was nothing I could do. The next voice I heard sent a chill though my spine.

"Book his partner here for attempted murder of a police officer."

When I looked up, the speaker was a Captain, Captain Murphy, Brendan Murphy's father. Revenge had been a long time coming and now it would be a long time gone. I couldn't have been more fucked. The worst crime imaginable was shooting a police officer. Fortunately, this one would survive, but that didn't lessen the crime. The only question was—would I survive the ride to the jail?

The "good" news is that I did survive, but barely. My eyes were swollen shut, my jaw was broken as were several ribs. They had done a number on me as Captain Murphy watched with glee.

My father had rushed to the jail as soon as he heard the news. There were tears in his eyes. He knew I wasn't guilty, but he also understood the anger that had been suppressed for three years by Captain Murphy and knew that he wouldn't be forced to stand down a second time—particularly as he had several "witnesses".

"Son, you just gotta pray as hard as you can. Pray to Grandma and Mama. They're up in Heaven and they'll look after you. I'm gonna go see the Colonel and see what I can do."

Chapter 5

Good News/Bad News

Freddy—Chicago 1960

My father went directly to City Hall and the Colonel's office. He was surprised when the Colonel said that the Mayor wished to see him first. They entered the Mayor's office. The Mayor stood and said (remember I said he had a genius facility for names and faces), "Lionel, I heard what happened and just want you to know that we know Freddy is a good boy who happened to be in the wrong place at the wrong time. I appreciate the good work you have done for the party and we'll do whatever we can to help. The Colonel will look after this for me."

They then proceeded back to the Colonel's office. My father felt better after speaking with the Mayor, but could tell from the Colonel's serious demeanor that this was a very difficult situation.

"Lionel, I've got some good news and some bad news. The good news is that the attempted murder charge isn't going to stick."

"Praise Jesus Christ."

"The bad news is that Freddy is going to have to do some time. That can't be avoided. Murphy and the police swallowed a bitter pill three years ago, but knew they had no choice. Freddy may be innocent of the charges, but we told you loud and clear that he had to walk the straight and narrow until this cloud was lifted."

My father had his head in his hands.

"Now, before you despair even more—there are some things we can do to help."

"Colonel, I'll do anything you ask."

"Yes, well—we'll get to that in a minute. Here's the deal on our end. Everybody has heard of Stateville, Alcatraz and Sing Sing."

My father winced.

"But, very few people know that the Justice Department also has a couple of facilities that are designed for—let's say friends who have made some poor choices or had some misfortune. Minimum security facilities that are more like a country club than a prison."

My father perked up.

"The one that Freddy will call home for the next five years has no fences. It has a running track, tennis courts, basketball courts and a library. The food is pretty good and Freddy will have a room to himself—like a dorm room. The only condition is he doesn't up and walk away. If he does—next stop is Stateville and twenty to life."

"God bless you Colonel. God bless you. What can I do for you?"

"We'll get to that. Now we know that Freddy likes to read. Everybody has to have a job of some sort. We can make him librarian. He can read all day and can even take some college courses offered by a local community college. Freddy could get himself in shape and even come out with a college degree. "

"Again, God bless you. Where is this place? "

"It's in Florida, but forget that I ever said that. Captain Murphy has agreed to the deal, but doesn't need to know where Freddy's going."

"And the deal is?"

"Ah yes, the deal. Lionel, as you know, this is a hotly contested presidential race. The Mayor is all in for Kennedy and will do everything in his power to see him get elected. He has already arranged to have Chicago's votes counted last, but nothing is certain as the race is a tossup. What you need to do for us is to deliver 25,000 votes for Kennedy in November."

My father appeared momentarily stunned.

"There must be some misunderstanding. My precinct only has approximately 2000 registered voters and I deliver all 2000—sometimes more."

The Colonel paused and looked directly at my father.

"I told you what we're doing for your son and you must understand that the police are our friends. I didn't misspeak. You need to deliver 25,000 votes for Kennedy—not 24,999. 25,000."

"How—how am I supposed to do that?"

"Lionel, that is for you to figure out. Every precinct in the city needs to perform if we are to get him elected. You have an extra reason to do so."

"Can you help me out here? Where do I find the bodies?"

"Perfect choice of words—bodies, and where do we find bodies? Now if we understand each other, I have to get back to work."

CHAPTER 6

The Dark Side of the Moon

Tommy—Chicago 1960

B y attending classes in the summer, I was able to get my degree in three years. The day I graduated from college turned out to be a day of healing and joy—great joy. During my time at Northern Illinois University my mother had visited me in DeKalb at least once a year, but my father had yet to set foot on the campus—still believing that my college experience was somehow repudiation of his career, his successful career, in the steel mill. Truth is, I had doubts he would attend the graduation, but there he was in all of his glory despite the ill-fitting suit and shirt that he couldn't button at the neck.

I spotted them as I strode to get my sheepskin, but when I went to join them, he was missing. My mother didn't seem to notice as she was literally on cloud nine. My disappointment was obvious.

"What happened to Dad? Did he reach his limit?"

My mother laughed—which I thought was curious. "Do you really want to know? He'll be angry at me for telling you."

"I really, really want to know."

Her smile turned a bit sad. "The King started blubbering, he was so proud. He left for fear that you would see him cry."

Just then I saw him returning and, sure enough, his eyes were red and puffy. With quivering lip he embraced me in a bear hug and I returned his hug with equal ardor. Something that I will never forget was feeling his heart beat against my chest. Neither of us wanted to let go and both were crying tears of joy.

We returned home for a celebratory dinner which included my girlfriend Mary Kay and the good Father O'Shea who was never known to turn down either roast beef or Jameson. After grace and a toast my father turned to me beaming and said, "Tommy, I had to start at the very bottom and work every shite job (my mother cleared her throat and Father O'Shea pretended not to hear) at the mill before I made foreman. With your college degree you will start in management. Imagine that!"

You could've heard a pin drop as I looked to my mother for guidance while the good Padre averted my glance. "Dad, I already have a job. I was waiting to tell you."

The King was clearly flustered. "You have a job? What job? You mean you aren't coming to the mill after all of these years of paving the way for you?"

"Dad, what you have done is incredible. Truly, I couldn't have done it." That seemed to mollify him a bit.

"It's just—it's just that it's not my calling. I have an opportunity to do what I want to do."

As I had kept this news secret from everyone—all eyes were on me.

'I studied criminal justice and liked it. Last year I took the entrance exam for the Federal Bureau of Narcotics and passed it. I have been engaged in a dialogue with them since then and in two weeks I leave for Quantico, Virginia where I will be in training to be a Field Agent."

My mother, Mary Kay, my younger brother Jamie and Father O'Shea all seemed impressed and it was clear that the King's wheels were turning as he processed the news. "So you'll be working for the government?"

"I will indeed with full benefits and pension." Said looking directly at Mary Kay—as it was accepted as fact that we were destined to marry someday.

"What exactly does a Field Agent do? Do you carry a gun?"

"There is a real drug problem in this country and it's not just the coloreds. In fact, the government thinks it will get worse long before it gets better.

I will carry a gun, which I will be trained to use. We'll be targeting the drug smugglers and dealers who are peddling this poison."

My Dad was pensive as he savored his next drop of the "nectar of the Gods"—clearly warming to this unexpected news. "Tommy, I never told you this before," true enough as we hardly ever spoke—about anything, "but there is a drug problem in Gary and even some of the steel workers are hooked."

"I'd only be surprised if there wasn't."

More often than not, Father O'Shea was invited to ensure the peace, but this dinner could not have turned out more enjoyable—made even more so by the Jameson which I shared in liberally. After dessert the phone rang and Jamie said it was my good pal, also named Freddy. It turned out that the usual suspects had gathered at Freddy's house and the coppers had already been called twice for the disturbance—which was par for the course for our parties.

I announced that I was going to fetch a light sweater from my room and pop over for a while. In my room, I noticed the notebook that I kept for favorite adages and bits of wisdom was open to the page listing the twelve stages of drunkenness. Numbers eleven and twelve were bulletproof and invisible. I wasn't close to either, but I was headed in that direction if I left to join my pals.

Just then I heard footsteps and turned to see my mom and Mary Kay standing in the doorway. Mary Kay's beauty was complemented by her superb wit. When I asked how I could get out of going, she replied, "Tell them you're too well to attend."

My mom then tossed me a Mason jar which was the vessel used for Jameson on the back porch, where the King and the good Father had reposed to. As she turned to leave, she literally twirled and I was almost dumbstruck by how happy and lovely she looked. If only for an evening, the household drudge had morphed into Cinderella and no one deserved it more. I had to laugh at the thought of my dad being Prince Hans, but Mother had always been blinded by love where he was concerned.

When I stepped out on the porch with my Mason jar, the conversation seemed to stop and I quickly realized why. The bottle was already half-empty and the extra jar would only hasten its demise. That would be no way to end such a wonderful day. I sat the jar down, "I think I've had enough whiskey for the night. Do you mind if I have a beer instead?"

My father jumped at the idea. "Fooking brilliant idea—ain't it Father?"

Father O'Shea, now three sheets to the wind, replied, "Fooking brilliant idea" before realizing what he had said. He crossed himself as we all three laughed.

Mother and Mary Kay were chatting away as they cleared the dinner table—probably planning the wedding. When I went in the kitchen to grab a Falstaff, Jamie was washing the dishes. I was halfway out when I turned and returned to the fridge and handed Jamie one too. It was likely his first beer. As he took his first sip and wasn't certain about the taste, Mother appeared in the doorway. She appeared to frown, but then came over and kissed us both. No one wanted the day to end.

Returning to the porch with my beer, Dad and Father O'Shea were standing at the railing getting the evening news from Riley, our neighbor. Long before the talking heads and twenty-four hour cable news, we got the news from word of mouth—particularly the local news.

By their collective demeanors the news hadn't been good. My father motioned for me to sit. "Two nights ago it sounded like World War III on the colored side. There were so many cop cars that they lit up the sky and the sirens went on all night."

"What happened?"

"What happened is that a couple of the coloreds got into a gunfight with the coppers. One of the coloreds was killed and one of the cops was wounded."

Father O'Shea shook his head.

"And guess who the other colored shooter was?"

I shrugged. How the hell was I supposed to know?

"Remember Fat Freddy?"

I did remember, but I was stunned. Mind you—I never knew him that well and a lot can happen in three years, but I couldn't imagine a fate worse than that facing a colored kid for shooting a white cop and they were almost all white at that time.

As I gazed at the full moon while digesting the news, I realized that the moon, like the neighborhood, had two sides to it. I was on the bright side winding down a perfect day, but Freddy was on the dark side of the moon and it was only going to get darker.

CHAPTER 7

A Rogue's Gallery

Gary, Indiana, 1940-1960

Carlo Gambino came to the US in 1921 at age nineteen and already a made-man from Palermo. Sicily. He went to work for his cousins, the Castellanos, in one of New York City's largest crime families. He quickly distinguished himself among a group of "young Turks" destined to take control of the American Mafia that included Lucky Luciano, Al Capone, Albert Anastasia, Vito Genovese, Meyer Lansky and Bugsy Siegel. Perhaps only Lansky rivalled Gambino in organizational skills, sheer cunning and instinct for self-preservation. Capone was convicted of tax evasion and sentenced to eleven years in prison. Gambino was convicted of the same crime, but his sentence was mysteriously suspended. In fact, it was Gambino who would seize control of the American Mafia Commission in 1957.

No one of that era was more opportunistic than Gambino and it was a combination of opportunity and that instinct for survival that led his attention to Gary, Indiana in early 1940. He had learned through contacts at the C.I.O. that the steel workers were expected to be unionized as early as 1942 and realized what a cash cow that could become. Particularly in a steel town, like Gary.

To get involved in Gary was a bold gamble, but a calculated one, as Capone was nearing the end of his prison sentence and his future was uncertain. Gambino devised a scheme to carve out a territory in Gary, even though it was certain to be opposed by both Chicago and Detroit mobsters. Capone was the wild card as Gambino was less concerned with Detroit.

That the world's most powerful man at the time, Julius Caesar, was stabbed by a friend is a lesson ingrained in the Sicilian DNA. Gambino's favorite saying was, "God protect me from my friends—I know who my enemies are." So it was that he had the perfect vehicle for his scheme in the person of Tommy Antonacci. He was a cousin from Gambino's mother's side, but his ambition was as outsized as his ego and neither had any rational justification. "Promoting" him for this mission was almost a win-win for Gambino. If Tommy A. succeeded, he was out of NY and Gambino would get his union prize. If he failed and created conflict with Chicago and/or Detroit, Gambino would disavow him as a rogue elephant.

The truth is that Tommy A. did succeed—actually over-achieved for a while, but by 1950 both Chicago and Detroit mobs were unhappy with their share of the union spoils (50% Gambino/25% Chicago/25% Detroit) and Gambino was threatened with a war over the territory. Tommy A. then committed the cardinal sin for a Mafioso—he went crying to Gambino for support. Weakness is a fatal affliction in the mob.

The crisis provided Gambino another opportunity to make lemons out of lemonade. Without showing his hand to Tommy A., this was an opportunity to be rid of him and replace him with the Vecchio brothers whose complementary skills definitely justified their ambition and that ambition could also prove a threat someday to Gambino.

Anthony "The Sheikh" Vecchio got his nickname from his resemblance to Rudolph Valentino. Two years senior to his brother Angelo, he was a charismatic figure who someone once said, could charm the skin off a snake. Angelo "One-Time" Vecchio earned his nickname by issuing only one warning and, sometimes none. Few people were more feared than "One-Time" and his mercurial temperament. Together, they were a formidable team and Gambino had no doubt that they could resolve the situation in Gary.

The Vecchios took the train to Gary with the clueless Tommy A. and arranged for a sit-down with leaders of both Chicago and Detroit mobs. Tommy A. was seated in the middle. Anthony "the Sheikh" addressed the group, "My brother and I are here at the request of Don Carlo Gambino to mediate this dispute." He motioned to Angelo who, in the blink of an eye, put a bullet in the center of Tommy A.'s forehead. Anthony walked around the table and used his foot to topple the very dead Tommy A. from his chair. He then sat down and addressed the two shell-shocked mobsters, "It's my understanding that the previous arrangement was 50/25/25. It's now going to be 40/30/30 and there will be no further negotiation. If anyone disagrees or is unhappy with that—speak up or keep your peace". Chicago and Detroit couldn't accept the terms fast enough.

The Sheikh would solidify the mob's position in Gary by bringing virtually all of the city and county officials, even the Judges, to the party. Narcotics distribution was a hard pill for most of them to swallow, but it was largely confined to the "colored" sections and the union money was too enticing to ignore. At the end of the day, the prevailing logic was "if you can't lick 'em—join 'em".

It was far from blue skies and clear sailing however, as, contemporaneous with Gambino seizing control of the Commission in 1957, James "Jimmy" Hoffa took over leadership of the powerful International Brotherhood of Teamsters, which would become the largest union in the country. His rise in power was made possible by his mob connections—particularly those with the Detroit mob, which created additional friction for Gary. But, at times, Hoffa seemed to have the ability to piss off everybody—even his close associates.

The seminal moment for the Gary mob came on a starless night in the summer of 1960 when a Teamster's semi crossed the median of a two-lane road outside of Hammond and crashed head-on into a car driven by Anthony Vecchio, who was killed instantly. The semi driver claimed he had swerved to avoid a deer in the road and lost control, but no skid marks were evident of any attempt to brake. Angelo wasn't buying any excuses and wanted revenge, but Carlo Gambino wasn't going to risk an all-out mafia war at a time when they were a mere few months away from getting the mob's hand-picked candidate elected President. Son of a bootlegger/contemporary of Luciano and Lansky, JFK was like family. The stakes were too high and the potential consequences too severe for a mob war at that time. It was only later noted that Anthony had been driving Angelo's car that night.

If Angelo "One-time" was a ticking time bomb while Anthony was alive, he was totally unpredictable without any adult supervision. Anthony did have a son, Richie "Gorgeous" Vecchio, who managed one of the mob's more valuable franchises, Vecchio's General Motors dealership, which had a no-bid contract to replace Gary's public vehicle fleet every two years. Richie's combination of charm and marketing skill had turned the dealership into one of GM's most profitable, even without the public contract, and he had never evidenced the desire to get more involved in the mob's business.

However, loyalty and tradition are twin pillars of the mafia and most of the Gary captains and soldiers had been loyal to Anthony Vecchio as the acknowledged leader of the mob. That loyalty was destined to be transferred to Richie, whether he wanted it or not. When you get involved in "this thing of ours" you are in for life and you do what you have to do, but Richie had never been close to his uncle Angelo (who had?). A transition to any type of power sharing agreement seemed like a pipe dream—and likely was.

The celebration of JFK's election would temporarily take people's minds off of their other problems, but "a funny thing happened on the way to the forum". JFK would appoint his brother, Bobby, as Attorney General and it wasn't long before Bobby made the mob and Jimmy Hoffa an obsession. Talk about "biting the hand that fed you!"

CHAPTER 8

St. Momo's Hospital

Freddy—Chicago 1960-1961

"The Boss" had a dilemma. He knew how critical my dad was to any hope of JFK getting elected. Our precinct on the south side was as far off the radar screen as possible and few would question how a colored precinct swelled from two to twenty-five thousand in a few short years. It would seem eminently understandable to the more urbane citizens of the Gold Coast and north side of Chicago—none of whom were likely to travel to a colored neighborhood on the south side to count noses. Benign neglect suited their purposes fine. Daley had no doubts that my father would deliver—particularly after the Colonel dispatched a fleet of empty school buses daily to the neighborhood, to pick up the cemetery "volunteers" paid five cents per name. But, who could the Mayor trust to protect me from retribution from the police until after the election and then deliver me safely to the facility in Florida?

The solution would involve a pact between three seemingly strange bed-fellows—Daley, Sam Giancana and J. Edgar Hoover, who bonded together for the common goal of getting JFK elected. While they shared the same goal, their motivations were uniquely personal. Quite simply, if Satan had declared himself to be an Irish-Catholic Democrat, Daley would have supported him. Giancana had an even more personal relationship with JFK—sharing a mistress in Judith Campbell Exner. Hoover's motivation, as like most of his motives, was purely political. Like Daley, his aphrodisiac was power—raw, naked power and blackmail was his instrument of choice.

JFK was almost too good to be true for Hoover, as few families, if any, were more morally bankrupt and ethically challenged than Joe Kennedy's clan. How far do the apples fall from a bootlegging, philandering tree?

It was decided that I would be moved immediately to the Little Company of Mary hospital in Evergreen Park where I would recuperate and be guarded around the clock by Giancana's soldiers. In Chicago, the mob and the police were often two separate branches of city government and the police had to back off—a retreat made a wee bit more palatable by a significant donation to the "Widows and Orphans Fund".

What happened next was right out of Lewis Carroll. The largest room in the hospital was set aside for me and my new best friends. Free of any interference by the police, the opportunity was too good for the mob to pass up and not only did the mobsters move in, but they installed a sports ticker tape and six telephones on their second day. For the next several months, the most successful bookie operation in Chicago would operate from the hospital whose new nickname was St. Momo's.

Out of boredom, I agreed to man the phones and, in fact, made $500 when Bill Mazeroski hit a walk-off home run to beat the hated Yankees in game seven of the 1960 World Series. It was an intuitive bet for me. Growing up near the river in Mississippi, we would pretend to be pirates and there was little love lost between the colored folks and Yankees. They may have "freed" the slaves, but they indiscriminately destroyed everything in their path including the crops and animals, which the slaves depended on for their subsistence.

If the bookie operation wasn't bad enough for the good Sisters, the leader of the crew, Johnny "The Italian Stallion" Santini made it a personal mission to bang every nurse in the joint and, as far as I could tell—he was successful. In short—St. Momo's was an absolute zoo.

CHAPTER 9

Club Fed

Freddy—Chicago 1961

If I had any concerns about the outcome of the election they were dispelled on election night when CBS News announced that the only remaining votes would be coming from Chicago. I can't remember what excuse they gave or if they gave one. The election of our next President would not be decided in the halls of power in Washington, a smoke-filled room in one of the private men's clubs, or a salon on the upper-east side of New York City. It would be decided in a humble bungalow on S. Lowe Street, in the working-class neighborhood of Bridgeport in Chicago.

Even if Richard Nixon had contested the election—which he didn't, he would have gotten little or no support from Republicans in Chicago. They tended to include wealthy property owners and the lever of power in Chicago, then and now, resided with the County Assessor who was a loyal minion of Daley. It was—it is quite simple: a handful of powerful Democrat politicians and power brokers specialized in property tax appeals. If you played ball and availed yourself of one of their services—your appeal would be successful. The degree of success would be a function of how well you played the game. "Sorry, Tricky Dick", they'd say. "It's just business."

I was packed, what little I had to pack, the day after the election and was getting a bit nervous as the "FIBs" didn't show up until the middle of January. The mob didn't mind, as basketball and hockey were in full swing and the phones were ringing off the hook. Living and operating in such close quarters with the "Italian Stallion" and his crew only served to re-inforce what I had come to believe: human nature is human nature and we have more in common than that which separates us. I even got used to being called "Snowball".

The day the FIBs did arrive was surreal. All of the phones were manned by mobsters and the Stallion was banging one of the nurses behind the curtains. They must teach a course in Quantico on how to display zero emotion, as they appeared oblivious to everything but me. I don't remember the agent's names. I referred to them as Smith and Jones. One other note—I don't know if they recruit one total asshole for each human being or if that's just a coincidence, but Smith was a total jag off and seemed to be proud of it.

I guess I had developed a false sense of security under the protection of my mob homeys, but I was quickly brought back to reality by the arsenal of weapons the FIBs had in their van and the fact that they insisted on shackling me for the ride. I was unnerved by the fact that they didn't relax a bit until we were well clear of the city limits. Jones said they had credible info that I still had a target on my back with some coppers.

When I asked where we they were taking me, Jones said Louisville. Smith told me to fuck myself—which I pointed out was impossible with the shackles. I was certain that Louisville wasn't in Florida—so was a bit concerned, but it was the end of the line for them, not me. In Louisville I was transferred to another non-descript van with another asshole/decent sort duo who would take me the rest of the way. The destination was on a need to know basis and Smith and Jones didn't need to know. Hoover was a stickler for secrecy.

It was late morning on the second day when we arrived at what I would come to learn was called "Club Fed". Neither my dad, nor I had any idea what a country club was like—just that anything sounded better than Stateville. The facility, however, is still hard to adequately describe. When we first arrived I literally thought I was either dreaming or had completely lost my marbles.

As part of a military base, there was a guard house that provided entry to the grounds, but nothing to stop you from leaving—save Stateville and twenty to life if you were caught. That wasn't going to happen because I wasn't sure I would ever want to leave. The grounds were manicured and included a running track, basketball courts, tennis courts and even a par three golf course!

There were separate group housing arrangements with one or two bed rooms that included a dinette, writing table and private bathroom. I had a single room to myself. That suited me fine as I had heard the rumors about prison life and, in fact, barricaded my door at night for months. The truth is, my fellow guests included a governor, elected officials and a fair smattering of judges and lawyers—all white. None would have been eager to share a room with me.

The food was better than average and if you had enough money in your commissary account you could buy and cook your own food. The only requirement was that each person had a job—a job per se. As the Colonel had promised, I became the librarian and couldn't have been happier. I loved to read—as did most of my fellow guests—and the library had a great collection of many different literary genres. I was in heaven, plus could be as engaged with, or removed from, others as I chose to be.

I would privately smile or laugh to hear someone from the manor born yearn for freedom. I knew something about freedom that they didn't. I did miss my father and female companionship, but they had a saying in Mississippi that most of man's woes could be traced to either a "wine glass or a woman's ass" and I could survive without either for five years—if I had to. In the meantime, I was going to eat right, get in shape and look into the college courses that were offered by a local community college.

CHAPTER 10

A Perfect Storm

Gary, Indiana

Although the Five Families appeared aligned in the Mafia Commission, a better analogy might be an alliance of five hungry wolves. As long as there was plenty of meat to go around—there was peace, a fragile peace. However, as the families grew there were more mouths to feed and conflicts were inevitable. As head of the Commission, a title he had claimed rather than been elected to, Carlo Gambino was a target, as much as a leader. It wasn't in a mob leader's DNA to relish being number two—let alone part of a lesser four.

In that regard, Gambino had another factor to consider in his decision making process—saving face. A loss of face was a sign of weakness and the four other "wolves" were alert for any sign of weakness.

As 1963 was coming to a close, it was apparent to Gambino that a perfect storm was brewing and it would require all of his finesse, skills and power to survive. His hands-on involvement in the Kennedy hit had been limited The main mob contribution was handled by Santo Trafficante and Carlos Marcello who had closer ties to the Cuban community, The "Company" did the rest, as Kennedy's Irish Mafia was perceived as an existential threat to the military-industrial complex's expanding adventure in South East Asia. There could be no repeat of the Bay of Pigs fiasco. Oswald was just one of hundreds of stooges they monitored daily. With connections to both Cuba and Russia, he was the perfect foil. Neither the CIA, nor the mafia would leave such an important message to the incredible chance of an almost impossible shot. There was no way that Kennedy was going to survive past the grassy knoll.

Two other "wild-cards" had emerged on the scene and both required an abundance of finesse, Bumpy Johnson and Jimmy Hoffa. Johnson was the colored face of the rackets in Harlem. In truth, he was a vessel of the five families—primarily the Genovese family where he had been a contemporary of Lucky Luciano. It was a perfect relationship—as long as it lasted. Johnson's out-sized ego was fed and was only rivaled by his guile and instinct for survival, while the mob floated under the radar screen and reaped the bulk of the profits.

The end came as it usually does, by a stupid mistake and this one led to a bust and indictment of Johnson on federal charges. The mistake, however, was made by one of Genovese's men—not Johnson. The feds were aware of the relationship between Johnson and his patrons and their real target was the five families. They were convinced that if enough pressure was applied to a colored man—he would give up the mob. The mob agreed.

Johnson was sent to Alcatraz where the feds were free of prying eyes. They would do what was necessary to get him to sing. The mob had gotten to one of his guards and he would die before the second note was warbled. Either way, Alcatraz was to be Johnson's last stop. However, and despite unspeakable torture and deprivation, Johnson survived and they were forced to release him in 1963.

He was received as Lazarus back in Harlem and the five families, particularly Genovese, made him untouchable after refusing to give them up. The problem was that no one expected him to survive, let alone return, and all of his rackets had been doled out to other gangsters. Despite appeals for Johnson's patience and promises to make things right, patience was a virtue that died in a dank cell at Alcatraz.

It wasn't long before Johnson provoked a war between the Genovese and Bonanno families that posed a threat to Gambino and the entire commission. Maybe an even greater threat was Johnson's boast that he would take over all of the rackets in every colored neighborhood in the country—which included Gary.

It seemed an idle threat until considered in the light of the disturbing phenomenon where Uncle Sam was drafting young Black men for Viet Nam fresh out of high school—at a rate of almost double their share of the population. The worst part of all is that they represented the best and brightest of a new generation of Black men, who possessed a great education and were on the threshold of the dream that America represented. They could have gone on to be Doctors, Lawyers, business leaders—the sky was the limit, but the ones fortunate enough to return from jungles thousands of miles away, were trained in only one vocation, "killer", and indoctrinated into only one philosophy, "might makes right". Can you imagine being in a snake infested, sweltering jungle in Viet Nam with people you knew nothing about trying to kill you, and when you ask "What the fuck are we doing here?" some 21 year old white Lieutenant tells you, "If we don't prevent the Commies from taking over this jungle—they will take over the jungles in Laos and Cambodia, too!" The mind would stop functioning rationally, even before wondering what the fuck Laos and Cambodia were.

Maybe there was gray area in re Viet Nam, but upon return, what the survivors found in the colored neighborhoods of Chicago, Gary and Detroit was starkly black and white. The victims were Blacks and the profiteers were white. Maybe Johnson's boast of taking over the rackets in every colored neighborhood in the country was hyperbole, but the war for the drug trade had already begun in Gary. That represented a trifecta of concern for Gambino: the loss of revenue, that would result in an inevitable accommodation with the Chicago street gangs; the attention the carnage was drawing from the feds and the potential loss of face, such an arrangement with the gangs would create.

If that wasn't enough, Jimmy Hoffa and the Teamsters were under investigation—had been almost continuously since JFK appointed Bobby as his AG and the Teamster billions were attracting sharks like chum in the water.

In the grand scheme of things, was Gary worth hanging onto, with its apparent diminishing fortunes, while there were bigger fish to fry? Gambino knew where to turn to for advice and counsel.

CHAPTER 11

The Fixer

Washington, D.C.—March 1964

Carlo Antonini was Gambino's son by his favorite housekeeper. The paternity was never in doubt and the only person who ever commented on it, disappeared. Maybe it was a coincidence, but likely not. That the child was male, healthy, above-average height and, soon to be understood, of substantially above-average intelligence didn't hurt.

It had stuck in Gambino's craw that Americans adored Italians like Valentino and Caruso, but regarded Italian-Americans, like Irish-Americans and African-Americans, as some inferior species. Sinatra's special status with the mob bosses was simply because he was beloved by Americans, but that was because of his God-given talent, not his ethnicity.

Gambino realized he had, in young Carlo, the perfect vehicle to prove that Italian-Americans, even a bastard child, could compete with the WASPS at any game given a level playing field and he had the power and the money to make it level.

Step one was to Anglicize his name. He was persuaded not to use Marc Anthony, his first choice, to remove any hints of nationality—in favor of Carlton Anthony. The requisite under grad Princeton and Harvard Law degrees would be easy to secure via Gambino's political "friends" and facilitated by substantial, anonymous donations to both schools.

His real education, however, began with tutors at an early age, with an emphasis on the classics and history, which is destined to repeat itself. He would learn how the world really worked, not how it could or should work according to some political ideology. He had four main references: *The Old Testament*, *Aesop's Fables*, Machiavelli's, *The Prince*, and Sun Tzu's, *The Art of War*. The latter two were the only books on either his desk or night stand.

The Bible and ancient histories taught him that human nature had never changed and would never change. It was simply as advertised—human nature. Understand the frailties and vulnerabilities of that nature—the seven deadly sins—and the keys to the kingdom were yours.

He also learned that every attempt by society to legislate morality had eventually failed. The real Golden Rule was, "He who has the gold—makes the rules!" One of his elder tutors actually prophesied that when the forces of socialism realized how much money was involved, that the state would legalize and operate the vices themselves. Gambling and narcotics? That could never happen—could it?

Like a "chip off the old block" Carlton inherited his father's hatred of hypocrisy and how it had been weaponized against his people. While he stood out with his movie star good looks, bespoke wardrobe, flawless manners and superior intellect—his "peers" considered him aloof—even arrogant for eschewing most attempts at socializing.

He, in turn, held them in contempt—the same contempt they would have for the bastard son of a mob boss, as opposed to the urbane heir to a mysterious fortune. They weren't at Harvard to learn the law. They were there to learn how to manipulate it for personal advantage. To them Lady Justice was blindfolded so that she wouldn't have to see what they were doing in her name. And, after all, what good was the law if a defendant's fate was left to a man or woman with feet of clay or, worse yet, twelve people who weren't smart enough to know how to avoid jury duty?

Upon graduation from Harvard Law, the Wall Street and D.C. law firms engaged in a bidding war for his unique talents, but he politely declined all offers. His practice was built around just one client, Carlo Gambino, who also spoke for the Mafia commission.

The infamous bank robber Willie Sutton, when asked by a Judge why he robbed banks replied, "You schmuck—that's where the money is!" It turns out that Willie was a piker. On a good day you might get ten grand from

a bank and on a bad day face hard time for doing so. The real money—
the real bank—is the U.S. Government that doles out BILLIONS, now
TRILLIONS per year, and if they need more—they print more!

Those funds are disbursed according to the collective will of otherwise
ordinary citizens who rely on money and support to get elected. The most
common ploy is called "pork" and comes in the form of a rider to a bill that
has overwhelming support to begin with. In this way tens of millions of
dollars in fees and projects can be diverted to their patrons, the mob, and,
it all appears legal. Is this a great country or what?

So it was, the day after graduation, a simple brass shingle was attached to
the wrought iron gate in front of a vintage, red brick mansion in the 3000
block of R Street, one of Georgetown's most exclusive neighborhoods. It
simply read: Carlton Anthony, Esq.

If "loose lips sink ships", an apt metaphor for the halls of power in
D.C. would be Pearl Harbor, the day after December 7, 1941. In contrast,
Anthony was the model of discretion, which only added to his reputation
and facilitated dialogue. He hardly ever spoke on the phone. He never
allowed notes to be taken or discussions recorded and nothing was ever
memorialized by hard copy. He didn't need a shredder. All agreements
were sealed by a handshake. The consequences of violation were implicit
and severe.

He assembled an experienced staff of former legislative aides and a few
ex-Congressmen to monitor and scrutinize every piece of legislation that
was introduced in Congress. It was akin to having a permanent seat on the
U.N. Security Council. The other seats would change with the political
winds, but Anthony was a constant.

He avoided the Capitol social scene and had no use for lobbyists. His
name was known to all who wielded real power. His protocol was clear and
succinct. His assistant would place a call, his number would be recognized
and the call would either be taken or returned quickly—even by the Oval
Office. Particularly by the Oval Office. The message never changed, "Mr.
Anthony will be pleased to receive your emissary at his residence at such
and such a time on such and such a date". At the precise time his gate would

swing open and the limos would proceed to the circular drive in the back of the mansion. A butler would escort the guest into Anthony's massive study, where Anthony would be seated behind an antique cherry wood desk. Little or no small talk would take place and the meetings were always brief and to the point. It helped that Anthony had a reputation for being a voice of reason, as well as keeping his own counsel. It was also well accepted that he never asked for something without offering something of value in return.

CHAPTER 12

The Call

Washington D.C.—March 1964

Johnson had been waiting for Anthony's call since the fateful event in November. Patience was not one of LBJ's virtues. In fact, that he possessed any virtues was a sentiment open to doubt. No one believed that Johnson shed any tears at Kennedy's passing, but Anthony, on behalf of the Commission, would be seeking a "statement" from the new President that he, unlike JFK, wouldn't forget from whence he came and who helped him get to the White House.

Pundits could debate for ages what had gone wrong and how Pompeii became a more apt metaphor for Kennedy's administration than Camelot, but the chief culprits were clear: the "old man" and JFK's self-absorbed "Irish Mafia" that held Rasputin like power over him. That Joe Kennedy knew the rules was indisputable, but which Joe Kennedy? The amoral, womanizing ex-bootlegger, or the Honorable Joseph Kennedy, Ambassador to the Court of St. James? The latter may have believed that the rules no longer applied to a President who was the son of an Ambassador.

The very public affront to Frank Sinatra in the Palm Springs affair was a bone-headed P.R. disaster as it was an affront to all Italian-Americans— particularly the Commission who would be responsible for his election. Had Mayor Daley not been Irish Catholic and/or the dead been able to change their votes—Nixon would have been President, as many in the mob would never forgive Kennedy for his incredibly hypocritical slight to their beloved Francis Albert.

The Bay of Pigs fiasco, however, could not be remediated. It not only meant that JFK's Irish Mafia had become an existential threat to the CIA on the cusp of the military-industrial complex's expansion in South East Asia, but it sounded the death knell to any hopes the Mob had of recovering their casinos and millions of dollars they had invested in Havana. More importantly—it destroyed their dream of Havana becoming the international Mecca for gambling and entertainment. It is a dubious achievement to make mortal enemies of both the CIA and the Mafia, but Kennedy's advisors had done so in just three years.

Johnson knew the drill as JFK had designated him to be his emissary in response to two invitations from Anthony. Both involved unusually stern warnings to be conveyed to the President, but in each case, on the limo ride back to the White House, Johnson decided that passing along the messages would only help Kennedy and not doing so might hasten his own ascendancy to the Oval Office.

It puzzled him, at first, that Anthony, regarded by many as "the smartest guy in the room", wouldn't understand that Johnson despised Kennedy. He would later come to realize that Anthony understood the relationship quite well and knew the messages would never be delivered. The messages were for Johnson not Kennedy. Anthony was preparing him for the Presidency.

While waiting for the call, LBJ gave serious thought, as he did to all political decisions, as to who his emissary would be. At first glance, his selection of Carl Albert, Congressman from Oklahoma, appeared a study in stark contrasts. Johnson was a Texan—Albert a Sooner. Johnson was six-four—Albert was a full foot shorter at five-four. Johnson had a well-earned reputation as a bully, while Albert couldn't have been less threatening. It was the one trait that they had in common that made Albert an inspired choice. They both knew how to acquire and wield power. They just did so in dramatically different fashions. As Majority Leader in the House, Albert was the perfect emissary, as the Commission was only concerned about "the Benjamins" and that meant legislation.

Anthony's Office

The call came in mid-March and Johnson immediately dispatched Albert to meet with Anthony. When Albert was ushered into Anthony's office he almost disappeared into the over-stuffed leather chair.

"Mr. Majority Leader, it's an honor to meet you."

"It's my pleasure Mr. Anthony and the President sends his kind regards."

"And mine to him."

Anthony gently pushed a thick binder across the desk. Albert had to struggle to get out of the chair to retrieve it.

"My staff has taken the liberty of preparing a draft of some legislation that we would like to see introduced and passed in this session. We believe that it will also be beneficial to the President's election."

Albert briefly leafed through the document. "Mr. Anthony—your staff's reputation for the quality of their work is well known, but I must caution you that even the most thorough document isn't immune to the committee process."

"Understood. That is why I have highlighted only one article—number ten. That article must survive the committee intact."

Albert raised his eyebrows at the blunt directive. "I'll relay that to the President."

"Please. Now, will you join me for some lemonade in the gazebo?"

"As enticing as that sounds, I think the President will want to give this his immediate attention."

"Perhaps another time. Good afternoon, sir."

"And to you as well Mr. Anthony."

The Oval Office

Upon returning to the White House, Albert was ushered right into the Oval Office. Johnson was seated with his cowboy boots resting on his desk. He motioned for Albert to take a chair—which he did after plopping the binder on the desk. Johnson sat up and glanced at the document—appearing to weigh it.

"Food Stamp Bill? What the hell is a food stamp?"

"I only had time to glance at it on the ride back, but I believe he is proposing to issue food stamps or vouchers to those living in poverty."

"Meaning the colored folks?"

Albert was relieved he hadn't used the N-word. "Primarily, but anyone under a certain income level."

Johnson mused for a bit. "So I'm giving food vouchers to the poor. I like that. Hell yes, I like that. "He then turned pensive, stood up and paced back and forth. "I get what this does for me, but what does that fucking guinea get out of it."

Albert braced for one of LBJ's frequent profane tirades. "You might check out Article Ten. It's very brief."

Johnson read it aloud. "These food stamps will be fully redeemable and transferrable."

Here it came. He threw the binder on his desk and was animated. "Those fucking greaseballs are brilliant! I'll give 'em that. You give a colored junkie a hundred bucks and what's he gonna do with it?"

Albert knew that was a rhetorical question.

"I'll tell you what he's gonna do. He's gonna sell it to the fucking Dagos for fifty bucks and then he's gonna buy fifty bucks worth of heroin from them. It's a win-win for the Dagos. They redeem the stamps for face value and sell them the drugs."

The President sat down again and banged his fist on the desk—still smiling.

"With all due respect, Mr. President—isn't that like throwing gasoline on the fire."

Johnson looked incredulous. "No—it isn't like throwing gasoline on the fire. It IS throwing gasoline on the fire."

"What happens when they realize what we've done to them?"

"Number one—they haven't yet. Number two—we give 'em more gasoline."

"So, you want me to take the bill to the House?"

Now Johnson was incredulous. "Have you been paying attention? Of course I want you to take it to the fucking House and get it passed, God dammit! And don't let them fuck with Article Ten. You hear me?"

"Loud and clear."

Carlton Anthony

It was a picture postcard day. Mid- 70s and a very light breeze. The trees were in blossom and the tulips were in bloom. After Albert left, Anthony changed into casual clothes and told his assistant that he would be having lunch in the gazebo.

"Any calls?"

"Only the Cardinal. He hopes he can count on you for ten thousand for his special appeal."

"Send him twenty-five with my regards. Oh—and find out where Judge Francis Xavier McMahon will be tomorrow."

He had just finished lunch with his beloved Golden Retriever Caesar at his side. His assistant rang him. "Judge McMahon is at Greenbrier for the ABA conference and will be there for the next two days."

"Perfect. Have Albert pack my clubs and tell the Judge to meet me on the first tee of the Old White Course at 8 A.M." Knowing that his requests were rarely declined. "If Jimmy is in the pro shop tell him that Mr. Smith needs a twosome at eight. Oh—and see if we have a bottle of Pappy Van Winkle for Jimmy."

"Anything else?"

"Just one—did we get the hammock fixed?"

"It's good to five hundred pounds now."

"Perfect. Tell Albert that if I fall asleep not to wake me, but cover me with a light shawl." He should have said us, as Caesar would be joining him.

"I'll have the jet ready in the morning and arrange for breakfast on the plane."

"Thanks."

Albert had been with Carlton since birth in one capacity or another. The master and his best friend were sawing logs by the time Albert arrived with the shawl. Caesar was probably dreaming about the French Poodle next door. Carlton was pleased that part one of his complex plan was in play and was likely thinking about the favors he would need from Judge McMahon Albert sat down and took in the scene. There rested a man with the power of life and death at his disposal, but Albert saw what he wanted to see—a boy nestled with his dog.

CHAPTER 13

Quid Pro Quo

Greenbrier Resort

White Sulphur Springs, West Virginia, March 1964

Honorable Francis Xavier McMahon II was a Justice for the Seventh District US Court of Appeals, which was second only to the Supreme Court in the US Judiciary system. In fact, Judge McMahon was rumored to be on a short list, of only two, with Honorable Thaddeus Wagner of the D.C. District for the next vacancy on the High Court.

Aware of each other's reputation, McMahon and Anthony met for the first time at the Old White TPC course at the Greenbrier precisely at 8 A.M. as planned. Anthony was well known at the resort as Mr. Smith. The starter had blocked out the start times until 9 A.M., which gave the twosome maximum privacy.

"Your Honor it is a pleasure to meet you."

"Likewise Mr. Anthony. May I suggest that for today its Frank and Carlton?"

"Works for me."

"Have you played this course before?"

"A few times a year. I play to a five handicap here. By the way, they know me as Mr. Smith."

"I caught that."

"Nothing nefarious, it's just that I generally have a high-profile guest and prefer not to have my name in print."

McMahon laughed. "You succeed so well that I was beginning to wonder if there was a Carlton Anthony."

"Ego is a luxury that I cannot afford."

"Back to important things—I played this course yesterday and shot an eighty-eight which is great for me."

"How about I give you six strokes a side?"

"Sounds fair. What are the stakes?"

"Things."

"Things?"

"Just things. Hopefully this won't be the last game we play together."

"How do you want to handle our discussion?"

"The start times are blocked out until nine, so we have no pressure. Let's enjoy the front nine and we can grab a snack and chat at the turn."

"You want to lead off?"

"Your Honor, it's your Honor."

They both laughed.

At the turn they each grabbed a donut and coffee. McMahon broke the ice. "So, Carlton—what can I do for you?"

"Frank, we prefer to think in terms of us, not me."

"Fair enough."

"You're aware of the war that's going on with the street gangs over the drug trade in Gary?"

"Acutely. Bad business."

"Bad business indeed—for several reasons."

"Do you—do we have a solution?"

"It's a bit complex, but I've put the first piece of the puzzle in place. What we need now is some help with the DOJ."

McMahon hesitated. "Any such help now would be very expensive for me, but now is a perfect time to tell you that I have decided to withdraw my name from consideration for a high court vacancy."

"You haven't even heard what we need."

"It has absolutely nothing to do with this matter. You see, I had an epiphany yesterday—right here on the front nine. I couldn't help but notice the buds flowering on the trees. Trees that were dormant were given another chance of life. I love what I'm doing and it has afforded me more time to be with my wife and family, from whom I was pretty much AWOL while I was climbing the layer cake and they were growing up. I missed that and can't get it back, but we've now been blessed with grandchildren and I've been given another chance of life and I'm not going to blow it this time—even for a Supreme Court seat,"

"Wow. Does anyone else know this?"

"I haven't even told my wife yet. Not sure if she can handle the news."

They laughed. "To be totally forthright, I didn't relish the thought of putting my family through the scrutiny. The stakes couldn't be higher politically as my record is bi-partisan, while Wagner is an avowed liberal."

"But you were confirmed unanimously by the Senate."

"That was then and now is now. I was a registered Democrat and appointed by Eisenhower because of my record which was devoid of partisanship. I was a safe pick for both sides."

"You're a brilliant jurist."

"Thank you, but so is Wagner and I doubt if his father was nicknamed "The Hammer" because of his choice of persuasive tools or if he acquired a million dollar estate on a government salary. Carlton—I've made some very good decisions in life and a few that I regret, but that's life and life has been very good to me. Now—what do we need at DOJ?"

"I have two asks, neither of which should be a reach—particularly when you let Wagner know you're withdrawing."

"Which will be this afternoon."

"He's here?"

"I speak tonight and he has the keynote address tomorrow night."

"Anything to be read into that?"

"Probably. The D.C. District carries a little more weight than the Seventh—at least in some minds."

"Number one is this: there is a rumor that the DOJ is planning to send an army of feds to Gary to address the violence and corruption."

"If they send a bunch of white agents to Gary right now—it will go up in flames and I don't live that far away."

"There's that, but we—emphasis on we—don't want an army of feds snooping around."

"You have a solution?"

"They can't just abandon the plan, but we are requesting they send a single agent to act as liaison with the local authorities—rendering help as requested or needed. In the meantime, we will bring the war to an end and hand deliver the feds some minor corruption victories."

"That sounds doable to me and the alternative would be a disaster. What's number two?"

"It's associated with the minor corruption. You're familiar with the Vecchios?"

"That's a rhetorical question. I had some interaction with the uncle before I was appointed to the Appellate Court where, thank God, I don't have to deal with him. As for Richie, I've bought all my autos from him for as long as I can remember. I think if he had the option, he would gladly walk away from this business."

"And if a pig had wings…. He doesn't have an option. Here's the rub—the uncle has to go and we have fed the DOJ with enough information to bring tax evasion charges against him which will be akin to a death sentence at his age. In the meantime, Richie is going to plead to a minor charge so that the uncle doesn't suspect his involvement and we need a place where he will be safe and warm while this plays out."

McMahon smiled. "Do you have a place in mind?"

"I've heard that there is a special place for special friends somewhere in Florida."

"We call it Club Fed. Ironically, a fellow associate of mine—and Ted Wagner, is there as we speak."

"What does it take to get Richie and four of his men an invitation?"

"It's all done on trust and goodwill. There is no application process. Someone with serious stroke has to make the request."

"Did you make the request for your associate?"

"No—I just seconded it. The request was made by Ted Wagner."

"So—if you asked Ted if he would reciprocate?"

"He would have to say yes—even without my withdrawal."

"Let me make sure that I understand. Are you telling me that each request should be a fait accompli?"

"I'll see Ted this afternoon—they like to do the high tea. After I give him my news—there is no way he will say no. Let me ask you a question. Has Richie signed on to this?"

"Like I said, no isn't an option. How are you getting home?"

"We're part of a bar association charter flight out of Chicago that leaves the day after tomorrow, but now that I have made my decision I'm going to look into leaving tomorrow. My grandson Frankie the fourth has his first t-ball game on Sunday afternoon."

"How about I give you a lift? My Gulfstream is parked here. I was planning on leaving after golf, but I wouldn't mind getting a horse ride in and spending the night. We could leave right after breakfast."

"That would be great and my wife has always wanted to fly on a private plane."

"I can arrange for Richie to meet the plane. After you make the introduction, you can head home and I will take it from there. Now let's grab some lunch."

Later that Afternoon

As expected, Judge McMahon was able to "run into" Judge Wagner on his way to tea.

"Ted, you're just the man I wanted to see."

"Hello, Frank. I'm looking forward to your speech tonight."

"Ted, I have some news that I want to share with you first. Can you give me a few minutes?"

"I'm meeting my wife for tea, but I'm a little early. How about we go out on the veranda?"

They chose a couple of chairs out of anyone's earshot. McMahon went first. "Ted, I have been honored and flattered to be mentioned on the so-called short list for the high court with you, but after much deliberation with my wife—we've decided that the timing isn't right for me and tonight I plan to announce that I am formally withdrawing my name from consideration."

Wagner took a deep breath and exhaled as he tried to suppress his elation at the news. The short list was now only one—Ted Wagner. "Frank—I—I don't know what to say. Are you sure you are making the right decision?"

"Absolutely certain."

"Frank—I don't know how to say this, but I hope there was no concern on your part of any non-collegial campaign on my part."

"My motivation is purely personal. I truly enjoy what I—what we are doing and, as you know, the Appeals Court provides us with free time that I have never had before. Therein lies the rub—I was married to the law and missed countless birthdays, ball games and proms while my children were growing up. We've now been blessed with grandchildren and I feel like I've been given a second chance and one that I intend to embrace. My family was always there for me and now it's my turn to be there for them."

"Frank—is there anything that I can do for you?"

"Ted—I do have two small matters that you can help me with so that I can clear my deck."

"Can you give me the Cliffs notes versions?"

"It'll just take a sec. The first has to do with a rumor the DOJ has some half-baked plan to send an army of agents to Gary—part of my district—to deal with the drug war violence and corruption. Ted—if they send a bunch of white agents into Gary at this sensitive time the city will go up in flames and maybe trigger a national reaction. It's the wrong idea at the wrong time."

"Even I get that. What's your proposal?"

"Send one agent to liaise with the city and DOJ and prepare an informed assessment of the situation. The city officials claim they have a plan that needs time to implement and massive intervention at this time will be counter-productive."

"Together, we can make that happen. What else?"

Frank laughed, "The other one is a bit more complex, but simply requires you to second my request to get a group of five into Club Fed."

"Didn't you second my request for Judge Jenkins?"

"I did indeed."

"Then you needn't ask, assuming they can take five."

"Thanks, Ted. Oh—by the way—now that we've made our decision, we'll be departing tomorrow after breakfast. I regret that we'll miss your speech. I know you'll make a splendid justice. Let me know if I can help in any way."

"Thanks, Frank. That means a lot to me."

CHAPTER 14

Give Me Your Tired, Your Poor

Michigan City, Indiana—March 1964

Richie Vecchio had received the summons from Gambino and was waiting by the tarmac as Anthony's Gulfstream taxied to a halt. Judge McMahon and wife exited first and exchanged greetings with Richie. The Judge then introduced Richie to Carlton before begging their leave to attend a t-ball game.

Carlton invited Richie onto the plane informing him that, as it was his home much of the time, it too was swept electronically daily. They were free to speak. Richie sat down in one of the plush leather seats and turned to Anthony. "Mr. Anthony, what can I do for you?"

"Richie, this is a good place to begin. This isn't about me—or you. It's about the family that you are part of—a family that still depends on you. That family is now beset with several conflicts and it is my job—with your help and the help of others—to try to resolve those conflicts."

"Mr. Anthony, you may not be aware that I have little interaction with my uncle and am quite happy with my very successful dealership."

"Richie, let's take a moment for a little history lesson. A romantic poet may pretend to be Lady Liberty and proclaim, "Give me your tired, your poor etc." but, in reality, that didn't include the tired and poor Italians or Irish or Jews and the Blacks didn't come here by choice. Your uncle is a problem, but your uncle and your father had to fight—literally fight—for every scrap they got. You wouldn't have that successful dealership or your comfortable life if they hadn't come to Gary and carved out this territory.

It wasn't just for them, or you, it was for the families of the men they brought with them and those families have grown like yours has and they still depend on Gary for their livelihoods. "

"Fair enough, but what can I do when my uncle doesn't even acknowledge me? And, with all due respect, with the territory under siege and the hit to its revenues from the war with the Black gangs—is it worth saving?"

"Richie—your uncle and the war with the street gangs is for me to deal with and I have a plan. You have a role to play in that plan."

"Which is?"

"I neither choose to, nor need to get too specific—so I'll give you the need to know version. While we're fighting the gangs on one side, the Detroit mob, now emboldened with their Teamster connection, has made no secret of their desire to take over Gary. Under the terms of Our Thing—they can't do that as long as a Vecchio is in charge, otherwise your uncle would have—um retired—long ago. The feds are building a tax evasion case against him that will put him away for his natural life, but that won't be ready for a couple of years. At that time you will step up and take control. In the meantime, your uncle can't suspect any of this. You must be above suspicion and safe and warm for the next eighteen months or so."

"Am I not safe and warm enough where I am?"

"Not even close and here's another piece of information you need to process. I told you the feds are coming after your uncle for tax evasion. Until yesterday, they were planning on sending an army of agents and going after the entire operation—including you."

"What happened yesterday?"

"Your good friend the Judge has intervened and instead of an army of agents—they'll be sending only one and his job will be to observe and advise."

"My only obvious connection—other than my name—is the no-bid contract I have with the city."

"If only they played that fair, but they don't."

"I'm waiting."

"We have a plan that kills two birds with one stone, so to speak—and hear me out. This is the plan, not a suggestion. We need to give the feds something to back up our assertion that the city has been doing its own investigation. You and a few associates are going to plead to a minor charge to do with that city contract. You're going to have to do some time."

Richie jumped up and started pacing.

"Richie—sit down until I finish. You're gonna like this."

"I'm going to like going to prison? You don't know me very well."

"Would we send you to prison? One of the best kept government secrets—and it must stay that way—is that the feds have a facility in Florida attached to a military base, which is designated for the fortunate few who have friends in very high places. It's where judges, governors, congressmen etc. serve their time. The feds call it Club Fed. If it was a resort it would have at least three stars. You'll have separate housing. There is a par three golf course, tennis courts, a running track, lap pool and library. You can bring in your own food and wine. You can have visitors until midnight. The only rule is that you can't leave. Now—I've only heard of it, but another reason for me flying here is that you and I are going to fly down and check it out. By the way—that's another thing you have to thank the Judge about."

"So—if I go down, so to speak, and my uncle is never mentioned—he will have no reason to suspect any ulterior motive?"

"Bingo."

"So—we work on our tans and chill out for—did you say eighteen months—while the feds prepare their case?"

"You have two important jobs you have to accomplish during that time. The first is—the Commission is giving every family, because this affects us all, two years to make an accommodation with the Black gangs—and that means some sort of partnership. You have to select one of the gangs for the deal and it will be up to them to deal with any others. We will continue to supply the product, but they will control the distribution."

"That's a huge hit we're taking."

"Number one—we have no choice. Number two, you will soon learn how we will more than make up for that loss. We are going to emulate the

Bumpy Johnson model, as he may have started this all. We need to find a Black guy to be our liaison with the street gang and appear to all to be the face of the business—our own Bumpy Johnson. It will appear that we have vacated the business."

"I wish we had long ago."

"Me too, but wish in one hand and shit in the other and see which fills up the fastest."

"When do we check the place out?"

"You have any plans for the rest of the day or tomorrow?"

"None that can't be changed."

"Do you play golf?"

"As much as possible."

"Grab your clubs and a change of clothes and meet me back here asap. I'll get us a tee time at Sea Island. We'll spend the night there and visit Club Fed in the morning. I'll have you back here tomorrow afternoon."

"My clubs are in my trunk with my golf clothes."

Anthony approached the cockpit. "Fuel up and head for Sea Island."

CHAPTER 15

The Swamp

Tommy—Washington, D.C., Early 1965

After graduation in 1961, I applied to both the FBI and the FBN, the Federal Bureau of Narcotics that would eventually morph into the DEA. I was accepted by both, but opted for the FBN as I was attracted to the more clearly defined mission. I began as a Grade Five—comparable to a grunt in the armed services, but was fortunate enough to be part of some very successful operations early on and caught the attention of my superiors—notably Jonathan "Butch" McCarthy with whom I shared much in common.

Looking back on that time, it was apparent that Butch's rise through the ranks to become Deputy Director had taken a toll on him. He seemed to have aged more and been drinking more than even I was—and I was the guy in the field.

We bonded even more as time passed and I was personally selected to run—even at my age and experience level—a major operation that in FBN speak was "off the books". Again, in retrospect, I was surprised that Butch's superiors didn't appear to be elated by the success of the mission. Not only was Butch passed over for the new Directorship in 1965 in favor of a junior bureaucrat, but I sensed that I was being given the silent treatment by the Ivy Leaguers whose motto was "See no evil, do no evil, hear no evil—and advance".

It was late spring 1965 when I answered the phone and it was Butch on the other line.

"Tommy, this is Butch McCarthy are you alone?"

"Hey, Mr. McCarthy. Yeah, I'm just catching up on some paperwork."

"Tommy—fuck the mister business, Butch will do. Do you have any plans for tonight?"

"Nothing that can't be changed. What's up?"

"Good. You remember where we had dinner the last time the Bears were in town?"

"Yeah, the ...."

"Don't say it. You remember, right?"

"Sure."

"Okay—meet me there tonight at seven. No—let's make it eight. Tell Mel, the maître d', that you're meeting me. I'll reserve one of the private rooms."

"Copy that."

"Good. See you then."

We had a sort of tradition of having steaks at Duke Ziebert's on 17th and L after a ball game when the Bears were in town. Any excuse to go there worked for me.

To say that my curiosity was piqued doesn't do it justice, but you hang around Washington long enough and nothing surprises you. Regardless, I went through my common diversionary tactics to see if I was being tailed and was as certain as can be that I wasn't.

When I arrived at the restaurant and was ushered into a private room in the back, the man waiting for me—the Deputy Director of the FBN—was just a shell of the movie star vision of a government agent I had been befriended by a few years before. His glass was empty and it was clear that had not been his first drink.

He motioned for me to sit down—barely looking up.

"Angelo, have them send in two double Bourbons—the good stuff. Wait, have them send in the bottle and some ice."

I sat down and started to talk but he waved me off.

"Wait until we have a drink. We've got a lot to talk about."

It was a bit uncomfortable—the silence—and I had a strange urge to tell him to stand up so I could give him a hug. His pain was that was obvious.

The booze was served and Butch poured the drinks. We clinked glasses without a toast. After savoring the whiskey he broke the silence.

"Tommy, how much do you know about me—about my life?"

What a curious question I thought, but I just shrugged and said, "I know you have ties to Chicago, you're a Bears fan and the Deputy Director of the Bureau—and that you have been a great mentor to me."

He suppressed a smile—a sad smile.

"Tommy, from the first moment we met—I saw myself—a young myself in you. I came from similar stock—the salt of the earth and I remember having the same red, white and blue idealism. The world was black and white. Right was right and wrong was wrong and the Lone Ranger always won in the end. You know that's bullshit now—right?"

I had no idea where this was going, but remembered my training and took a drink before I replied so that I could collect my thoughts.

"Let's just say that the more I'm around Washington, the more gray and less black and white I see."

He laughed and clinked my glass. "Diplomatically spoken. Well done, but tonight I have to speak frankly with you—as there are things I need to say and have no one else I can trust. Can I trust you, Tommy?"

"You have my word and when …."

He cut me off. "That's good enough for me."

He replenished our drinks and with a button on the wall paged our waiter.

After we had ordered and our waiter departed, he spoke again.

"Tommy, I will be sixty next month and will be soon forced out of the bureau—something that being passed over for promotion failed to do. This is it for me, but I have been tasked with one more project and it can involve you. First of all—do you know how or why I came to the FBN?"

Again, making a practice of taking a drink before replying, I sort of shrugged and said, "I think I heard that you were a decorated FBI agent.

I believe 'Golden Boy' was the phrase someone used—and you decided to transfer to the FBN, which, I heard, surprised a lot of people."

He laughed—again a sad laugh. I'm not certain there wasn't a tear in his eye. "Oh, I was a Golden Boy all right. I was married to the Bureau and soaring through the ranks because I made the Bureau my life. Problem was, I had another life, a wife—a beautiful wife and a very handsome son."

That's when he stood and turned around so that I couldn't see his very real tears, but his heaving shoulders gave them away. I stood, but was paralyzed—not knowing how to react, when the waiter brought our steaks and a bottle of Chateau Margaux, compliments of the owner.

After composing himself he said, "Let's have something to eat. This may be a long night and, Tommy, thanks for coming."

When we had finished our steaks with only very casual talk of the Bears and, now, St. Louis Cardinal Football team—traitors—he resumed the conversation. "Tommy, I believed in all of the bullshit about honor, duty and country"

I raised my eyebrows, but he said, "Let me finish. I'm going to tell you some things I've never told anyone else. I thought a father's job was to set a good example for his son. Work hard, sacrifice and pay taxes so that you could afford a nice home and private schools. Set an example for him to emulate—a template. My father never played catch with me—never took me fishing or asked how I was doing. I thought that was the way things were. Here I was a skilled analyst, a super star investigator of other's lives, but I was totally oblivious to what was happening with my own son!" He had to pause.

"Even a fucking blind man could have seen that there was something wrong looking at pictures of a smiling, clean cut Little League baseball player and then the same kid as a teen ager with long hair, trench coat, jack boots and a tattoo. How the fuck did that go unnoticed? It didn't happen overnight, but my wife said, 'It's just a phase that kids go through—he'll be okay'. Deep down I knew it wasn't okay, but believing otherwise would have created a conflict with my career—my 'Golden Boy' career."

That may have been one of the best steaks I've ever had and was definitely the best bottle of wine I'd ever had, but their memory faded quickly as I braced myself for an ending to a story that would be no surprise.

"Tommy, I swear to God that I continuously planned how my son and I were someday going to do this or that. It was just a matter of having the time. Then the call came ...."

By now tears were running down his cheeks—mine too, as I knew what was coming and pretending otherwise was futile.

"Then the call came. They found his body in a flop house in the projects. He had overdosed on some bad heroin which, apparently, he had been addicted to for some time. My wife blamed me and she was right. After a few months of almost total silence—she filed for divorce. She was lucky in a way. She escaped from the villain, but I couldn't."

He stood and walked aimlessly for a few minutes, but then seemed to compose himself a bit.

"The Bureau, the FBI, was very supportive—even gave me time off, but they were part of the problem not the cure. It was then that I started to do a little research into the FBN and beguiled myself into believing that my mission in life was to try to prevent others from experiencing the heartache that would haunt me forever. I notified my superior of my desire to transfer and he asked me to hold that thought until I had spoken with others in the bureau hierarchy. They took me to dinner and told me that 'no doors were closed to me' and that I was on the short list for higher promotion, however, my mind was made up and my only hope of penance was to make a difference in the war on drugs."

I tried to think of something to say to assuage his pain and could only fumble the words, "That seems like a noble thing you did."

He looked at me with proper disdain for the platitude. Before I could try to do better, he held up his hands. "I had to get that off of my chest as it is germane to what we need to talk about."

I didn't reply as I didn't have one.

"Tommy—I have been tasked with one final project. At first glance it seems like it is one that an ambitious agent would want to avoid, because it is way off the radar screen and it is clear that the bureau is going to obstruct it if possible, rather than support it. If you're thinking about your career and advancement—this isn't for you."

Wild horses couldn't have kept me from hearing more.

"Butch, you saw my tears when you told your story and I didn't try to hide them—if I could. My relationship with my father was similar, but I think that had something to do with the war and the effect it had on everyone. I'm married and we want to have children—as many as possible—so I needed to hear your story. I just wish you didn't have to pay the price you did, but admire that you are honoring your son's memory by trying to save others."

He laughed, "Trying is the key phrase. I always believed I was a smart guy. I got good grades in school and so forth, but I was blind. I believed what I was told and it was all bullshit. I failed to recognize what was happening to my son and then I took comfort in transferring to a bureaucracy whose sole mission is self-preservation and politics."

He was on a roll and I needed to make sure it wasn't a rant.

"Are you telling me that the FBN's mission isn't to fight the drug epidemic? We're all friends aren't we?"

He laughed, "If I give you one piece of advice that you take to the bank it's this: if you want a friend in Washington—get a dog!"

"Tommy, the powers that be think I am a naïve motherfucker and they are right. Actually—they are wrong. I was a naïve motherfucker. I'm just a real slow learner. I had an opportunity to advance to Director each of the three times I was passed over for promotion, but each time I refused to play ball—to play politics and let the bad guys go for the sake of some greater good—which generally meant campaign contributions."

He laughed again. "Can you imagine how stupid they thought I was that I didn't get it the second or third time?"

I was puzzled. "Then what is so different with this last project that is low priority?"

He smashed his fist on the table, knocking over the wine glasses—which fortunately, were empty—and leaned forward.

"That's the point. It isn't low priority. In fact it's very high profile. The agency was going to make Gary, Indiana a template for their war on drugs. They were planning on sending an army of agents and requesting marshal law if needed."

"Whew—was that a good idea at this time?"

"I actually argued against it as being excessive, but supported the idea that something needed to be done. Then, all of a sudden and after almost a year of planning, the powers that be did a 180 and declared it a low priority mission to be handled by one—by a single agent—who would act in an undefined role with local authorities.

"They have given it to me because they're convinced I'm naïve and because they know—they think they know—that no one agent can make a difference. I'm calling in all of my markers and I know what is going on in this case. I'm only lacking an agent—the only agent they will provide me with. I need someone who will do the right thing regardless of how powerful or well-connected the bad guys are and, in this case, everybody is on the take."

"Wow. If you are naïve, maybe it's something to do with our backgrounds as I am as guilty as you. Having said that, in a few short years I've seen a lot of things that don't add up and too many Ivy League pukes who act like their asses are in a tub of butter. What might be different about us is that I have never dreamed about promotion or running the bureau someday. Who knows—maybe that doesn't speak highly of me. My dad became a foreman in the steel mill and never spent a second wishing for more. I've always felt lucky to be an agent and I swear I never dreamed of more."

He leaned forward. "Tommy—do you want to make a difference? Do you want to save lives?"

"What part of what I just said didn't you hear?"

"Then you're in?"

It was my turn to laugh. "All I need are some minor details about what I'm signing on to?"

We both laughed.

"Here's it in a nutshell. If you're in—we'll do a full briefing after we've had a good night sleep, but everything will be off-campus and for our eyes and ears only. I assume you're familiar with Gary?"

"Butch—don't tell me you don't know that's where my father works."

"Sorry, but this has little to do with the mills. Gary has a severe drug problem. It's not just the hundreds—if not thousands—who have died drug related deaths. They don't seem to count as mostly are poor Blacks, but now there is a war for control of the narcotics distribution. The mafia, a branch affiliated with the Gambino family, has had a vice grip on all rackets, including drugs, since the steel workers became unionized. Some of the Chicago street gangs have decided to challenge their control over drugs and the more rational voice of the mob passed away a couple of years ago. The smart thing would be for the mob to give up the drug trade, but the current Don is old school. Here's the rub, since Gary was off the radar screen and so much cash was being generated—eventually everybody had their hands out and I mean everybody—the police, the city officials, the politicians and the judges."

"Wow, I had no idea."

"No one did, as even the press was controlled, but some young Black kid got a scholarship to study journalism at NYU and wrote a series of articles that attracted national attention. The politicians and judges have used their influence to stymie a full-blown intervention, but they know that they have to appear to be doing something. Hence, they turned to Mr. Naive to select an agent—a single agent, with limited resources—to investigate the situation. Unbeknownst to them, there are others within the bureau who know what's going on and will help, but they need to keep their heads down."

"I gotta ask. Is this a suicide mission?"

"I wouldn't ask you if I thought it was. In fact, the compromise with the so called hawks was that if anything happened to the agent the original plan would go into effect. So you can actually push the envelope a bit. We've got some pretty good intel that the judges and politicians regret ever getting involved. It won't be pretty. A few might face some time, but those who cooperate will be better off than those who don't and they might be able to keep their off-shore bank accounts and homes in Florida. It will be a domino effect. The key will be finding a mole in the drug trade who is in a control position. That is something that one guy, one special and motivated guy, can do. You focus on him and let us handle the rest."

Neither of us spoke for what seemed like a long time, but was probably only thirty seconds.

"This is what I signed on for. If you've got my back—I'm in."

"It seems like hours ago, but I told you what this means to me."

"Let's do it. One little problem—or big, little problem—neither of us should be driving tonight."

"I have a limo waiting and drivers who will drop our cars off in the morning."

CHAPTER 16

Surf and Turf

Freddy—Club Fed, Early 1965

As the New Year, 1965, dawned, I was pretty much settled into my routine. I'd been on a little bit of a health kick—watching my diet and jogging daily on the running track. When I arrived I tipped the scales at almost 250, but over four years had lost almost forty pounds and never felt better. I spent most of my time in the library either as the librarian or working toward an associate degree with the local community college's "home-study" program.

I successfully completed the program in a little over three years and for the past six months had been mailing out my resume to a list provided by the college. I was excited when some responded with application forms, but that excitement quickly waned when I ran into the double-whammy of "Race?" and "Have you ever been charged with a felony or misdemeanor?" I was now an educated, Black felon and there didn't appear to be great demand for that category at this time.

I'd be lying if I didn't say that my spirits hadn't been dampened, but it forced me into confronting the world as it was—not as I, and many others, dreamed that it would or should be. On the plus side, four years had seemed to fly by and I had only one left to serve. The irony was that many of the comforts that I enjoyed at Club Fed weren't going to be readily available on the outside—when I was "free". In short—I had no idea what I was going to do when I was released. My father was now an influential member of the party—of which there was only one, but Chicago wasn't a viable option as long as Captain Murphy was afflicted with "Irish Alzheimer's" where you forget everything except your grudges.

Like almost everyone else, I had kept pretty much to myself by choice and observed that the social relationships that did exist had mostly to do with shared interests such as golf, tennis or gin rummy. It was an unwritten rule that you didn't inquire as to someone's past and there was no guarantee that they were who they appeared to be. A case in point was "David" who supervised the mail service and all deliveries and whose facility shared a wing with the library. Even with the close proximity, our relationship developed very gradually—in fact, took all of three years. If I had a mentor it was "David" who may have been from Louisiana or Mississippi or Boston for that matter. It was clear that he was educated and, in fact, urbane in his unique manner. Perhaps what I admired most about him was his ability to "see no evil, hear no evil and speak no evil" which is harder than it seems. I had a naturally inquisitive nature, but learned from David's tales, real or imagined, that curiosity could kill more than cats. I believed him.

Other than David, my interaction with fellow "club" members was generally limited to casual conversations about literature during visits to the library. In all other instances, benign neglect was a safe policy. David re-emphasized the wisdom of such with the arrival of five Italians a couple of months ago. It wasn't hard to avoid them—at first—as they had their own facilities on the opposite side of the property and didn't appear to be literary buffs. Thus, I took little note when two of them just happened to appear in the bleachers near the running track while I was doing my daily laps. That it happened once, twice or a few times could be a coincidence, but it was now a daily routine and now a third person had joined them and he was clearly the boss. When I confided as much in David he doubled-down on his philosophy. In fact, he almost doubled over laughing at my implication that they had an "unusual" interest in me.

"Freddy, as you may be aware, visitors are allowed until midnight and even that is not strictly enforced. It is a rare night that the Italians don't entertain the finest—shall we say, 'ladies', the local madam has to offer."

I was relieved to hear that, but even more puzzled as to their interest in me. I was soon to find out first hand. David handed me an envelope that had been dropped off while I was at lunch. It was addressed simply to Freddy. It read: "Please join us for cocktails and dinner tonight at Six P.M. at our residence. Casual attire." It was signed, "Richie"

When I showed it to David he said, "Lucky you!"

"Lucky me—why?"

"Because you're having surf and turf and the lobster was flown in this morning from Maine. Not to mention a case of expensive wine."

"What's surf and turf?"

He laughed, "Only prime filet mignon with lobster. I wish I could join you."

"But—why me?"

"You'll find out tonight—and guess who also got a delivery of steak, lobster and wine today?"

I shrugged.

"The warden. Some coincidence—ey?"

That Evening

Casual attire was no problem for me as that is the only attire I had, but when I arrived everyone else were in sport coats and slacks. The host, Richie, greeted me wearing a madras sport coat, which was all the rage, white shirt and dark slacks.

"Freddy, welcome. I'm Richie Vecchio and I'm glad you could join us. We have a real feast planned. Let's grab a cocktail and get this party started. I'm having a vodka martini—what's your pleasure?"

"I'm not much of a drinker—what do you suggest?"

"How about a mimosa—champagne and orange juice?"

"Sounds ok, but I have a question for you."

"Freddy, we have all evening to talk and lots to talk about. Let's relax first and have a drink and some appetizers."

Richie had all of the social graces and charm out the wazoo. After the mimosa—which was great—I started to relax and go with the flow.

If I live to be a hundred—I may never experience a feast like that one. The surf and turf was incredible—my first time having either filet mignon or lobster and the pairing (as my hosts would say) fuggetaboutit! After we finished our dessert of tiramisu, I was toast, but Richie suggested we move to some lawn chairs where we could have cigars and port and speak in private. It was then that alarms went off in my head. How naïve was I to allow myself to be wined and dined and forget why I was there in the first place? I tried to shake the cobwebs loose, but the silk had morphed into cement—wasn't gonna happen. I realized that I was a babe in the woods compared to my host who had plied me with drink, better said—played me, like a violin.

We settled into our chairs and enjoyed a bit of our cigars and port—both incredible, like everything else, before Richie broke the ice. "Now Freddy, it's time to talk. Or should I say, 'Fat Freddy'?"

I couldn't have been caught more off guard. I tried to compose myself—as best I could—before responding, but Richie must have read my mind or body language and pre-empted me. "You're wondering how we found out? Truth is—it wasn't that difficult with a little deductive reasoning. For a Black man to get into this facility—and I'm certain you are the first—you would have to have friends in very—let me stress that—very high places. So I started with the premise that you had to come from a place of power and that winnows things down to New York and Chicago, pretty much, and you don't have a New York accent.

"So we asked our friends in Chicago if any Black men had been convicted of a high profile crime in the last few years and then disappeared into the justice system and, maybe, with the name Freddy? They replied that there was a Freddy whose father was well respected in the local party and who was convicted on some trumped up charges relating to the shooting of a policeman. Apparently the father played a big role in getting Kennedy elected—the friends in high places—and no one was sure where Freddy was doing his time. There was one problem, though. That Freddy was named Fat Freddy.

"We were trying to reconcile things while taking a stroll one day and happened to see you doing road work on the running track. If Fat Freddy had been doing serious running for the past four years—he would be the picture of health, as you are. Fat Freddy would be only a memory."

"May, I ask. How many people know?"

Richie smiled, "Only us. You see, as you will find out, we have a vested interest in your survival. And, by the way, our friends in Chicago spoke very highly of Fat Freddy. It seems that they had looked after him while he was recuperating from his arrest."

"You know, Richie, before we go any farther—it might be best if we spoke tomorrow as I'm a little muzzy headed from the wine."

"You'll be fine. There is a saying, 'In vino veritas' ".

I replied, "In wine there is truth."

Richie leaned over to clink our port glasses. "Good for you, but I'm not surprised. It's obvious that you are intelligent. There's another reason, and a good one, that I wanted to spend some time with you before I brought up business. I'm about to make a proposal to you. A proposal that would make you a partner of sorts and that's not something we take lightly. We have to respect and enjoy the company of our partners and you have checked all of the boxes so far."

I glanced around, "Won't I stand out a bit?"

Richie laughed and we clinked again. "Let me cut to the chase and you'll understand why our partner must be Black. Some of the things we'll talk about—I'm not proud of, but I didn't make the rules and I am powerless to change them. Capiche? That means...."

I cut him off, "I know what it means. Capiche."

"For many years the mob has been supplying drugs to the inner cities."

"You mean to the colored folks."

"Touche, but there are poor white users as well. To make a long story short—there is a relatively new phenomenon of well-organized Black street gangs in Chicago and Detroit who don't like the idea of Black users and white dealers. I get it and stopping them from eventually taking over the business is like trying to stop the tide from coming to the shore. It's gonna happen. I get it, but the old mob bosses refuse to accept that fact and their only answer to violence is more violence. And that's what we have in Gary. A war between the mob and the street gangs that, if left unchecked, will destroy everything."

"I'm aware of the situation, but don't see where I fit in."

"I'm not going to get into family business, so to speak. Let's just say that the solution is that we have to replace the old bosses with a generation that understands the new realities."

"Replace like—forever?"

"Forever, but not like you think. This is real life, not the movies. There is a better way to do things and we have a genius who has designed a plan. Very simply, we—" he gestured to his men, "—entered into a plea agreement that got us out of Dodge for eighteen months, during which time the Feds will be bringing a tax evasion case against the boss. When he goes away, as he will, I will step in and take his place—a place my father once held."

"Are you saying the feds are part of this plan?"

"Freddy—look around. This isn't Kansas, Toto. You have friends in high places and we have friends in high places, also. Friends who have a vested interest in our survival."

"Again—where do I fit in?"

"During out time of—how do you call this incarceration? During our time here we have two missions to accomplish. We're already engaged in conversations with one of the Chicago street gangs. We're going to turn over the distribution business to them, but we will be the sole supplier. It will be up to them to make peace, or whatever, with the other gangs. The war has to stop. It's brought too much attention and attention is never good. Your role, if you accept it, will be the overseer—the face of our end of the business. "

"So—to anyone on the outside, it will appear that you're out of the business?"

"We are out of a significant portion of it, but we have a model they used in Harlem and we're willing to pay handsomely for you to handle that end of the business for us."

"What do you call handsomely?"

"How does ten percent of the gross sound?"

"Twenty per cent sounds better, but even twenty per cent times zero is zero."

Richie laughed. "In a bad year—you're talking seven million gross. Can we shake on fifteen per cent? That would be over a million a year and it's about to go up in a big way pretty shortly."

"I have just one question. Why are you so confident I will do this—even for that type of money?"

"I'll give you two reasons. Number one: you're a great guy—good looking, well mannered, highly intelligent and now, I understand, with a college degree. Those are all good things, but when you fill out the job applications, you're going to add that you're Black and a convicted felon. We know it's bull shit, but that's reality and it sucks sometimes."

"I'm finding that out. What's number two?"

"That's where you and I have something in common. This plan allows us both to play a role in stopping the bloodshed and, unfortunately, there is a lot of collateral damage when bullets start to fly. A five year old child was killed the other day while jumping rope."

"How about the people who will die of overdoses?"

"Freddy, for thousands of years people have tried to legislate morality and no one has ever figured out how to do so. You and I together can't stop the flow of drugs. What we can do is put an end to this war."

"Where would I live? And, when I leave here I'm flat broke."

"We'll get you situated and money will never be a problem. It's best if you avoid Chicago and it's best for all of us if no one knows who you really are. We need to come up with a new name. Hey, how about Cool Freddy?"

I smiled. "I can work with that." I stuck my hand out. "Did we say fifteen per cent?"

As I said, my mind was far from clear, but what he said about my job prospects was painfully true. Unfair, but true. He was also right in that saving even a few lives, particularly innocent victims, would appeal to me. The analytical side of my brain was in rationalization mode and was wondering if I could make enough money to disappear and realize my dream of sharing my dad's last few years together on a remote island somewhere. A couple of years with this kind of money and it could work.

We shook hands just as the party had entered a new phase with the entrance of the "ladies". What they might have lacked in class and bearing they made up for in other ways—the only ways important under these circumstances. I did a quick head count and there was one for each of us, including me, and one stunning brunette who did exude bearing and class and appeared to be their leader. There was no way to hide the fact that I was mesmerized by her. She could have been anywhere from nineteen to late twenties—an absolute goddess with a remarkable skin tone that I had never encountered.

The goddess approached us and greeted Richie warmly. He turned to me, "Freddy, as guest of honor—you can have your pick. That is, except for Jasmine here—she's not for sale."

Without forethought, I blurted out, "There isn't enough money in the world. As for the others—no offense, but I have a lot to think about and it's best I do that alone."

I thought I detected a slight smile on her face as I turned to take my leave. By the time I reached my room I was kicking myself for turning down some primo booty—particularly after four years of abstinence, but even the best of the rest would have been a letdown after seeing Jasmine.

My sleep was fitful and I thought I heard a slight tapping on my door. When I realized it was real, I got out of bed warily and peered through the peep hole. I couldn't have been more stunned or paralyzed as Jasmine stood outside my door. I had to be dreaming, but when I opened the door—she was very real and very there.

I was dressed only in my shorts. She closed the door and guided me back to bed. When I tried to speak she put her finger to my lips as she disrobed and joined me in my bed. Neither of us spoke a word as we experienced ecstasy beyond my wildest dreams—maybe hers too. If this was a dream—I didn't want to wake up.

Finally, when the "storm" did pass, we laid there silent for a while until she broke the ice. "My name is Jasmine and I'm not for sale. I am what is called an octoroon—one eighth Black and a descendant of an African Queen—a very proud descendant. My grandmother is my guardian and the Madam. I love her dearly, but this is no life for me and I couldn't have been more impressed—maybe even surprised—by the nobility and restraint you displayed tonight. It's funny what motivates people, but—" she laughed, "—that turned me on."

I turned to her, "Had I not seen you—I wouldn't have been either noble or restrained, but after seeing you—I lost my appetite, you could say, for anything less. I guess I've always been a dreamer."

"Well Mr. Dreamer—share your dreams with me and I will do the same with you. My grandma reads Tarot cards and tonight my card was The Lovers. I have to confess that I believe in fate and believe that we were meant to meet."

There would be no more internal debate in re Richie's offer. It was now a done deal as it was the only conceivable way for Jasmine's and my dreams to become a reality as none of our dreams were pedestrian. In fact, I would be saving two more lives—Jasmine's and mine.

CHAPTER 17

You Don't Get a Second Chance to Make a First Impression

Tommy—Gary, Indiana, December 1965

Other than the bureaucratic paperwork, which we expected to be part of the DOJ's effort to obstruct the project—without appearing to do so, my biggest problem was what to do with my wife Mary Kay. She had a great job teaching at Sidwell Friends, an exclusive private school in nearby Bethesda, Maryland.

I was less concerned about the risk to either of us, but since it was doubtful that anyone truly had my back and since the duration of the project was up in the air, we decided that Mary Kay should stay put and I would come home as often as possible.

I departed for Gary on Pearl Harbor Day, hoping that wasn't an omen of things to come. The plan was to get situated and return for the holidays. Now, if there's one thing that I learned in my young life—it's that you only have one chance to make a first impression. A corollary of which is—if you can't avoid a fight—make sure you get in the first punch or kick. I won a couple of fights as a lad by following that advice.

I was pretty confident that the powers that be in Gary, a substantial part of whom must be on the mob's gravy train, were complacent in the fact that I was just one man and a young man at that. On the long drive, I played several scenarios out in my mind as to how I would either dispel that notion or make it a sentiment in very much doubt. In short—I was an Irishman with a bad attitude or is that being redundant?

I followed what directions I had and wound up at the Municipal Building. Months earlier, when the operation was being planned it was communicated that I would need a reserved parking space and an office with a desk and filing cabinet. As I pulled into the parking lot I didn't expect to have either and, sure enough, there were several reserved parking spaces, but none for me.

There was little snow on the ground as I scanned the spaces, most of which were empty. I decided on one that said, "Guest of the Mayor". After all, wasn't that what I was? I no sooner parked than an armed deputy confronted me uprooting the sign.

"Hey, what are you doing?" said as he put his hand near his holstered gun.

I replied, "What the fuck does it look like I'm doing. This is going to be my space and I'm removing the old sign."

I could tell he was nervous as now he had a grip on the handle with the gun still holstered. "Stop what you're doing or I'm going to arrest you for destroying public property."

I turned now to face him and opened my jacket displaying my holstered Glock. It was hard for me to suppress a grin as this was playing out even better than I had hoped. "If you pull that gun, you better be prepared to use it."

His hand was shaking as he removed it from his gun, but he was still trying to cop an attitude. "What, you're going to shoot me over a parking space?"

"There's only one way for you to find out."

"Man—you crazy. You are a crazy motherfucker. Who the fuck are you?"

"I hear that a lot. My name is Tommy O'Brien and I'm with the Federal Bureau of Narcotics and this will be my reserved parking space until further notice."

I flipped open my wallet, displaying my badge.

"Wh-wh-why didn't you say so in the first place?"

"You didn't give me a chance. What's your name?"

"Otis."

"Otis—it's nice to meet you. You can call me Tommy. Now, will you do me a favor and get rid of this old sign?"

I handed him the sign and proceeded into the building. As I entered, I turned to look back and Otis was still standing there with the sign trying to figure out what just happened.

I approached the information desk and announced myself. "Hi, I'm Special Agent Tommy O'Brien. Can you direct me to my new office?"

The name plate said she was Dora and Dora was a bit flustered. "Can you hold on just a minute?"

She got up and dialed a number, stepping back and turning to shield the call. All I could make out was, "I'm telling you he's here. Here. What do I do?"

Composing herself a bit, she reached in a drawer and handed me a key. Clearing her throat she said, "Mr. O'Brien, take the elevator there to the basement level and your office is—is B-4. Here's the key."

One other thing I learned along the way is to never over estimate human nature. It will only lead to disappointment and heartache. As I headed to the elevator to push B, I wasn't so concerned about not having a view. That is actually a blessing in Gary. I was only wondering how bad it would be. B-4 was actually the plumbing closet—a maze of rusted, hissing pipes many of which were patched together with duct tape. In their defense, there was a desk or what might pass for one if all of the legs were the same size—and a rickety chair. No sign of a filing cabinet. This was war and I couldn't be happier.

I surveyed all of the pipes and my attention was drawn to one that said, "Danger. Do Not Touch. Building sprinkler control." Building sprinkler control. Hmmm. I didn't touch it. I wailed on it and if B-4 was any indication—the entire building was experiencing Monsoon season. As I left, I broke off the door handle to frustrate anyone trying to enter and rescue the situation. I took the stairs up to the lobby and smiled at the pandemonium. Dora was drenched as she saw me emerge from the stairway. I walked over and said, "It's a wee bit damp in my office. I think I'll come back tomorrow and hopefully it will have dried out a bit."

Dora was speechless and the lobby was now a zoo with people running around like rats—like wet rats. Very, very wet rats.

Otis was still in the parking lot trying to process what was happening as I casually walked to my car. I backed out and rolled down my window. "Otis—I wouldn't go inside if I was you. I think they're having a fire alarm. The sprinklers seem to work fine for an old building. I think I'm gonna like it here." I waved as I drove away. How's that for a first impression?

That Night

I was not surprised to receive a call from Butch McCarthy around 11 p.m., but had to wait for Butch to stop laughing before we could speak. "Sorry, Tommy—I've never laughed so hard in my life."

"I assume that means you've heard from our new best friends in Gary."

"Heard from them—" still laughing, "—I listened to a fifteen minute rant from the Mayor about how you threatened a deputy and then almost destroyed the Municipal Building and they haven't even met you yet."

"You want to hear my side of it?"

"I don't need to." Laughing. "I just wish I had been there."

"What's the upshot?"

"Well—after his rant, I calmly replied—which was hard to do and suppress laughter at the same time—that I was afraid something like that might happen, as you were young and I apologized profusely. Then I told him that I had serious doubts that Plan B with just one agent was going to work and I would suggest to the DOJ to revert to the original plan. You could have heard a pin drop—and then he said, 'The original plan?'"

I replied, "Yeah, you know—fifteen or twenty agents so that we can do a thorough investigation. I'll pull O'Brien out tomorrow morning. He must have had me on conference call because I could hear a real ruckus after I said that. He claimed he had an emergency call that he had to take and asked if he could call me right back. I replied that I'd be standing by. Ten minutes later, my phone rang and it was a totally different person on the other end. Same Mayor, but different persona."

"Listen, Butch—I owe you an apology and one to Agent O'Brien as well. I've just been informed that the sprinkler problem was a mechanical problem—no one's fault, and I'm to blame for not having his parking space and office ready for him as promised. I must have misunderstood and thought he was coming after the holidays."

"Understood and the apology was unnecessary, but accepted. What do you want me to do about O'Brien?"

"I really would like if we could forget this call even took place. We need to give the plan a chance and give Agent O'Brien a chance before we take more drastic measures. I don't know if we told you, but we were successful in convicting five of the mob guys and they will be eligible for parole on Jan. one. I'm confident they got the message and will spread the word. We need to give that a chance."

"I was having a real problem not breaking out laughing. I replied, whatever you think is best, but if you have any problems with Agent O'Brien, you let me know and we can switch back to Plan A in a heartbeat."

"N-n-no that won't be, um necessary. Please have him introduce himself tomorrow so that we can welcome him to the team."

"I'll be happy to do so. Don't hesitate to call me if you need anything."

"So, Tommy. They will have the welcome mat out for you tomorrow and I'd give a thousand bucks to be a fly on the wall. Call me after your meet. And Tommy—this is the best I've felt since I've been at the bureau. Well done, Tommy. Well fucking done."

"Thanks, Butch. It's gonna be hard to beat the first Act, but I've got time to prepare. God bless."

"God bless you, Tommy. Good night."

The Following Day—Late Morning

Whatever else they do in this godforsaken town—they can get signs made overnight. Otis was beaming as I pulled into my space, where the sign read: "Reserved for Special Agent O'Brien". I parked and exited the car. "Good morning Otis."

"Good morning Mr. O'Brien."

"Tommy to you."

"Thank you Mr. O'Brien—I mean Tommy. They all waiting for you in the Mayor's Office."

When I entered the lobby, Dora was not a happy camper. She was wearing a scarf to cover up a bad hair day caused by the sprinklers. As I waited for the elevator, I had an idea and pivoted and approached her desk. At first she tried to ignore me.

"Dora, I'm authorized by the DOJ to take care of minor expenses. I noticed that your lovely hairdo was ruined by the sprinklers yesterday. How much does it cost you to have your hair done?"

Her mood seemed to change a bit. "Twenty-five dollars. Why do you ask?"

"So I can get the DOJ to reimburse you." I pulled out my wallet and gave her a twenty and a five.

The scowl had now disappeared. "Wh-why would you do that?" Spoken as she took the money.

"Because I want to and we're gonna be neighbors so to speak. I want to be a good neighbor. Oh—do you have another key for B-4?"

"I—I've been advised that I made a mistake yesterday. Your office is upstairs. The Mayor is expecting you and will give you the key. And, Mr. O'Brien—that was unnecessary, but greatly appreciated. It's tough making ends meet these days."

"Please call me Tommy and I know from my wife how important a good hairdo is."

The Mayor's Office

When I entered the Mayor's spacious office, there were six people, including the Mayor, seated at a conference table with one empty space for me at one end. They all stood and feigned smiles as if happy to see me. The Mayor spoke first. "Special Agent O'Brien—you make quite an entrance."

I let it slide as we all sat down.

"I'm Mayor Richards. I'll go around the table—that's Deputy Mayor Smith; Alderman Peters; Alderman Trachuk; Fire Chief McNally and seated next to you Chief of Police West. Gentlemen, this is Special Agent O'Brien." Nods all around, but no smiles. All but Deputy Mayor Smith and Aldermen Peters were white.

"What? No plumber?" My attempt at humor elicited some clenched teeth.

The Mayor replied, "Agent O'Brien."

"Tommy."

"Very well, Tommy. Look—speaking for all of us, we got off to a bad start and we apologize for that."

I just nodded.

The Mayor waited for a response, but when one wasn't forthcoming he cleared his throat and continued. "We weren't ready for you, but we're getting a proper office prepared for you now."

Alderman Peters interjected with a frown, "What was the Aldermen's Office."

The Mayor shot him a look, "Bob—we've covered that. Until we find another space you can use my office, okay? This is just going to be temporary—right Mr. O'Brien—I mean Tommy?"

"Not more than five years I would guess."

Alderman Trachuk spilled his water and the Chief of Police almost fell out of his chair.

"Just kidding. Truth is—there is no time limit that I know of, but I'm as anxious to get out of here as you are to have me leave. It will all depend on the cooperation I get."

The Mayor seemed a wee bit appeased by my comment. "Tommy, I think you'll find there isn't that much for you to do. We were successful in convicting five mob associates including Richie Vecchio who is reputed to be the new boss now that his Uncle has been indicted. They will be returning after the holidays and I suggest you meet with Richie yourself to confirm that they got religion—so to speak."

I nodded. "May I ask what he was convicted of?"

They all exchanged uncomfortable glances until the Chief of Police replied. "It had something to do with corruption in regards to his no-bid contract for the City's vehicles. Richie runs the big auto dealership in town."

I was wearing a blue windbreaker with the initials FBN, Federal Bureau of Narcotics on the front and back. I looked at the initials on the front of the jacket. "Gentlemen, maybe there's a misunderstanding here—another one. See these initials. They don't say AAA, the American Automobile Association. They say, FBN. That stands for Federal Bureau of Narcotics. I don't give a damn about your automobiles. I'm here to stop the flow of drugs. Period."

There was an uncomfortable silence broken by the Mayor. "Tommy, what do you expect from us in that regard?"

I turned to look straight at the Police Chief. "Well let's see. I guess I could start by reviewing all of the Police files having to do with drugs—and I mean all."

The Police Chief jumped up and pounded the table. "This is outrageous. Those files are confidential," he said while looking around for support, but seeing only averted eyes. "Most of them have been—have been placed in storage." Realizing the scene he made, he sat back down.

I waited a bit to reply—just to see him squirm. "Let me re-introduce myself. I'm here representing the DOJ and I will get those files one way or another. If you refuse to produce them—I will have them subpoenaed."

The Police Chief got up abruptly and stalked out of the room.

Alderman Peters spoke, trying to appear the voice of reason. "Tommy, the Chief has been under a lot of stress. I will be surprised if some of those files still exist—" meeting nods from around the table, "—but if I may say—I think you'll get more in Gary with honey than with vinegar, so to speak."

"Alderman, I appreciate the advice, but honey, so to speak, is sweet and one thing I've never been called is sweet. You do your job and I'll do mine. Now, Mr. Mayor—I was told I could select any deputy I wanted to assist me."

Again, uncomfortable glances around the table. "I'll try to arrange for you to meet several of them."

"No need. I already know who I want."

They all looked puzzled. How could I know any of the deputies? The Mayor asked, "Who is that?"

"Otis."

A few of them actually broke out in laughter. The Mayor suppressed a grin—or tried to—sorry the Police Chief hadn't hung around to hear this. "Do you mean Otis in the parking lot?"

"The very same."

"Well, I think that can be arranged. Now, if you'd like, I'll show you to your new office."

As I exited the building I motioned Otis over to my car to tell him of the new arrangement. "Otis, I just spoke with the Mayor, Chief of Police and others and they have agreed to let you assist me as needed. There will be some extra money in it for you."

At first he had seemed dubious, but he warmed up at the mention of some more green. "Tommy, or do I have to call you Mr. O'Brien now?"

"It's still Tommy."

"Tommy, I hope I didn't make you think I'm some kinda tough guy. I wear a gun, but I've never fired one—so I'm not the man for you if rough stuff is involved."

I suppressed a grin. "Otis—you really had me fooled there, but what I need you for doesn't involve any rough stuff. In fact, you won't even need the gun."

He smiled. "That's great news and did you say there's some extra bread in this? I sure could use it and, if you don't mind, can I still wear the gun?"

"There is some extra dough and it's probably a good idea for you to keep the gun. I mean—just in case."

"Yeah—just in case."

"Now, if you're ready—I've got your first assignment for you. Did the Police Chief leave the building yet?"

"He left about ten minutes ago. You just missed him and he didn't seem too happy."

"Did he have any boxes with him?"

"Just a briefcase."

"Good. Now Otis, he might come back after the building clears out and remove some boxes—maybe a lot of them."

"What do you want me to do?"

"I want to know where he takes them. You ever tail anybody?"

He thought for a moment, squinting his eyes—"I followed my ex-wife Lisabeth once. She'd been messin around with a gambler named Leroy."

"And what happened?"

"Well, sure enough—she went straight to his home on the other side of town. She never saw me followin her."

"And?"

"Shortly after that she died. She got that gonorrhea."

"I didn't think you died from gonorrhea."

"You do if you give it to Leroy."

"Otis—I think we're gonna get along just fine. Good luck tonight and be careful."

CHAPTER 18

Exit Strategy

Freddy—Club Fed, December 1965

The Vecchios and I had been notified that we would be released early so that we could spend the holidays at home—wherever my new home would be. My last few days at Club Fed were a time for reflection and anticipation. I learned a lot during my time here, but, and ironically, it wasn't from the three years of correspondence courses. They were a waste of time in the grand scheme of things. I've come to believe that if you seek wisdom—not to be confused with intelligence—find yourself a Jewish grandfather and a Black grandmother. Collectively—they have seen and done it all. I have been fortunate enough to have had both—my Granny and David.

As afore stated, it took me the better part of three years to get close to David. We both had instinctively kept our distances and, also as previously mentioned, to this day I'm not confident that David is his real name or where he's from. Neither really matter. I am pretty confident that he is Jewish because too many Yiddish phrases would slip out in our conversations.

It was David who eventually took me under his wing and guided me through my Club Fed experience. I was properly daunted by his confidence in his philosophy of life—which was based upon experience. David was quick to point out, you learn more from your failures then your successes. It was David who ingrained in me that you should never let anyone else—anyone else—know all of your thoughts and plans and that if something didn't need to be said—don't say it.

But what occupied my thoughts these last few days were the discussions that we had had in regards to what he called an "exit strategy". He recounted chapter and verse of stories about failure being snatched from the jaws of victory because someone either stayed at "the table" too long or didn't make adequate plans for their getaway. It was obviously more of an art than a science, but he hammered home the idea that "failure to plan is to plan for failure".

Like with Aesop's Fables his messages were reinforced by actual events that were described in the Bible, history books and countless biographies and autobiographies I read. Having said that, some things are easy to say, but almost impossible to do.

Let's start with the concept of an exit strategy. From the very evening I first met Richie Vecchio I had been thinking about how you let go of a tiger's tail and live to talk about it, but it was another event from that evening that complicated that thought—meeting Jasmine. If I truly heeded David's advice I couldn't let her know the entirety of my plan. The more I pondered it—the more I rationalized that it was in her best interest not to know.

I had had only sporadic contact with Richie during the months that followed our introduction. Friday night dinner was our opportunity to get even better acquainted and for me to learn exactly what was expected of me. If I understood things correctly—they were granting me quite a bit of autonomy in exchange for distancing themselves from the business.

I had more—a lot more—contact with Jasmine during that period. It was rare for her not to visit late at night, which was truly out of sight, if not out of mind, to the Italians. My residence was on the opposite side of the grounds and hadn't I turned down the free trim when it was offered. They believed I was all business. What they didn't know and didn't need to know was that I now had a business partner—if a silent one.

Jasmine's grandmother blessed the union—ironically believing that anyone at Club Fed must be an important man and one with big ideas.

Oh—I had big ideas, but they needed to be further refined. I couldn't and wouldn't keep Jasmine in the dark about my deal with the Italians whom she liked and respected, by the way. But, I had to let her know there was an end game, lest she think I sanctioned that activity. I didn't—it was just a means to an end and a life with Jasmine was the end.

I did share with her my original dream of escaping to a remote island in the Bahamas, of which there are thousands, and living out my days with my father. It was a dream that she fully bought into and one the money from the deal with the Italians could make possible. There were just some gaps to fill. How do we get from here to there? And how do we let go of the tiger's tail when I know so much? Were there islands that remote?

The picture started to get a bit clearer when Richie explained that I would be travelling to New Orleans every other week to pick up the drugs and deliver them back north. I would be assisted on my journey by Gary's Chief of Police which would make it appear official business. There had never been any problems.

That got me to thinking. If I was going to spend half my time in New Orleans, why not make the Big Easy my base? That would allow Jasmine to be with me free from the madding crowd and prying eyes. Richie said that while in New Orleans I was under the protection of the mob boss Carlos Marcello who was friends with both Carlo Gambino and Sam Giancana.

Jasmine liked the idea and we agreed that she would leave for New Orleans around the same time I left for Gary. I would still have to find a place to hang my hat up north, but didn't Richie say that even he didn't want to know where? Truth is—I just needed to be in Gary twice a month to get the money and bring back the drugs.

We spent our last week debating the merits of the French Quarter versus the Garden District and generally getting psyched up about the move. Florida was warm, but the humidity of the Delta, which was offensive to many, warmed the soul of anyone who grew up there and I was looking forward to feeling it embrace me once again.

I was getting too complacent—forgetting David's admonition that change is as certain as death and taxes. I was thinking that the exit plan

I was formulating, and keeping to myself, was relatively uncomplicated. Well—it was soon to become a lot more complicated, but only time would tell if it was in a good or bad way. It happened in a casual conversation I was having with Richie Vecchio as we were planning our exits from Club Fed.

"You'll be flying back to Gary with us on a private plane. When we get there I'll get you twenty-five g's to get you started. Oh, by the way—I got some news from home. It seems like the new drug agent, a guy named Tommy O'Brien, has shaken things up a bit. The Chief of Police stormed out of their meeting today. If he gets spooked that might complicate things a bit.

I was momentarily stunned. Had I heard right? "Back up a minute. What did you say the agent's name was?"

"Who—the agent? They said Tommy O'Brien. He's just one guy. No problem."

"See if you can find out where he's from."

Richie looked at me. "Why—you know a guy named Tommy O'Brien?"

"Let's say I knew one once. Probably a coincidence."

It was way too late to bail now and what would I do? Jasmine had left yesterday for New Orleans. She had some money of her own to get us situated. The $64,000 question was, how did this affect my exit strategy?

CHAPTER 19

From Ashes to Ashes

Tommy—Gary, Indiana, The Following Day

left Otis to his first task and had time to make it home to Chicago for my brother Jamie's graduation party. Jamie was a brainiac and had earned a scholarship to Illinois State where he would major in education.

The King and my sainted mother had decided to spend their last years in Florida after my father's imminent retirement. Jamie, being a dutiful son, had decided to seek a teaching job close by in Florida.

It was a festive occasion being near to Christmas. I don't know how she did it, but my mother could decorate our humble home to rival a mansion.

I was a bit surprised to learn of my dad's retirement. I always thought he would die in that mill. I was even more surprised at his vitriol that prompted his retirement.

"Tommy—the US steel industry is doomed. We can't compete any more. Get this—we're still use ropes, fooking ropes, to operate one of our furnaces! Every day when I arrive for work I go past the plaque that commemorates employees who lost their lives in the war. The war we, supposedly, won and then totally rebuilt Japan and Germany's steel industries with 1950s technology—while were still using fooking ropes! Now the Germans and Japs are kicking our ass and we can't compete with them. It's time for me to leave before the whole thing goes into the shitter."

Although I was taken a bit by surprise, I wasn't unhappy to see them move from the old neighborhood as many of their neighbors already had. For the first time, even our side of the tracks was being integrated. They called it redlining—prompting the whites to flee in fear and then burdening the poor Blacks with onerous mortgages. We both lost again.

I was late returning to my rented home in Hammond which backed onto the fairway of Woodmar Country Club. I had just fallen asleep when my phone rang. I looked at the illuminated clock and it said 3:15 A.M. Who the hell was calling at this hour? It was Otis.

"Otis, do you know what time it is?"

"Tommy, I debated whether to call, but supposed you'd want to know."

"Know what?"

"The Police Chief's house is burning down and I mean burning. I think I know what happened."

"Otis—hold on a minute."

I got out of bed and tried to shake the cob webs loose.

"Okay—start at the beginning."

"I waited around the building as you told me to and, sure enough, around 8:30 the Police Chief showed up with another man and they took out several boxes."

"Did you recognize the other man?"

"Nope. He looked like one of them Mexican farm workers. Oh—and he had a limp."

"Where'd they take the boxes?"

"They drove them straight to the Chief's house. I saw the route they was taking so I figured where they were going and laid back a bit—just like when I was following Lisabeth."

"That's good Otis. That's very good. What then?"

"Well, I parked up the street where I could see the front of the house. They pulled the Chief's car in the garage, but they left the door up so I saw them take the boxes into the house. I was gonna leave, but I was listenin to the Piston's game on the radio. I grew up in Ft. Wayne and I'm a die-hard Pistons fan—even though they havin a tough time right now. They were playin the Celtics and it went into O.T. I was so into the game I hadn't noticed that I'd been sittin there for more than an hour. It was just after ten when I saw the garage door close and the Police Chief—he comes out the front door with two big suitcases and, get this, he gets into the other guy's car and drives away."

"Did you see the other guy leave?"

"He never left the house."

"What'd you do then?"

Otis hesitated before answering.

"Otis—you there?"

"I thought my job was done for the night, so I paid a visit to a lady friend of mine. I was drivin home about one when I saw the fire trucks—several fire trucks and decided to see where they were goin and guess what? It was the Police Chief's house and I've never seen flames like that. It was burned up before they even got there. I came right home to call you. I thought you'd want to know?"

"You did good Otis—better than good."

"You want me to meet you over there?"

I thought for a moment. "Otis, I want you to stay away and Otis—don't breathe a word about what you saw to anybody and I mean anybody. I'm afraid this might get rough and I'm not sure how to play it, but the bad guys don't know there was a witness and let's keep it that way."

"I'll get that, whatta you call it? Amnesia."

"Good. Now get some rest and we'll talk tomorrow. You didn't see anything. Oh, Otis—one more thing. Did you notice what kind of car the other guy had?"

"It was a '55 Chevy. I had one just like it. And it had Michigan plates."

"You did good Otis."

I pondered the news as I got dressed. I had gotten unbelievably lucky with my call on Otis and the overtime ball game. They were gonna find a dead body in the house, burned beyond recognition, and the Police Chief's car in the garage. If the files were in the house, they were now ashes. I say, "if", because the contents of the suitcases were still a mystery.

If it was a migrant inside—good luck with that, as most were illegal and wouldn't cooperate with authorities, particularly the DOJ. The other mystery was—did anyone else know about the Police Chief's plans? The former Police Chief who no longer existed.

I decided to drive over to the fire scene and sniff around a bit.

When I arrived, the area was cordoned off and what once was a house and garage had been reduced to ashes. It didn't appear that much water had been used by the fire department. I counted four trucks, but the firemen were standing around drinking coffee as if enjoying the view.

I spotted the Fire Chief, McNally, whom I had met in the Mayor's office and approached him.

"Well if it isn't the special agent. O'Brien isn't it?"

"Tommy. I was in the neighborhood and decided to stop by. Looks bad. Isn't that the Chief's house?"

"Was the Chief's house, with the Chief inside" He smirked, "If I recall right—he used to keep his files in the garage."

"You know for certain that was his body inside?"

He stared at me, "Who the fuck else would it be? He lived here alone and it was his car in the garage. Now—why the fuck are you so interested in fires as I recall you saying your only interest was drugs? No—your only interest was drugs—period."

"I guess I'm just a curious sort."

"You know what happened to the cat, right?"

"Yeah—he died, as I recall, but don't cats have nine lives? I wonder how many lives Police Chiefs have?"

If looks could kill—I'd be dead. "Tommy, I think it's time for you to go home and go to bed. You're over your head and you don't know it."

"You'll let me know about the funeral arrangements?"

He just stared, but I had my answer to the question, did anyone else know?

CHAPTER 20

The New Don

Freddy—Club Fed & Gary, Indiana, Christmas Eve 1965

Our exit from Club Fed was delayed a couple of days so that Carlton Anthony could dispatch his Gulfstream to pick up Angelo Vecchio's underboss Ralphie Pisani and Consigliere Nunzio Pacori and fly them down to Florida to meet and bring us back to Gary.

To say that a lot had happened in the meantime would be an understatement. As expected, the Feds had taken Angelo Vecchio into custody to be arraigned for tax evasion. A death sentence in his case. Richie Vecchio, also as planned, automatically became the new Don. A position more thrust on him than sought after.

What was not expected, was that the Police Chief in Gary, instrumental to the mob's drug distribution scheme, would stage his own death after, apparently, destroying all incriminating files and then disappear.

As a new addition to the team, I was within ear shot of many conversations that took place as we waited for the plane, but I wisely pretended not to be aware—recalling the advice of my mentor David.

What I did glean was that it was important for Pisani and Pacori to join us, although I didn't know why, and that the jury was still out on the Police Chief's unsolicited and unapproved actions.

It was generally believed that he would seek refuge in New Orleans, where he had been an integral part of the mob's drug transport scheme. I heard it expressed that his actions, although unapproved, removed evidence that would have been harmful, if not devastating, to the mob and, with his public burial, it appeared that he executed the perfect getaway.

I also heard the concern that he might now possess that information which could be used as leverage against the mob and that a violation of the rules is a violation of the rules, whose punishment was implicit. He knew that. Not to mention—it wasn't certain that the getaway had been perfect.

Which begged the question, would he seek and receive the protection of Carlos Marcello who might then be the holder of the leverage? If he did so, that would present a problem.

I was impressed with the fact that meaningful actions were very rarely impulsive, rather a subject of careful consideration of all potential consequences.

It wasn't clear at that time what his presence in New Orleans would mean to my situation. I understood that Richie expected to hear from the ex-Chief in the coming days. Failure on his part to reach out and explain his actions would be a violation of the rules that even Marcello wouldn't countenance.

It was clear, to at least me, that the Chief's exit had been brilliant, but that wasn't the point to Richie and the others. It hadn't been approved.

When the jet arrived, Pisani and Pacori never deplaned. Richie entered first with his men next and me pulling up the rear. The curtain was pulled closed right before I entered the cabin. Although I couldn't hear what was spoken, I could see through a slit in the curtain as first Pisani, then Pacori, then each of Richie's men bowed their heads and kissed his hand.

In that most solemn moment, I witnessed Richie transform from the "hail fellow—well met" into the new Don. A man with the power of life and death at his discretion.

When they opened the curtain, I tried to act like I was oblivious to what had just happened, but I can't imagine I succeeded. Regardless, no one seemed to notice or care. I could never be part of "Our Thing". Champagne was served and there was a festive mood for the rest of the trip.

Richie and his men spent Christmas with their families as I checked into a Holiday Inn and spent the day scouring the real estate section for a rental property in the area. One suitable for my purposes.

I did speak with Jasmine—several times. She found an apartment on Royal Street in the Quarter with a courtyard and a balcony. It was pricey, but money wasn't our problem.

It was very difficult, as every Christmas tends to be, not to be with my father, and I did bend my rules, this once, by calling him. I told him that I was safe and well, but that I couldn't disclose my location—at least not yet. I told him about Jasmine and that I was working on a plan so that we could all be together someday soon. We were both blubbering by the end, but I was glad I called.

The following day I was in Richie's office at the dealership with Pisani and Richie's men present when the call came in from the ex-Chief Ed West. No Judge in the area would approve wire taps on his phone without his knowledge. Not to mention that he had just been released from federal custody. Today, he could use his phone.

Richie's secretary told him an old friend was on the phone. He picked it up and put it on speaker for all to hear. I guess I was included because this had an effect on the drug distribution business which I now oversaw—supposedly.

Richie answered. "I understand this is an old friend, but one who leaves town without telling me. Is that what old friends do?"

"Richie, I didn't know what to do. That new agent was going to subpoena the files and I couldn't let that happen, but the others said we can't whack him or they'll send twenty more to replace him. I've been working for your uncle and didn't know how to get in touch with you so quickly. I came up with the plan and it worked. They've already buried me."

Richie paused before replying. "I assume you're down south?"

"I didn't know where else to go and if need be maybe Mr. Marcello will give me protection. I mean—until things get sorted out."

Richie raised his voice a bit, "Don Carlos has offered you protection?"

"I haven't asked, but—I mean—I was working with his men on our deal."

101

"And what is going to happen now to our deal, as you say?"

"I can still help organize things on this end. I just won't be able to protect the shipment back north. I understood you were going to turn over the operation to a spook."

I pretended not to hear the slight.

"I've already done so. In fact the—ah—spook is sitting right here. His name is Freddy. Cool Freddy."

"Hey—I didn't mean nothing. I'm just—this has been a stressful time for me."

"So let me ask you this. Are you working for Marcello, now, or me?"

"Richie—I was hopin to work for you. I know I have to take a cut in pay due to my reduced role, but I'm the one who has all of the contacts down here."

"How much of a cut in pay?"

"I was hopin we could discuss that in private."

"Let me sleep on it. Cool Freddy will be making his first run next week. I'll get one of my men to accompany him. Call me tomorrow and we'll set up the meet."

"No need for you to use one of your guys. I've got a man who can handle the job. Tell Freddy I meant no offense."

"You can tell him yourself next week."

When Richie hung up, Pisani spoke first. "If Marcello gives him protection, we can't touch him, but why would Marcello do that?"

Richie answered, "Why does anybody do anything? Greed."

"But think of it—Marcello is getting street tax off the suppliers. It ain't close to what we're getting, but we take all the risk up here. If he ups the tax, maybe we buy from a different supplier and maybe in a different territory. He'd be cutting off his nose to save his face—so to speak. If Marcello wants part of the bigger deal he would approach you, not Tom Sawyer—the guy who organizes his own funeral."

They all laughed—even me.

"No, there has to be something else involved. Let me ask you this. How do we know that all of the files burned up in the fire? Or this—how do we know there were no witnesses? Somebody out walking their dog."

Richie was pensive and I gained an appreciation for the role of the consigliere.

Richie replied, "Short answer—we don't. Right now, he's the one with the contacts. I think we have to go along until we get a better handle on things. Plus, from talking to the others—people are sleeping better now that he's dead."

They laughed again.

"What about the agent who's causing so much trouble?"

One of Richie's men chimed in, "McNally said the agent was nosing around at the scene of the fire, but nobody's heard anything more from him. Why would he suspect anything? A body was in the house and the Chief's car was in the garage?"

I had to bite my tongue not to say, "You might not have heard anything from him for a few days, but if Tommy O'Brien was snooping around at that time of night—he suspects something."

CHAPTER 21

It's Elementary, Dear Watson

Tommy—Berrien Springs, Michigan, January 1966

After the scene with the Fire Chief, I was so pissed at myself for going off half-cocked and letting him know I didn't buy that it was the Police Chief's body in the ruins. I am typically more disciplined and would never give away the advantage of knowing something they didn't think anyone knew. Sun Tzu would have lopped off my head for that unforced error!

I could only think that I had been roused out of my sleep and didn't take the time to get my head clear before I rushed into "battle" The other excuse is that I'm Irish and I wanted that s.o.b. to know that I knew. The other Irish s.o.b.

I forced myself into seclusion until after the funeral. It gave me time to plan my next moves carefully. One of my greatest assets is my ability to reason. I excelled at logic at the academy—reason and logic being a large part of an agent's job.

A lot of that I attributed to my love of anything to do with Sherlock Holmes. I read Doyle's, *The Complete Works of Sherlock Holmes* and some of the stories several times. It helped me to hone my deductive reasoning skills. Thinking of that, I had to laugh—the first humor in weeks,—at the thought of Otis being my Watson. But it was Otis who had provided me with the clue that might help me crack this case.

The Police Chief and his cronies were probably smug right now—believing that people bought into his death and the destruction of incriminating evidence. The Achilles Heel to that train of thought was that he, the person at the nexus of this conspiracy, was very much alive. If I could capture him alive it would automatically prove that he was guilty of murder and he might trade a high-voltage ending for testimony against the others. It's a powerful and persuasive tool.

The weak link in my plan was identifying the victim. The Police Chief, my "Moriarity", had chosen well. There were migrant communities for seasonal farm workers scattered all over Michigan—many of them trailer parks. Chosen well, because even the grieving spouse would be reluctant to go to the police and report her husband missing for fear of being deported herself.

I had to put my figurative Holmes hat on, not the Deerstalker. If Moriarity was confident that he could get away with it, why would he travel a longer distance, as opposed to a shorter one, to find the victim? He wouldn't.

I discovered that the nearest migrant enclave to Gary was near Berrien Springs, Michigan in the southwest corner of the state. One more problem. My Spanish was just good enough for me to order food and "dos mas Margaritas".

Ergo: I couldn't communicate in Spanish with people who wouldn't speak to me anyhow. What to do? It was then the answer came to me. What are Mexicans known for? Hard work—you'll never see a Mexican pan handler—and also for being a very devout people.

I needed to find the Catholic Church that tended to the communities spiritual needs and then appeal to a Priest for assistance. A Priest who would be bi-lingual. It's elementary dear Watson—er, Otis.

The Church was St. Gabriel's which advertised Spanish Masses. I parked in the lot and walked over to the rectory. A housekeeper let me in and I gave her my card. I asked to speak with the priest who officiated at the Spanish Masses. She escorted me over to a sitting area and went to fetch the priest, Father Thul.

The good father was tall, but slight of build. What was remarkable about him, which I will never forget, was the warmth of his smile. As he approached he was looking at my card.

Smiling, as he said it, "Tommy O'Brien—what a wonderful name. My name is Father Bob Thul. What can I do for you Tommy O'Brien?"

I swear I saw an aura around this man and felt totally at peace in his presence.

"Father, thanks for seeing me. I have a delicate, but important mission. I've been sent by the government to try to disrupt the drug epidemic in Gary."

He smiled, "Good for you and good luck with that. What is it that I can do to help?"

"Father, just before Christmas the home of the Police Chief in Gary burned down with him, supposedly, inside."

"How terrible."

"Forgive me for saying so, but what's terrible is that it wasn't him inside. The world is better off without him." The only time Father Thul frowned. "He was involved in the drug trade. What's terrible is that I have reason to believe that the victim was a Mexican immigrant who had a limp and drove a 1955 Chevy with Michigan plates."

Now Father Thul's expression went from frown to pensive. "So you're wondering if the victim might be one of my parishoners?"

"Precisely. I know the sensitivity involved. The victim's wife would be fearful to report him missing lest she get arrested and deported and, besides, my Spanish isn't good enough for me to communicate with someone who may not speak English."

"Tommy, you are quite right in regard to the migrant's fears and please understand—my job is to tend to their spiritual needs. I work for the Lord and our Lord and Savior Jesus Christ was concerned with the spirit as well as the letter of the law. Maybe more so. I can't do anything that will imperil my flock."

"Nor would I ask you to. I simply want to know if we can identify the victim. If yes, you can keep his name confidential until such time that I can provide you with assurances that his family won't be harmed and that the information will help bring a killer to justice. How does that sound?"

"So, I have your word that all you are seeking now, is that if the victim can be identified?"

"That's all. Unless I can capture the killer, his identity isn't of value to me. If—and when—I do capture him, the victim's identity will be needed to convict him. At that time, I assure you that the government will be willing to help, not harm his family."

Father Thul was looking at my card again and smiling. He looked at me, "Tommy, are you from Chicago by any chance."

"Ninety-second and Wallace."

"Where did you go to high school?"

"Calumet. We were the poor Irish. We couldn't afford Leo, but there were so many of us at Calumet that we used to call it 'Our Lady of Calumet'."

Father Thul smiled. "Tommy, I taught advanced math at St. Ignatius for several years." St. Ignatius was the Jesuit high school where the joke was you had to be a genius to get in. Not sure if it was a joke. "I was also the Chaplain for our wrestling team and I remember being at Leo's Invitational in Nineteeen Fifty—"

"1956."

"That's it, 1956. I saw a kid named Tommy O'Brien break the arm of the undefeated champion of the Catholic League. He had to be carried off on a stretcher."

"Actually, I dislocated his shoulder, but I would have broken his arm if I had to."

"As I recall, Leo's little bandbox of a gym was packed when you two wrestled and despite the fact that you destroyed him—you were disqualified and he was still undefeated. What was his name?"

"Jack Muldoon, Father, and I knew what the outcome would be going in. Muldoon's dad was a copper as was the referee, but I wasn't going to let Muldoon walk away from the mat. Is that a confession?"

Father Thul laughed, "None needed Tommy. I have to confess I enjoyed watching it."

"Well, Father—what do you think of my proposal?"

"I can't afford to have you dislocate my shoulder if I say no."

We both laughed.

"So, I'm inclined to say yes. And Tommy—there is a victim and he left a wife and four children. Anything you can do to help them will be appreciated."

"Let me see, Father. Thanks for meeting me. It's been a real pleasure. Will you do me a favor?"

"What's that, Tommy?"

"Will you give me your blessing before I leave?"

Father Thul blessed me and I left knowing that I could take the Police Chief and all of the other conspirators down, if I could capture him. I couldn't wait to call Butch.

By the way, I think of Father Thul frequently. He was as close to a Saint as I ever met.

That Night

I called Butch to report what I found out and he was elated at the news.

"Tommy—do you know what this means? You find the Police Chief and all the other bricks fall into place. This is incredible news. Someday you'll have to tell me about how you found your sidekick. What a find?"

"Butch—you won't believe me when I tell you, but you do have to hear how his wife died!"

CHAPTER 22

The City of New Orleans

Freddy—Gary, Indiana & New Orleans 1966

I decided to stay at the Holiday Inn until after my first run to the Big Easy, as I didn't know how long I would be staying there with Jasmine. Truth is—I was getting nervous about the first run itself. When I signed on, the protocol seemed safe enough. I'd be accompanied by the Police Chief of Gary on both legs of the journey, which gave it the appearance of an officially sanctioned trip.

Subsequently, the Police Chief, the provider of protection, had engineered his own death and funeral, and wouldn't be making either leg. That's not an incidental change and I couldn't help but recall David's comments about changes.

It didn't help that, despite the trip being scheduled as planned, the main talk of conversation was the status of the Police Chief—now that he was officially "dead".

I had five days to sort my feelings out and make a decision whether to fish or cut bait. Were it not for the fact that Jasmine was now ensconced in a luxury apartment in the French Quarter and that she had totally bought into my exit strategy—my decision would be-easy. I'd be out of here in fifteen minutes—never to look back. But there would be no exit strategy, hence no Jasmine, without the money this deal represented.

David was paroled at the same time I was and had given me a contact number if I ever needed him. I never needed anybody as much as then. I looked up the prefix and noted it was a Palm Springs, California number. I

didn't know much about Palm Springs other than it was an exclusive location—which didn't surprise me knowing David. A man of wealth and taste.

I dialed the number and another older man answered—one with a gruff
voice. "Yeah?"

"I'm trying to reach David. Is he there?"

"David who?"

It was then that it dawned on me that after a four year relationship I
didn't know his last name. It also occurred to me that whatever name he
might have given at Club Fed was likely an alias.

"If he is there, tell him it's Freddy and I need some advice."

"Freddy who?"

"Please just tell him. He'll know."

"Hold on."

There was a long pause and a muffled conversation before David answered
the phone. "Freddy, my little boychik, I didn't expect to hear from you so
soon. Is everything okay?"

"That's why I'm calling. I need some advice—your advice. Everything
was okay, but there've been some changes, big changes, and I remember
what you told me about changes."

"Start at the beginning."

"I don't know how to make this a short story. Are you busy right now?"

"Am I busy? Yeah—I'm busy playing cards with a bunch of supposedly
big machers who tell bad jokes and cheat at poker."

That unleashed a torrent of insults from his partners—all talking over
each other.

"Yeah, fuck you too. I'll sit out the next game. Steal from each other for
once. Sorry Freddy—where were we?"

"You better get comfortable. Here goes."

"Freddy—hold on. If this is important—you know, business related, I
want you to go to a pay phone and call me with the number. I'll go to one
nearby and call you back."

That's why I needed to talk to David. He was the model of discretion.

"I'll call you back within five minutes. David—I'm sorry about taking you away from the game."

"Sorry—you just saved me a bundle. These assholes are a bunch of thieves."

There were more catcalls as he hung up.

When we finally hooked up, I told David the whole story and why not? He was aware of my meetings with the Italians and knew something was up as I had no other place to go when I left. What he didn't know is what I had signed on for.

I had to ask a couple of times if he was still there as he was so silent. He would just reply, "Keep talkin."

When I finished, he took a deep breath. "Freddy—I'm not a fortune teller and I can't see the future. What I'm gonna tell you—advise you—is based upon experiences that either I was involved in personally, or knew someone who was. And I can tell you two things. Change does exactly what it says—it changes things. What you bought into is history. The risk just ramped up exponentially. Number two—this Police Chief is like a wounded animal. Everyone's basic instinct should be self-survival and that's bad enough, but this chumbelone is dangerous, because his very survival is in doubt and if you succeed without his help—that might be the nail in his coffin, his real coffin. He'd be expendable and he knows too much. Knowledge is a dangerous commodity to the mob.

"Know this—that man is not your friend and you don't know who his allies are. It's always a dangerous time when there is a change at the top of a mob and it's not just from the inside. Carlos Marcello is no one to fuck with and he's no dummy. You're talking about millions of dollars and that is too big a prize to ignore. At minimum, he might want a piece of it and, if he's got the Police Chief, he's got a lotta leverage. You, my friend, are a pawn in a very dangerous game. If you can—take a pass on this. You may not live as well, but you'll live."

I then explained to David about Jasmine and our dreams and told him I couldn't walk away if there was a way to proceed.

He sighed, "Okay—let me ask you. Who is going to take the chief's place on the trip with you?"

"I don't know the guy. He's one of the ex-Police Chief's men."

"That's not good. Here's what you have to look for. If he suddenly gets the flu or for any other reason can't make it—you're being set up. Not saying it's gonna happen, but just remember that. He also may make a play on the train to make you look bad. How much time do you have?"

"I've got five days."

He paused before replying. "How much money are we talking about?"

"A hundred grand in c-notes."

Without hesitation he answered, "That's a little over two pounds. Okay—here's what I would do. You listening?"

"You know I am."

"Okay—they're gonna give you a briefcase or satchel probably with the money inside. This is very important. You count, and I mean count, the money to make sure it's all there. Don't take anything for granted. You hear me?"

"Loud and clear."

"Where are you staying?"

"A motel." I must be learning fast, because I didn't even tell David that it was a Holiday Inn.

"Good. Now Freddy—you're gonna need your lady friend's help. Have her take the train up to Chicago tomorrow. Meet her there and you two find an Abercrombie and Fitch store. There's probably one on, or close to, Michigan Avenue."

"What's an Abercrombie & Fitch store?"

"It's a clothing store that sells clothes for safaris and such. How well does this guy, the one who's supposed to protect you, know you?"

"I doubt if he does."

"Good. I meant to ask—you have some money? Because those clothes won't be cheap?"

"They gave me an advance of twenty-five grand."

He whistled, "That's plenty. Now, buy each of you matching khaki outfits and, this is very important, walking shoes, so it looks like you're on a trip. Get each of you one of those floppy hats and buy yourself a pair of reading glasses. You writing this down?"

"I am. So we're gonna look like a couple of tourists?"

"You're gonna look like a couple of well-to-do African Tourists. Nobody will give you a second glance. In fact, get a couple of nice leather or fabric duffel bags for your clothes and stop by the Rand McNally store and get some country stickers to put on them."

"Do I switch the money to the duffel bag?"

"Buy a roll of good medical tape and some cellophane. Have your lady friend tape the packets of bills to your torso. In fact, your safari jacket should be a size larger than usual."

"What do I do with the briefcase they give me?"

"Toss it. You're going to pick up the money and go directly to the motel and change before heading to the train station. Buy two coach tickets and wait till the last minute to board. The only way they can get the money is by taking you hostage and they won't risk a war with the new boss by doing so. He's the only one I can say for certain is on your side."

"What if I run into the guy at the gate—waiting for me?"

"Freddy—no offense, but you people do look a lot alike and nobody wants to stare at a Black person. You two will be walking fast and engaged in conversation. He's not expecting a couple and certainly not in safari clothes. Not to mention the hat and glasses. I'll bet I wouldn't recognize you."

"What happens when I get to New Orleans?"

"Go straight to her place. They don't know about it, right?"

"No one does."

"Keep it that way. When you're settled in—call your boss and tell him you made it. Tell him you must have missed the other guy. When they set up the meet, call me."

"David, I couldn't do this without you. What can I do for you?"

"You got some walking around money, right?"

"Plenty for right now."

"Okay, do this. Go to a Western Union office and wire two grand to Mr. David at the Palm Springs Western Union Office. There's a horse running at Santa Anita this weekend. I'll put one grand on it for me and one for you. Trust me on this one."

"Is it good enough for me to wire you four grand and double the bet?"

"It's that good."

"Consider it done."

"When you call from New Orleans—follow the same protocol. Call me with a pay phone number."

"Thanks, David."

"Oh, Freddy—one more thing and it may be the most important thing. Do not and I mean do not carry a gun. If this guy was an ex-Police Chief he knows that would be a parole violation and you'd be facing some hard time. You can't afford to take that chance. You understand me?"

"Loud and clear."

CHAPTER 23

The Best Laid Plans

New Orleans, January 1966

I t had all seemed logical, if not brilliant, to the ex-Police Chief. After all—he was the essential cog in the wheel of the multi-million dollar drug trade between New Orleans and Gary, but he was getting a small piece of the pie and Carlos Marcello, the boss of New Orleans, was only getting crumbs in the form of street tax on the supplier.

That thought had been grating on him long before Tommy O'Brien arrived on the scene. One thing was certain, he wasn't going to be the fall guy for the Gary mob—not in exchange for peanuts. He could take them all down.

The Mayor, the Fire Chief and others told him to chill out, but they weren't the ones threatened with subpoenas and this fucking O'Brien guy was crazy. Before he even introduced himself he almost destroyed the entire municipal building.

He'd been thinking about his exit for a long time and there were plenty of wetback victims to choose from. If anything, he regretted that he waited so long. After all, wasn't he the one with the leverage? He would have been a fool to burn up all of the incriminating files. They were his insurance policy and they could be worth a fortune, the drug trade fortune, to Carlos Marcello.

For years the drug trade had been a well-oiled machine. He would escort one of the Vecchio soldiers down to New Orleans, make the contact and bring the drugs back to Gary. But now, because the fucking natives were trying to wrest control of the trade from the Italians, the mob had capitulated and agreed to turn the distribution over to the spooks.

That was bad enough, but he was then informed that they were going to find their own spook to handle the supply end! Where the fuck did that leave him? But—but—what if the new guy fucked up? Gary had already given up half of the business. What if the supply side was delivered to Carlos Marcello on a silver platter—by his new partner—50/50? It would be found money to Marcello, found millions, and Gary couldn't touch him if Marcello offered protection. Why wouldn't he?

It seemed easy enough. He had already made the overture to Marcello's under boss Dante Colangelo. He would deliver the hundred grand the young spook was entrusted with in exchange for protection and the proposed partnership. Gary would realize they couldn't handle the business without either the contacts or the cover that, only he, could provide.

A couple of weeks later, however, the new spook not only made it to New Orleans without incident, but with the hundred grand intact. The hundred grand promised to Carlo Marcello. The only saving grace was that Gary was never aware of his scheme.

The same wasn't true of Carlos Marcello. The ex-Police Chief, who had been counting his millions a few days earlier, was now a nervous wreck when Dante Colangelo and two of his soldiers picked Glen Martin, nee Ed West, up at the Café du Monde adjacent to the French Market.

They drove in virtual silence to a warehouse on Tchoupitoulas Street. The only light inside the warehouse was what came through the windows. Colangelo motioned for the ex-Chief to sit.

When the ex-Chief started to speak, Colangelo raised his hand. "Mr. Marcello has been wondering where his hundred grand is? The one you promised him."

It was stifling to begin with inside the warehouse, but now the ex-Chief was sweating bullets. "I—I don't know what went wrong. My guy fucked up. He was supposed to handle it."

Colangelo cut him off. "I don't give a fuck about your guy—whoever he is. It wasn't your guy who promised the hundred grand to Mr. Marcello. It was you. Now, I'm gonna ask again. Where's the fucking money?"

"I—I don't have it. I'll get it—I swear."

Colangelo stood up and stretched before sitting back down. "Listen, Ed "

"It's Glen now."

Colangelo laughed and the others followed in, "You are some kind of fuck up—you know?"

"I have the—the files. And I'm the one with the contacts for the drugs. Gary can't do it without me."

Colangelo stood up and beckoned the others off to the side for a brief confab. They sat back down. "Tell me about the files."

The ex-Chief was now animated. "I've got enough to take the Vecchios down. The files are my life insurance policy."

Colangelo paused before replying, "I don't want to bust your bubble, but last time I checked—the only way to collect on a life insurance policy is if you die. And If Gary doesn't know about your brilliant, fucking, foolproof plan—" the soldiers laughed, "—are you still part of the action?"

"Yeah."

"And what's your cut?"

"Well—we haven't finalized that, now that I have a reduced role, but I'm still on the payroll."

"Okay—here's the deal and it ain't negotiable, so don't say nothing to piss me off or the deals off and the last sunlight you'll ever see is that coming through that window. Are we clear? Nod, don't speak. I don't want to hear your fucking weasel voice again."

Now drenched with sweat and trying not to shake, the ex-Chief nodded.

"By tomorrow noon, you will deliver whatever files you have from Gary. Maybe, just maybe, Mr. Marcello will accept the files in exchange for the hundred large. Maybe. That'll be his call. One more thing. You aren't under the protection of Mr. Marcello. He doesn't want to hear your name again—either of your names."

The soldiers laughed again.

Colangelo and his men got up to leave. When the ex-Chief started to follow them, Colangelo turned around. "Where the fuck are you going? Find your own way back."

If things weren't bad enough, the ex-Chief looked down and his crotch was soaked. He sat by the curb and tried to collect his thoughts. His man swore he was at the gate for the train and no single Black guy with a briefcase or satchel boarded the train. It was a moot issue now. The spook was here and he had the money.

However, Gary shouldn't suspect anything so he would go ahead with the meet as if nothing happened. He had to. The only other person who knew about his plan to hi-jack the spook was his own man, the one who fucked up, and he was still in New Orleans. He'd give that job to the deal-ers—tell them he's a rat. After all—how could you not spot a spook with a brief case or suitcase travelling alone? How many could there have been?

As for the spook himself, maybe he needed to take him a little more seriously. Prejudice might be a vice he couldn't afford right now.

CHAPTER 24

Tinkerbell

Freddy—New Orleans, Later that Day

What a whirlwind and adrenalin-charged few days it had been. The truth is—they had enjoyed their shopping trip on the Magnificent Mile and their stay at the Drake Hotel. Even though they were both light skinned, they were met with polite indifference until Freddy issued some more than generous tips. They even got into the Cape Cod Room after putting a smile on the Maitre'd's face. They were seated at a table as remote as possible, but who cared? The ambiance was romantic and the Lobster Thermidor was to die for. Freddy was now an expert on Lobster and even knew how to pick out a nice Chardonnay to pair with the entrée. He laughed, "Listen to me—pair with the entrée!" His time with the Italians hadn't gone for naught.

The train trip had been uneventful. Freddy was certain that he spotted the man who was supposed to be his escort—pacing fitfully at the gate. They had to suppress laughs as he had totally ignored them—not looking for a handsome African couple on safari, apparently.

Same, same when the train arrived in New Orleans. There was one person conspicuously anxious about those departing the train and Freddy decided to have some fun. He approached the man, who definitely fit the profile of a Police Chief—I mean an ex-Police Chief and feigned an African accent, "Excuse me, good sir. Can you kindly direct my wife and me to the limousine stand?"

The ex-Chief could not have been more perturbed—still rubber-necking to eye each passenger. "Do I look like the fucking information booth? Can't you see I'm busy?" He waved them away thinking, "Here I am looking for a fucking spook and Prince Mumbo Jumbo and his wife are looking for a fucking limousine!"

Just then he spotted his man, who appeared just as frantic and just as empty handed.

Freddy and Jasmine took a cab, not a limo, to the apartment on Royal Street and Freddy was absolutely blown away by how beautiful it was— everything was. The courtyard, the lush vegetation and flowers, the fountain, the apartment and the balcony. He was thinking to himself that this was all too good to be real when the buzzer on the front gate sounded.

Freddy wondered who it could be, but Jasmine just smiled as she buzzed them in. If Freddy thought the apartment was a bit surreal—he wasn't prepared for Tinkerbell.

Tink was a well-known denizen of the French Quarter and if he could have been any more outrageous—he would have been in a New York second. He defied description—which seemed to be his goal. He was ubiquitous in the French Quarter. Tink was a homophobe's worst nightmare or a subject of blind indifference. It depended on your perspective and New Orleans, particularly the Vieux Carre (French Quarter), was a live and let live kind of place. He was a threat to no one with a sense of humor. He was only slightly more bizarre than the Black photographer who walked around with a lamb on a leash.

He seemed to know everything and everybody—even those who ignored him. If you were a bit broad-minded, or had a sense of humor, you would know that Tink would have had to be created if he didn't already exist. The Quarter was definitely not Kansas.

Apparently he had latched onto Jasmine when she first arrived and was a great and humorous help with her chores. Tink made her and others laugh. That they were as often, as not, laughing at Tink as with him, didn't seem to make a difference to Tink. The only way to possibly slight Tink, was to ignore him.

I have to say, Freddy thought to himself, this is the first time I can remember being greeted with, "Oh boy, let's eat!" Jasmine just laughed and I was willing to tolerate anything to see her in such a state of happiness. If it could only last.

That was not to be, however, as the phone wakened me from my brief stupor. Jasmine had the phone installed before she left for Chicago. I had called Richie to tell him that I had arrived. I, not us, as he was still oblivious to my relationship with Jasmine. There was no reason, that I was aware of, not to tell him, but I yielded to David's general wisdom that there was no need for him to know.

It was Richie informing me that the ex-Chief and his supplier would meet me that evening at eight at the Olde Absinthe House on Bourbon Street—one of the French Quarter's historical landmarks. I didn't tell Richie that we had already met.

The Olde Absinthe House

Tinkerbell directed me to nearby Maison Blanche, the upscale department store, where I purchased some new duds, so that I didn't have to wear the safari suit to the meeting. I wasn't through fucking with the ex-Chief.

When I arrived, promptly at eight, I was wearing casual attire, navy blue crew neck sweater, white Levis and cordovan Bass loafers with no socks. The southern, frat boy look of the times. I had also jettisoned the reading glasses.

I spotted the ex-Chief and three others at a table. I walked right to it and sat down in the empty chair. I could tell he was a little puzzled at how I recognized them and couldn't seem to take his eyes off of me.

"Hi, I'm Freddy. You must be the Chief and I'll let you introduce your friends."

The ex-Chief was now flummoxed. He leaned forward, "Have we met before? You look awfully familiar?"

"Not that I know of—unless you were on the train yesterday."

At this, the ex-Chief's man jumped in, "I was on the train yesterday, but I didn't see you. You were supposed to meet me at the gate."

I held my palms out. "I waited at the gate until the train was about to depart and had to run to catch it."

If his fate wasn't sealed before—it was sealed now. The ex-Chief shot him a look that could kill as he protested, "I swear—I was at the gate. He's lying."

I gave my best puzzled look, "Why would I lie? What's the problem? I'm here aren't I?"

It turned out the other two were one of the dealer brothers and one of their enforcers who was planning on taking the rat on a one-way trip to Algiers. The trip just got expedited as the ex-Chief nodded to the enforcer and he escorted the protesting victim out.

The French Quarter is the quintessential "see no evil" place and none of the other patrons appeared to notice. Having said that, the Quarter was Disneyland compared to Algiers. They said that even the devil, himself, avoided Algiers.

Still staring intently at me, the ex-Chief asked, "Why then didn't I see you get off the train. I was waiting for it?"

I laughed, "How long did you hang around?"

"What's so funny? I was there for at least a half hour after the train arrived. I saw everyone depart. That is—everyone but you."

"It's funny in an embarrassing way. I fell asleep on the train. I was awakened by one of the clean-up crew. They asked if I was spending the night. Said the train had been there more than an hour. Now, are you gonna introduce your friend?"

Truth is—I had laughed because I couldn't help it. The ex-Chief was totally at sea. His mind told him that he had definitely seen me before, but try as he may, it didn't compute. He finally gave up trying as the dealer was getting nervous.

"Sorry. Actually that happened to me once, but not for that long. Freddy—I mean Cool Freddy, this is Ramon Garcia. Ramon and his brother are our suppliers. Ramon, Cool Freddy will be handling the shipment from now on. I'll continue to assist where I can."

I stuck out my hand, "Ramon, mucho gusto. And just call me Freddy. I can't be as cool as you guys in the Big Easy."

Ramon ate it up. "Freddy, I think we'll get along just fine. You have the money?"

"I have it, but not with me. It's safe."

"When do you want to make the swap?"

The ex-Chief chimed in, "How about we do it tomorrow?"

I looked first at him—then at Ramon, "I want to do a little sight-seeing as this is my first time here, plus I want to sample some of your world famous cuisine. How about you give me your number and I'll call you in a day or two?"

The ex-Chief tried to speak, but Ramon held up his hand. "That works for me. If you'd like to sample some authentic Cajun cuisine, how about I take you to dinner tomorrow night?"

The ex-Chief jumped in, "I've got plans tomorrow night."

Ramon looked at him, "I didn't invite you. I invited Freddy. You made the introduction. What do we need you for?"

As much as I enjoyed seeing him get his balls busted, I saw an opportunity to create some good will with a potential enemy.

"You don't need to join us tomorrow night as we need to get to know each other, but Ramon—I want to keep him in the loop. You know, coordinate things with you on your end. Let's see how that works out?"

I had no knowledge of what had transpired with Marcello's men, but I just threw the ex-Chief the only life-line he had right now. He might not have been happy at the turn of events, but knew it could have been worse.

Walking the short walk home I realized that I had promised to call David before the meet. I was getting a little big-headed because of my success so far, but that was due to David's advice. I needed to be a lot more careful as I was a long, long way from the goal line and, in this game I was playing, there would be no do-overs.

When I arrived at my gate, Tinkerbell was waiting for me. "Tink, what's up?"

"We need to talk."

"Okay—come in and we'll have a night cap with Jasmine."

CHAPTER 25

Looking for Answers without Any Clues

Tommy—Gary, Indiana

'd purposefully kept my head down after the incident at the fire. I used my office infrequently, as I was getting the silent treatment from everybody but Dora.

My meeting with Father Thul had buoyed my spirits. It confirmed that the ex-Chief was still alive and guilty of murder one, which was enough to make anybody flip. Problem was—I had no clue where he had sought refuge and this was a big country. That is, if he stayed in the country. I had my work cut out for me.

I slipped into my Holmes alter ego and wondered what Sherlock might have done. I chuckled to myself that maybe I needed a pipe and a violin. The seven per cent cocaine solution I could do without.

I was relaxing on my back patio, watching the golfers come up the fairway when I heard a door shut in my driveway. How appropriate—it was my Watson, Otis. Just the man I needed to speak with.

"Otis, what a beautiful day?"

"It sure is boss." Boss—not Tommy anymore. "I was wonderin if you needed me for anything more today?"

"Otis—pull up a chair. If you want coffee—grab a cup in the kitchen."

"I'm good."

"Otis, I was just thinking. We don't know where the ex-Chief has fled to and the answer probably has something to do with the drug trade that he was obviously tied up in."

"Boss—I got news for you. If you're in a position of authority around here—you somehow tied up in the drug trade."

"I don't doubt that, but some were more direct than others and the ex-Chief is the only one who bolted so far. To me that says he was very directly involved, but how and why?"

Otis appeared deep in thought before answering. "I don't know if this means something or not, but—you know how I look after the parking lot? The Chief's spot would be empty every couple of weeks like clockwork—for two or three days."

"I think that means a lot, Otis. That might mean that he was physically involved in the shipment of the drugs."

"Who's gonna stop a Police Chief?"

"Otis—you missed your calling. I think you nailed it, but where did he go to get the drugs? Had to be the south, right? We find that out—we go a long way to finding him. I want you to do some snooping around and find out who's running the drugs now that he's out of the picture and the mob boss is in custody. There had to be a changing of the guard."

"I can do that. People talk in the hood, but they talk even more freely if a bottle of Ripple or some Colt 45 is involved."

"Otis—I'm glad you mentioned that. I'll be right back."

I went in the house and retrieved two-hundred dollars in twenty-dollar bills from my "snitch stash."

I went back outside and handed the envelope to Otis. "Here's a little walking around money. I've put in a requisition for your payment and that should be coming in the next few days."

Otis couldn't have seemed happier. "This'll work, just fine."

"Now—one more question. What do you know about Richie Vecchio—the guy who was just paroled for the auto business?"

"Everybody knows Mr. Richie. We all buy our cars from him. If you get in trouble and miss a payment—he don't get mad or re-possess your car like some others. You know what he does? He asks you if you need any help with groceries and stuff. And when my son, little Otis, played Little League, he bought the uniforms, bats, gloves, hats and pizza after every game. Mr. Richie ain't like his uncle. His uncle is pure evil—bad to the bone. Good riddance he gone."

"I think I need to drop by and introduce myself. He may be the nicest guy in the world, but his last name is Vecchio and the way the mob works is that when the uncle goes away, Richie is odds on favorite to replace him."

Richie Vecchio

Vecchio motors was a huge and impressive operation and it was a beehive of activity when I pulled in. Cadillac, Buick, Oldsmobile and Chevrolet. As I walked into the show room my heart skipped a beat to see a fire-engine red 1966 Corvette convertible on display. I had always dreamed of owning a Vette, but I had to choose between Mary Kay and the Vette and no car is that good. Dreams don't die easily though and I was mesmerized gazing at the car when I was approached by a grinning salesman.

"She's a beauty isn't she? Wanna take a test ride?"

I snapped out of my reverie. "Would I? I'd give my left nut to own this car, but I'm not here to shop for a car. I'm looking for Richie Vecchio if he's here."

The salesman's demeanor changed instantly. "Is he expecting you?"

"He is, but not necessarily today. I'm Tommy O'Brien."

"He was here, but he might have left. Let me check for you."

While I waited, I sat down in the Vette and went back to my dreams. Next thing I knew, Richie Vecchio got in on the passenger side. If charm is ever an Olympic sport—this guy would take the Gold medal.

I started to get out, but he grabbed my arm and pulled me back down. He smiled and stuck out his hand. "Tommy O'Brien—I was hoping to meet you. Let's go for a spin."

I was literally speechless for a moment. I'd lost the high ground and this was Richie's show.

"Richie—can I call you Richie?"

"Of course."

"Richie, I can't afford this car. I came to talk with you."

"Tommy, my guy said you would give your left nut for it. We don't take nuts, but you can at least get to drive one. We can talk while you drive."

I probably should have said no, but I was totally off my game and the thought of just driving a new Vette was too enticing. I turned it on and put it in gear as the show room door was raised.

"Tommy, before you start—I gotta tell you—I never laughed so hard when I heard about the municipal building flood. That was good stuff and we don't have a lot of humor around here these days."

I smiled, "My mother used to say, 'You don't get a second chance to make a first impression'."

I had no sooner uttered that, then thought of the moment. Richie had blown me away.

"Yeah, well those assholes know who you are now. What did you want to talk to me about? I did my time."

I was in seventh heaven—not just with the ride, but the looks—the stares we were getting as I was tooling around in the Vette. I was starting to get my bearings again, however.

I glanced over at him, "So that we get off on the right foot, and I do appreciate you letting me drive the Vette—the rap—the auto rap was bogus and we both know it."

His smile faded, but he would be a good poker player as he betrayed no other emotion.

"I appreciate you speaking frankly and I don't know what you know, but the time I did was real. You got a family Tommy?"

"I've got a wife. We want to have a family."

"You'll be a good father. I can tell. Try being separated from your wife for almost eighteen months and then tell me it was bogus."

"Fair enough. I should also add that the people I've spoken to all speak highly of you."

"Tommy—since we're speaking frankly—man to man—I was born with the name Vecchio. My father and my uncle ran the mob here. I can't run from that or hide from it if I tried. And there's no fucking way I would ever change my name. I loved my father. He did what he had to do. I assume you're Irish and they didn't have it any better."

"Richie—I understand you went to college."

"I didn't just go—I graduated. I have a bachelor's degree from St. Joe's in business."

"When you were in college did you read 'Les Miserables' by any chance?"

"Who didn't?"

"Good. Richie—I'm an agent with the Federal Bureau of Narcotics. I have a job to do, but I'm not Inspector Javert. I don't have a mission to rid the world of vice. I am only focused on trying to mitigate—mitigate, not eradicate, the damage that drugs are doing to this community. What happens after I'm gone won't haunt me. So—in this regard, you're either with me or agin me, as they say."

He was quiet for a moment. "Tommy, let's start heading back. I don't know what you may have heard, but I have a very successful dealership, a great wife and family and life is good. I don't do drugs. I don't like drugs and I wish they never happened. I don't see how I can help you."

'How about this? What can you tell me about the ex-Police Chief?"

"You mean other than he's dead and the world's a better place without him? Not much."

I had trouble not responding, but was glad I held my tongue. I cleared my throat—another delaying device—before speaking. "It appears that West, the ex-Chief was involved in the drug trade."

"I've heard that rumor and don't doubt it."

"Well, if he's—dead, didn't you say? If he's dead, who takes over his spot?"

I finally got him to blink at my implication that I didn't necessarily buy into the fact that he was dead.

I pulled the car up to the show room door.

"Tommy—I'm afraid I can't help you in that regard. I just hear rumors and the rumors are that the Blacks have taken over the trade. I'm just surprised it took them so long to do so. If you need anything don't be a stranger."

We exited the car and one of the runners came to get it.

"Richie—you're a nice guy. If you are involved in some way—get out. You don't need this."

"Tommy, at St. Joseph's we were taught what they called 'The Serenity Prayer'."

"I know it well. It's my mother's favorite."

"Sometimes we have to accept the things we can't change. The wisdom to know the difference is the hard part. In my experience, wisdom comes from experience and it's generally the bad experiences we learn from."

"Richie—I really hope we don't ever have to butt heads."

"That makes two of us."

As I drove away, the picture was becoming a little bit clearer. It was true that the Black street gangs were involved and that there had been a change of leadership in the mob. What was hard to imagine was that the mob walked away from the game entirely. Even harder to imagine, was that someone as charismatic as Richie wouldn't be the new natural leader. I would follow him anywhere. I mean—if I was on the other side of the street.

CHAPTER 26

Coon-Asses

Freddy—New Orleans

Jasmine had waited up for me and was relaxing with a glass of wine on the balcony, watching the festive revelers. She was surprised to see Tinkerbell with me.

"Hey, Babe. Tink was downstairs waiting for me. Said we have to talk. Is there any more wine?"

"You may have to open a new bottle."

I turned to Tink, "Will you have some wine? I'll see if I can find an umbrella to put in it—and a cherry."

"Honey—I lost my cherry a long time ago. Do you want to hear how?"

"Stop right there. That's way too much information. I hope that's not what we need to talk about."

Tink smiled. "What we need to talk about may save your life."

Both Jasmine and I perked up. "Let me pour the wine first. In fact—let's move inside as noise travels."

We moved into the living room. The apartment came furnished and the interior decorator knew what they were doing. There definitely is something to be said about southern style.

Jasmine sat on the Spanish leather sofa with Tinkerbell and I sat in a deep leather chair facing them.

Jasmine asked how the meeting went. I replied that I thought it went very well. I reached out so that we could clink glasses and then turned to Tink.

"Tink, you have the floor. "

"I saw who you were meeting with at the 'Absinthe House'. He's a bad man—a real sicko. He's into a cult that's into B & D—only they take it to the extreme. I know for a fact that people have died—a lot of people, from their games."

"Whoa. Slow down a bit. What's B & D?"

Jasmine answered, "bondage and discipline. You'd be surprised how many people—men mostly and powerful men—are into it, but there are varying degrees. Mild, so to speak, B & D can be tying someone up and maybe spanking or a light whip. I've heard rumors, however, of even torture being practiced. Brrr." She shivered.

"Tink—are you telling me that Ramon Garcia is a sadist?"

"Not Ramon—he's harmless in comparison. The other man."

My mind was buzzing now. "Tink—how do you know this?"

"Honey, there isn't much that goes on that I don't know about. They recruit their victims by offering them money and most of the victims are migrant workers who need the money desperately. They have an almost endless pool to pick from. They take them to a home on Lake Ponchartrain. It's gated and guarded."

"And you know this, how?"

Tink sniffled, "Because one of my best friends was into B & D, but not the torture, and was lured into going. He—I mean she, had been a champion swimmer when she was younger. When she figured out what was going on she freaked, broke away and dived into the lake. It was dark and she said they scanned the water with search lights and even fired shots—one of which almost hit her. She escaped by being able to hold her breath for long periods of time and escaping.

"Several months later we were together at Mardi Gras and we ran into the man—the man you met with. He recognized her and, with the help of two others, took her away by force. I never heard from her again."

I was thinking—maybe the incident in Gary wasn't the Ex-Chief's first barbeque. I'm sure this would be news and not well received by either

Richie Vecchio or Marcello. It definitely made him expendable and he had shown no remorse at disposing of his friend.

The question was, when do I play that card? I needed to run that by David.

I turned back to Tink, who was crying now.

"I'm sorry if we brought back bad memories. What about Ramon Garcia? You indicated you know him."

"Ramon and his brother were just punk kids before they became drug dealers. I even know the guys they buy their drugs from."

I perked up, "Hold on a minute. What do you mean—the guys they buy their drugs from? You mean they are just middlemen?"

"Their source is a pair of Coon-ass brothers from back in the Bayou. The drugs come directly from Mexico. They stash them in the swamp where you don't go and live to tell about it."

I bristled a little at the Coon-ass part. "You mean, Blacks? Like me?"

"Coon-ass is another term for a Cajun—an authentic Cajun."

Tink took a deep breath. "I'm a Coon-ass. I was born in Thibodaux, but they aren't exactly welcoming to queers. I think I'm actually a cousin of the brothers who run the show, but it's hard to tell as it seems like we're all cousins."

"Tink, if I wanted to meet the brothers—how would I go about it?"

"Just go to the Seven Seas bar over on St. Philp. It's not far from here. Ask for a bartender name "Little John" and tell him I sent you. Tell him you want to meet the Coon-ass brothers. He'll tell you he doesn't know who you're talking about, but he'll ask around and you should come back in a couple of days. In the meantime I'll vouch for you."

"Tink, thanks. Hey—did Jasmine pay you for helping her move?"

"I didn't expect anything. I just love her—she's so beautiful."

I reached in my pocket and pulled out a hundred dollar bill. "You've been very helpful—please take this. It's not much, but it's some walking around money."

His eyes bugged out when he took the money. 'Thanks, I need it, but I was trying to help because you're both so nice."

I turned to Jasmine. "I just remembered that I have to call someone on a pay phone. I won't be long. "

Tinkerbell left with me and led me to the nearest pay phone. I realized I needed some change, but there was a bar next door. The bartender was only too happy to give me five dollars of quarters in exchange for a ten spot.

CHAPTER 27

The Mentor

Freddy—Palm Springs

I followed the protocol—calling from a pay phone to give David the number, which he could call back from another pay phone. Truth is, it wasn't that cumbersome and avoided a ton of stress.

It sounded like it was the same dude who answered the first time, but this time when I said it was Freddy for David, he said, "Hold on a minute and I'll get him."

I gave David the number and he returned my call in a matter of minutes. There must have been a pay phone nearby.

"You're still alive?"

"Thanks to your good advice."

"When is the meet?"

I then explained all that had happened since arriving in New Orleans— omitting the part where I fucked with the ex-Chief when I departed the train. That was just ego and David might have given up on me, which I couldn't afford right now.

I further explained what I had learned about both the ex-Chief and Ramon Garcia.

I was getting used to David's pregnant pauses and this was a long one as he digested this information.

"Freddy—I gotta ask you a simple question. What's your end game? If you could make a wish—how would this turn out?"

I pondered the question. "David, I remember one time you told me that true wisdom is knowing what you don't know. Truth is—there's a lot I don't know and you're the only person I can turn to. That's meant to be a compliment, but I know you didn't adopt me and you probably have your own issues, but everything you've told me so far has been good advice."

There was another pause before he replied and I could tell he was trying to compose himself. "Freddy—there's a lot you don't know about me. It would be false humility if I tried to act like I didn't understand this game of life and humble isn't an adjective that anyone who really knows me would use to describe me. Having said that, I read once, 'If you think education is expensive—try ignorance!'

"The wisdom I've acquired has come at a steep price. That price included losing my business, my friends and my wife. Those are terrible prices to pay, but I paid them—in full. The price I couldn't pay—I'll never be able to pay—is the loss of my son. I rationalized that he would have a leg up on this game of life from the wisdom that I'd acquired at such a steep cost.

"I was doing my first stint in 'college', as we called it, and counting the days to when we would be re-united and I could impart this wisdom to my beautiful boy. But, 'Man plans and God laughs', as they say, and my son was killed in a car wreck a week before my release. A drunk driver had crossed the median and hit his car head on.

"I've never told anyone this, but the drunk driver died a slow and painful death, but even that left me wanting. I realized what was missing was someone to benefit from my painful experience. Then I met you. I had to laugh at first. I thought—God has a sense of humor. He's given me a Schvartze to be heir to my wisdom. I now realize that it's God who has the wisdom and I who need the sense of humor."

"David—I don't know what to say. I don't know what Schvartze means, but I can guess. No problem. I've got nowhere else to turn. I can see the end game, as you say, but don't know how to deal with this new information."

"Freddy—it's like this. Except for my advice—you are alone in a very dangerous game. Let's take the ex-Chief first. It's way too obvious that your best interests and his don't coincide. You have the advantage knowing that. Knowledge is power and what you know would be a death sentence for him, with either your boss or Carlos Marcello. The question is—is he worth more to you alive then dead? I would argue he is at present.

"I guarantee he's scheming how to get back in the game, but, without you right now, he's on the outside looking in. As we've discussed, change isn't always a good thing and you are too new to the scene to affect change."

"I could tell the ex-Chief was relieved when I said we'd keep him in the loop. What about the Garcias?"

"Assuming what your friend told you was right, both Vecchios and Marcello have been shortchanged and neither will be happy with the news. Vecchios have been overpaying and Marcello is getting street tax while the Garcia's are getting the middle. Question is—does the ex-Chief know? If he does, he dies twice—if that's possible. If I understand you right—you may have to burn somebody to buy your exit from this game. Don't throw away cards early that you may need later on. You hear me?"

"So what's my next move?"

"Meet with the Cajuns. What'd you call 'em, Coon-asses? If you can cut a better deal, that would be a gift to Marcello. One he would very much appreciate. You could offer him the mark-up and Vecchios wouldn't know the difference. When you do that, though, the ex-Chief is a dead man. Really dead this time. He was either crooked or stupid and neither is a good excuse. I'd hold onto that card for a while."

"Makes sense, as I need to get some money flowing before I upset the apple cart."

"Talking about money—whatta you want me to do with the thirty grand?"

"What thirty grand?"

"The horse. Did you forget?"

"Are you shitting me? The horse won?"

"Freddy—I told you it was a lock."

"I know—I know, but this is—this is great news."

"So what do I do with it?"

"What do you suggest?"

"You ever hear of the Cayman Islands?"

"You got me."

"They're small islands in the Caribbean. Great for scuba diving, but not much else. Not much else, except some very discreet banking. How about I open a numbered account for you? You're gonna need one if your plan succeeds and it's best that it's as discreet as possible. If you'd like—I'll deposit twenty-five g's and put five on an interesting horse this weekend."

I laughed, "How interesting?"

"Even more so than the last one."

"David—I don't know how to thank you."

"The thirty grand that I won went a long way in that direction."

After I hung up, I realized I forgot to ask him the most important question of all. Now that I got the money down to New Orleans—how do I get the drugs back to Gary? I needed the extra time to figure it out.

I noticed that Tinkerbell was still hanging around nearby and motioned him over. "How about we expedite matters a little and go have a night cap at the Seven Seas? That way you can introduce me to Little John."

"You don't mind being seen with me?"

"Tink, I'm proud to be seen with you."

"You're really cool."

"That's my name—Cool Freddy."

CHAPTER 28

Checking the Boxes

Freddy—New Orleans, Two weeks later

As it turned out, Tinkerbell was an even greater asset than appeared possible. Like life in general, it's all about who you know and Tink seemed to be one degree of separation from most of the denizens in the French Quarter.

It was fortuitous that we stopped by the Seven Seas. I was introduced to Little John and he was going to arrange for me to meet with the Coonasses on my next trip down. Maybe of even more timely importance, Tink introduced me to another friend of his who happened to be in the bar.

Louis, pronounced Loo-ee, was as diminutive as Tink and Little John, but that was a problem when you work on an off-shore rig with guys twice your size and who don't see land for weeks at a time. To make matters worse—Louis had attractive, feminine features.

He had signed on with SIU, Seaman's International Union, seeking the solitude of being offshore and away from judgmental people, but he received even more attention on the offshore rig and the wrong kind of attention.

Dreading going back to the rigs, he saw an ad for long-distance truckers and answered it. The net-net is that Louis wound up driving a truck load of fresh shrimp and oysters from the gulf to—get this—Chicago, every other week!

I couldn't believe my good fortune. That is—if I could convince Louis to carry some additional cargo. I didn't want to lay too much on him at first meeting, so we agreed to have coffee and beignets at Café du Monde the next morning.

Turns out—it wasn't that hard a sell. Louis was burned out and his dream wasn't too different than mine, both of which required money. When I offered him five grand cash per trip, he jumped at it. His island was apparently smaller than mine.

He explained that his truck was refrigerated and that the shrimp and oysters were packed loosely in boxes. It would be easy to designate a few boxes to include my cargo. It wouldn't be that hard for Louis, Tink and me to repack the boxes. Tink got to earn a little dough for his help.

I told Ramon that I would take a rain check on his offer of dinner and that I wished to move the swap up a day as Louis was ready to roll.

I was checking my boxes, so to speak. The next one was the ex-Chief who, from now on, was referred to as Glen Martin. He had given me his contact number at the Absinthe House. I called to set up the meet—wanting to see him in advance of Ramon, in the event we had any issues to resolve.

The following day I met Glen at a Po-Boy shop on Decatur. At least the window said it was a Po-Boy shop—maybe had been at one time. Glen let me in and we sat down. Ramon was due in approximately thirty minutes.

I broke the ice, "Chief.."

"It's Glen, now."

"Okay, Glen. I don't know what went down up north and don't want to know. I didn't choose to be in this role—I was recruited. I don't want to cut you out, but I'm not sure where you fit if you can't offer protection."

He appeared nervous. "Like you told Ramon—I can help coordinate things down here. Make sure this end runs smooth. That's got to be worth something."

I purposefully appeared pensive. "Let me ask you this. How did you find Ramon?"

"Through some mutual friends."

That meant that Marcello's men weren't involved. That was even better.

"Okay—let's talk turkey."

I assumed he had no idea the deal that Richie had offered me, the fifteen per cent of gross. Richie would later claim it was of net, not gross, but it was still a shit load of money.

"What do you think that—ah—coordination is worth?"

I could tell that he was visibly nervous. "Freddy—it's like this. Five g's every two weeks is good with me, but I had to—ah—hock some property that I need to get back and it's gonna take a hundred large with maybe some vig to retrieve it. If you can figure out how to help me with that—maybe an advance—then we are really cool."

"Can you tell me about the property?"

"I can't and you don't want to know."

I remembered the conference call he had with Richie and the speculation afterwards about the ex-Chief's files. Whether they had burned up in the fire or whether he kept them as potential leverage.

We saw Ramon pull up in front. "Okay—I'll agree to the five grand every two weeks. I'll have to think about the advance. If I can figure a way to do it—it's done, but right now I don't know how to do it."

This was the second time I'd been in the Ex-Chief's presence. He was a tough hombre. If he was nervous about owing somebody a hundred large—that had to be someone even tougher and in New Orleans that meant Carlos Marcello. If I was right, and Marcello had the files, a plan was forming in my mind.

The swap with Ramon went seamlessly. I gave him the hundred g's and he gave me a suitcase full of uncut Mexican brown heroin.

When Ramon departed a happy camper, I gave Glen his five g's.

"So, how are you gonna get the drugs back north?"

I would have been a fool to trust him and I'm no fool. I've done some dumb things, but my idol Muhammad Ali once said, "A wise man can act like a fool, but a fool can't act like a wise man!"

"It's just a suitcase. I'll take the train. There was no problem coming down."

Just then I noticed him staring at me. "You sure we never met before?"

"Glen—you know what they say, 'We all look alike'."

Most racists are satisfied with that answer and he was a cracker, mother-fucker if I ever met one.

The following day, I took the train with the suitcase in hand, but the drugs were keeping some shrimp and oysters company in Louis's truck. The train ride was uneventful. The ex-Chief, Glen, had a reason to keep me alive if I could help him get his property back.

I had phoned ahead and arranged for two of Richie's men to meet me at Union Station in Chicago and take me to a freight yard on the southwest side, where we would pick up a couple of boxes of shrimp.

We then drove to a motel near Midway Airport, a no-tell motel, where the rooms were let by the hour. Richie's men dropped me off so that no white faces were involved and I waited for the leader of the street gang to make the exchange.

I was naturally nervous. First off, I couldn't carry a gun, but the gang would be foolish to kill the golden goose—or so I hoped.

As fate would have it, the leader's name was Bobby Valentine and—get this—he had worked for Mr. Big. Bobby pulled a Glen on me and kept staring at my face.

"My man—we ever meet before? You look mighty familiar."

"I get that a lot."

"Check this out. I knew a cat one time named Freddy, but he was Fat Freddy."

I patted my flat stomach. "This is as fat as I've ever been. Sorry."

"No—no dis. Fat Freddy was a righteous dude."

We made the swap. The drugs in exchange for four hundred grand. The money was insane. The mob would net a cool three hundred g's and the street gang, after cutting it, would turn it into a fortune. Even after five to Louis and five to Glen plus something for Tink, I was netting over thirty g's twice a month. This train was rollin!

"Oh, Freddy. This food stamp thing is insane. We gonna need more product. Add half as much to the runs and let's see how that goes down."

Cha, fucking ching!!

144

The last order of business prior to heading south again, was to meet with Richie and sort out the money. I had kept the room at the Holiday Inn and waited there for Richie's driver to pick me up. He drove me to Richie's lake house in Michigan which was only accessible via a gated driveway.

Richie couldn't have been more pleased that my first run, which was his first run, as well, went off without a hitch. I didn't share many of the details about the diversion.

I didn't protest—other than look disappointed, when Richie said I misunderstood about the net versus gross, but, like I said, it was still a lot of dough and made my exit strategy feasible. That is—assuming everything else went smoothly, as it never does.

"Freddy, I gotta ask you about the ex-Chief. What's he call himself now?"

"Glen Martin."

He sniffed. "So—what's your impression of whosit—Glen?"

I realized I had to tread carefully so I paused before answering. "I don't know him well enough to comment. He's not the kind of guy I want to go drinking with."

Richie laughed.

"Did he ever mention anything to you about any files he may have?"

I feigned surprise. "No—why would he?"

"No reason. I was just wondering? Did he try to make a deal with you?"

"He said he could be helpful coordinating things down there for me and I agreed to give him five g's a shipment for his help. He accepted."

"Is that five g's out of your share?"

"Yeah—I don't mind. We'll see how it goes."

"So, if he isn't providing protection—how are you moving the product?"

I smiled, "The details I'd prefer to keep to myself—at least for now. I didn't think you wanted to know."

"You're right. I don't as long as things go smoothly."

We divided up the money. Out of the four hundred gross, I got fifteen per cent of the net of three hundred large, forty-five gs less the twenty-five that had been advanced. I had paid Glen and Louis out of the advance funds, so was left with twenty grand—which still looked good, but was soon to get better.

Richie gave me my twenty plus one hundred and fifty for the next run. I would get the additional fifty per cent from the Coon-asses. As far as Glen Martin knew, it was still a hundred grand transaction. That would add another twenty-five to my take and the Coon-asses were another card I could play with Carlos Marcello.

In fact, no sooner had I thought that, but Richie added, "Have you heard from Marcello yet?"

"Not a word."

"Well, that will happen one of these days. They like to know who's operating in their back yard."

"Should I be concerned?"

"Nothing to be concerned about. It's just a formality, but I'll be interested in hearing how it goes."

I couldn't wait to return to the Big Easy and see Jasmine and Tink and Louis, believe it or not. I was also eager to make the next run and start building my stash. David had given me the name of a banker in New Orleans who could wire my funds into the Cayman account for an eight per cent fee. Everybody had their hands out. If my calculation was right—I would get sixty-seven five less the ten to Martin and Louis—hey Martin and Louis!! And another twenty-five from the Coon-asses. A cool eighty-two large and that was large. And I was just getting started.

CHAPTER 29

The Phantom

Tommy—Gary, Indiana, Summer 1967

More than a year had passed and I was no closer to finding either the ex-Chief or the mysterious new drug lord. Meanwhile, the food stamp program had been an absolute boon to the drug business. I thought the government wanted to halt the drug trade, but, in reality, they were funding it.

Otis had bought enough Ripple and malt liquor to float a boat, but all we ever heard was that the new boss was a guy named Cool Freddy. The natives called him Cool Freddy, but Otis and I called him the Phantom—which seemed more appropriate.

We must have followed a hundred false leads and gone up countless blind alleys. The strange thing is that he didn't appear to want to be found, but someone seemed to want to keep his name in the public arena. Why?

The best answer I could come up with is that it was a classic diversionary tactic. Maybe there was a Cool Freddy and maybe there wasn't. Either way the drug trade was booming thanks to the millions from the food stamp program. If we were convinced that there was a Cool Freddy, maybe the real boss was getting a pass as we chased our tails.

If—If there was a Freddy—excuse me—Cool Freddy and if—he did run the show, he would be raking in millions of dollars. Too much to hide and it's more typical of their ilk to flaunt it, than hide it.

But, try as we may—we couldn't find a gold-plated pimp mobile or a multi-million dollar yacht. We did notice, however, that the known mob associates were living very well. Very, very well.

We knew who Bobby Valentine was, but he rarely ventured across the state line and, despite the usual rap sheet, our little Valentine had yet to spend a night in jail. There were a lot of politicians on the south side who drove new Cadillacs and sported expensive watches.

I was starting to get some pressure from above. This hadn't turned into a good investment of time or money in their eyes. The powers that be in Gary couldn't have been more smug as the drug trade reached tsunami proportions. They were resting easier now, confident that the ex-Police Chief either didn't retain any incriminating files or wouldn't use them if he did.

I was no closer to finding where the drugs originated from. We just knew that Valentine's crew brought them into Gary. That didn't help us get closer to the ex-Chief or the elusive Cool Freddy.

I didn't envy Freddy—if he did exist. There were countless John Doe warrants out for his arrest all dutifully signed by a District Court Judge. Even one implicating him in a drug related murder. He was the proverbial man who knew too much.

I thought it might be time to pay a call on Prince Charming and at least rattle his cage a bit. He must have known I was coming because there was a brand new Vette gracing the showroom. This one a midnight blue. Be still my heart.

As fate would have it, Richie was talking to a customer in the showroom when I entered. He was good. He excused himself and almost rushed over as if he was happy to see me.

"Tommy—how do you know when we get a new shipment of Vettes? Will you buy one for chrissake and put us both out of our misery?"

"Richie—I wish I could. Now, if I had Cool Freddy's money."

He was animated, "Don't tell me—you caught him!! Good for you."

"Richie—if bullshit was music, you'd be a brass band."

"Tommy—ouch! What'd I do?"

"I don't suppose you've heard from the ex-Police Chief, either?"

"In fact I did. I went to a séance the other night and had a long chat with him and Napoleon. Why do you keep bustin my balls? He's dead, Tommy. Deal with it. Now if you want to talk about baseball or golf or—or fucking anything except Cool Freddy and a dead guy—I'll hang around. Otherwise, some of us have work to do."

I walked back to my car, my government issue Ford, not a midnight blue Vette. I felt like banging my head on the steering wheel. This is the second time I humiliated myself in front of him and on his turf! What rule hadn't I broken?

Maybe it was time for me to recite the Serenity Prayer.

CHAPTER 30

The Summer of Love

Freddy—New Orleans, Summer 1967

Jasmine and I were having coffee on our balcony as we pored over our finances. The drug business had doubled in the past year. Doubled from the one hundred and fifty percent where we were a year ago.

The business was a well-oiled machine. As far as Glen Martin knew, it was still a hundred grand per shipment business, but I could tell he sensed differently. If he had any communication with his old cronies, they would tell him that drugs had flooded the market.

Each shipment was now three hundred grand worth of product. One hundred from Ramon and two hundred from the Coon-asses, who supplied twice the amount for the same price.

On the Gary end, the take was an astonishing one point two million—every two weeks! Nine hundred g's net to the mob. That meant that yours truly was knocking down a hundred and thirty five fucking large every fortnight. I'd bought a little peace by bumping Martin up to seventy-five hundred, but I told him I couldn't help him with his other problem. More on that later.

I had given Louis a well-deserved raise to fifteen grand per trip—thirty g's per month. He was on cloud nine.

We figured we had easily over a million and a half in the Cayman account. We were close to our target of two million and I had an idea about how to make that three in one move.

That wasn't counting any money David wired in, which wasn't chump change. I don't remember him losing a horse race. It wasn't luck.

The potential game changer had come shortly after I returned from my second trip. Jasmine and I liked to have coffee in the morning at Café du Monde. We were enjoying the scene. It was 1967, the Summer of Love, and Scott McKenzie's, "San Francisco" was beckoning people to the west coast, but there were plenty of flower children from all over the world passing through New Orleans.

It was quite a scene. Something was definitely happening. Even the music was a bit different. The Beatles had just released their revolutionary "Sgt. Pepper's" and "The Letter" by the Box Tops and "Ode to Billy Joe" added to the eclectic mix. Change was in the air and it felt good.

Our reverie was broken by a well-dressed man who approached our table. He couldn't have been more polite.

"Excuse me. I'm sorry to interrupt, but may I have a word with you, Freddy?"

I put two and two together very quickly and told Jasmine that I would see her at home.

We walked outside where a car was waiting. "Freddy, I'm Dante Colangelo." He didn't offer his hand. "I work for Mr. Marcello and he would like to speak with you if we're not interruptin anything."

"Nice to meet you Dante and I've been looking forward to meeting Mr. Marcello."

We drove to an estate out on Lake Ponchartrain that was fit for an emperor, but that's essentially what Carlos Marcello was. I was escorted to his patio overlooking he lake. Mr. Marcello rose to greet me.

"Freddy—or is it Cool Freddy?" He smiled. "I've been hearing good things about you and thought it was time we met."

He motioned for me to sit. "It's my pleasure Mr. Marcello."

"So Freddy—how do you like my city?"

"What's not to like?"

He smiled. "I'm gonna be frank with you. I wasn't sure what your relationship was with the ex-Chief whatever the fuck he calls himself now."

"I met him for the first time when I came here."

"So—is he working for you?"

"Let's put it this way. I pay him, but I'm not sure what he does. He was originally supposed to give me protection, but that was before he faked his death. I'm new to this game and wasn't sure who I could trust—so I guess you could say I thought paying him was a good investment until I sorted things out."

"And, have you sorted things out?"

"I'm getting there."

"I gotta tell you. I don't trust the guy."

"That makes two of us."

"Good. So tell me this. Am I getting shortchanged in this business? I get some street taxes while others appear to be getting fat."

Now was the time to play the Coon-ass card. I was saving a cool hundred large every two weeks by buying from them without anyone else's knowledge. I had to tread carefully here.

"Mr. Marcello—when you asked me earlier if I had things all sorted out, I replied, I'm getting there. I'm trying to figure out what the proper relationship should be. Now—you know there's been a change of leadership in Gary."

"About time. Angelo Vecchio was a senile old prick. He caused a lot of problems."

"That's precisely why I was brought in—to deal with the Black gangs and give the appearance that Blacks run the whole show, now."

"I got the same problem down here. I wanna talk to you about it, but go ahead."

"Okay—and please understand. I'm not accusing anybody of anything. I don't know enough to do so."

He motioned for me to continue.

"It's like this. You're getting street tax on the amount Gary is paying the dealer, but I may know how to buy the same quality product for a lot less."

"You think somebody is screwing me?"

"I'm not saying that sir and I have no way of knowing. If I find out—I'll tell you. I happened to make a connection by chance and I've made a trial run to test it out. Everybody is on the level. So, here's what I think is the right thing for me to do. The cheaper price saved me fifty grand and will save me the same every two weeks unless they change the deal."

"Who's they?"

"With all due respect, let's talk about the money. When your driver takes me home, I'll give him twenty-five g's—" his eyes lit up, "—representing fifty per cent of the first shipment and I'll give you half of everything I save from now on—which is now twenty-five g's."

"Twenty-five every month?"

"Twenty-five every two weeks."

Marcello perked up. "And where's the other twenty-five go?"

"That I work out with the new boss. He's the one who recruited me."

He started to laugh. "Go fucking figure. I've got people whose lives I've saved who try to fuck me and a fucking moulinyan, no offense, who I've never met—comes in and treats me with proper respect!"

He beckoned to his butler. "Bring us some champagne and get us some lunch. Freddy—I accept your gesture. What can I do for you?"

"Well, and with all due respect, there is something I would like—that I believe you have?"

He furrowed his brow. "Which is?"

"Mind you—I'm just guessing, but the ex-Chief—" Marcello pretended to spit at the mention of him, "—wanted me to loan him a hundred large. He said he had some property that he wanted to get back." Marcello now stiffened. "I'm guessing that it might be some files from Gary that would be harmful to some people up there."

"What did you tell him?"

"Nothing, but there's no way I'm giving him the money and letting him keep those files."

The champagne was served and we clinked our glasses. He savored his first taste before he replied. "And you want me to give you those files?"

I feigned surprise. "No sir. I don't expect you to give me anything. What I propose is that I give you an additional twenty-five every two weeks until it totals a hundred and then you give me the files, but you don't let him know."

He took a more generous sip. "Freddy—I like you. You have manners, that's a lost art, and you show respect, but there's some interest due on that loan also."

"How about we make it one twenty-five and you keep the files until you have all the money? And, I may pre-pay the money if I can."

"But, with the interest."

"Of course."

He stuck out his hand. "You have a deal. The files don't mean anything to me anyway. There's nothing in Gary that I want. There is a favor I want to ask of you."

"Name it."

"Like everybody else in this fucking country—I've got problems with the coloreds. Just like Gary. They don't like the idea of Italians profiting off their people." He held his hands up. "Before you say anything—I get it, but I like what they did in Gary with you appearing to be in charge."

"What do you want me to do?"

"I want you to meet with this guy—the chief troublemaker. His name is Robin. He's got a bar in Algiers named The Robin's Nest. See if you can talk some sense into him—maybe make the same deal as Gary. Whatever you decide, I'll approve. What do you need to do that for me?"

"Sir, it will be my pleasure to do a favor for you. Maybe someday I'll need a favor."

"Freddy—where have you been? I'm surrounded by morons. I hope you like Crab Louis salad?"

"It's my favorite."

We had a great lunch and parted on the best of terms. His driver and Dante drove me home where I gave Dante an envelope with fifty grand in it. Twenty-five for his split and twenty-five toward the files.

The biggest obstacle now standing in the way of my eventual exit was Tommy O'Brien. The files could be the Holy Grail for him. Plus, I would deliver the ex-Chief. If that doesn't get me out of jail for free, maybe I could do some short time. Maybe another stay at Club Fed? Maybe pigs have wings.

Part of the deal would have to be that Richie and Marcello aren't implicated. They could re-start the trade with the Coon-asses and nobody would be the wiser. I'll let them sort things out.

We had a regular table for four with Tink and Louis at The Court of Two Sisters to celebrate each successful trip. Tonight was our night and I was looking forward to it. After dinner, Jasmine and I would discuss her departure to look for an island for us. Little did I know that she would announce at dinner that she was with child. Now, there was a sense of urgency to our plans.

CHAPTER 31

Blue Bayou

Tommy—Gary, Indiana, Summer 1967

I was contemplating my navel on my patio, watching the golfers chase their balls up the fairway. I envied them that they could keep score of their progress, even if they cheat and lie as most golfers I know, do. At least they had some basis for judging their progress, or lack thereof. I had none at present and that bothered me. My tantalizing leads had only taken me so far and I was at an impasse without a break through, which seemed to be elusive.

I had been dispatched to this hell hole to try to at least mitigate the violence, if not put a serious dent in the drug trade. The only substantive accomplishment thus far was a dramatic drop in drug related killings, but that was a dividend of the détente between the Black street gangs and the mob—which led to an even greater influx of drugs into the community. I could prove murder one against the ex-Police Chief—if I could find him in some place other than the local cemetery. And the source of the drugs, which might unlock many secrets, continued to elude me. To make things worse—if I were to choose someone to have a drink with and share some company, it would be the new head of the mob, who was engaged in a campaign to mislead me. Go fucking figure.

My phone rang and when I answered it was my trusty side kick, Otis. It was Otis who deserved credit for the few breaks we had so far. It was probably his TGIF call.

"Hey boss: It's the Friday that Big Judy has that shrimp deep-fried in her special buttermilk batter that you like so much. I thought I'd grab a mess of shrimp, some cole slaw and hush puppies and drop by and cheer you up a bit."

I don't know what it says about me that the thought of food could bring me out of my funk, but this wasn't just any food. This was jumbo shrimp, deep-fried in a special batter and the shrimp tasted like it had just been caught. It was that fresh. There would be cars lined up for a block at Big Judy's waiting for take-out.

Otis brought the food and I had plenty of cold beer. We ate on the patio. Truth is—I was gonna miss Otis. He was a good man and a great companion. He was the only entertainment I had. "Otis—we ought to go into the food business and franchise Big Judy's. This shrimp is incredible."

"Yeah, but the problem is—she can only get a delivery every other week."

I digested my hush puppy and washed it down with beer. "Otis—say that again."

"Say what? You mean she only gets deliveries every other week?"

"Now, Otis—think for a minute. This shrimp is fresh right?"

"Like it jumped out of the water and onto the plate."

"And, where does shrimp come from?"

"The gulf."

"Now think for a minute. How often do the drugs hit the hood?"

"My people say there's a new supply every other week."

Suddenly, Otis' eyes got big. "You think there might be a connection?"

"It might be a stretch, but think about this. What if the drugs come in with a shipment of shrimp? How come she only gets the shrimp every other week? How well do you know Big Judy?"

Otis smiled. "She wasn't always Big Judy. When she was younger she was prime tang, if you know what I mean, and she had a Jones for me. She wasn't the only one."

I loved Otis. "I have no doubt, Otis. You don't do so bad these days—I've noticed."

"These pants I wear. Know what they call 'em?"

"I have no idea. They look like brown slacks to me."

"Uh huh. These are my Burger King pants. Home of the Whopper. You dig?"

"Otis—I'm sure gonna miss you, but let's get back to business. See if Judy has a box that the shrimp came in. It might be in the garbage, but that won't be picked up till Monday. I want to know the name of the company that sells the shrimp."

"I'll swing by there and see. By that time I'll be ready for round two if she got any left."

"Any what? Shrimp or tang?"

"Boss—she ain't never gonna run out of tang!"

My mind was racing—considering various scenarios while Otis was on his mission. All roads led back to the purveyor of the shrimp. It would have been an incredible coincidence for the drug schedule and the shrimp schedule to happen to coincide. Particularly when both had to come from the south—and I didn't believe in coincidences. It was clever, actually—very clever. Chicago's restaurants would have been receiving regular shipments of shrimp and other seafood for decades. As an investigator, you look for anomalies and shipments of shrimp wouldn't have been an anomaly. Not to mention—the drugs would obviously be in boxes on the bottom and who wants to assume the liability for spoiling a truckload of shrimp in search of some potential drugs. Try to get that warrant signed. Particularly by a Judge who enjoys seafood at one of the restaurants the purveyor supplies. To get that warrant signed by a Judge who likes shrimp and is getting fat envelopes periodically—fuggetaboutit!

Otis returned with a heavy duty corrugated box emblazoned with, "Blue Bayou Seafood, Inc. Purveyors of the Finest Shrimp and Oysters since 1919. Fresh from the Gulf to your table!" The address was a New Orleans warehouse on Tchoupitoulas Street, hard by the Mississippi River.

Otis was animated. "What do we do now, Boss?"

"Otis—we have to really think this through. Do NOT breathe a word about this to anybody. I think we're on to something, but I need to sleep on it. Come over for coffee tomorrow and we'll make a plan."

CHAPTER 32

Rockin Robin

Freddy—New Orleans & Algiers

There just can't be another place on earth like New Orleans. The world isn't big enough. Even the indigenous peoples are unique. It isn't the Tchoupitoulas tribe—it's the WILD Tchoupitoulas tribe as we're reminded every Mardi Gras. Throw in the original settlers—French criminals and prostitutes, the pirates, the Irish, the Acadians (Cajuns) and the slaves—none of whom were welcomed. Put the blender on frappe and voila: The Big Easy!

I mean—what other city in the world, where everyone knows it's below sea level (which is why the friggin graves have to be above ground) do tens of thousands of people live in houses protected only by a levee made of dirt? Talk about "laissez faire"! Just one time—just one time does the levee have to fail for a disaster to happen, but tonight, Cheri, "laissez les bon temps rouler!" (Let the good times roll) They may eventually drown, but stress ain't gonna kill 'em.

I was in Marcello's car with the driver and the ever present Dante, heading to Algiers to meet one Rick, nee Dudley, Robin—Marcello's current source of angst. Rumor is that Robin owed his toughness to being born Dudley. I get it. But it wasn't toughness that kept him alive and he knew it. The Crescent City had almost gone up in flames two years earlier in the copy-cat Watts riots. More than two-thousand years ago Sun Tzu figured out that you don't gain anything by destroying that which you hoped to conquer. Marcello was no dummy, but neither could he afford to let a piss ant like Robin flaunt his control.

I didn't fear for my safety, being an emissary of Marcello. I guessed that Robin would leap at a "golden bridge to retreat across". I simply dreaded every moment I spent in Algiers. That is a scary fucking place. The driver dropped me off at Robin's bar, "The Robin's Nest". It was apparent from Jump Street that Robin was trying to posture. No sooner had we sat down than he started, "So you Marcello's house n****r?"

He was obviously playing to his entourage who enjoyed his slight. I simply got up and started to walk out without saying a word. The tables were turned. "Hey—where you goin? You can't leave without talkin."

I turned as I kept walking, "Watch me—Dudley."

I had reached the door when he rushed up and pleaded with me to stay. His entourage melted away. Round One to me. He invited me to a booth in the back of the bar. "Look, Freddy—do me a favor and don't call me Dudley in front of my homeys."

"Look, Rick, do me a favor and don't call me n****r—ever. You understand?"

"Word—it's just—it's just—how can you be representin Marcello against your own people? What's up with that?"

I looked him in the eye. "I'm sorry—have we spoken yet?"

"Not yet."

"Then I have a question for you. You ready?"

"I'm waitin."

"If we haven't even spoken yet—how the fuck do you know who I'm representing? Wouldn't it be helpful to hear what I have to say, first?"

"But—Marcello sent you."

"Marcello's a smart man. He can read the writing on the wall. Unless you start to rally before I leave here—you might be one of the dumbest assholes I've ever met." Said loud enough for his peeps to hear.

"Freddy—you can't dis me like that in my place and in front of my homeys."

"You want to be treated with respect—you gotta earn it. Now do you want to hear what I have to say?"

He was so at sea that he didn't know how to get back to land. He made his best effort, feigning a laugh. "I was just testin you." As he smiled to his sycophants. "You alright Freddy. Lay it on me."

I paused, letting him know that I knew his pivot was bullshit, but this is what I came for. "Rick—Mr. Marcello knows that the old way of the Italians running everything doesn't work anymore. It's not just here—it's all over the country. We—I said WE—have to have a seat at this table. If it doesn't work for all of us—it works for none of us and—and the table is a big fucking table. If everybody is reasonable and nobody gets greedy—we can make a new deal and stop this senseless bloodshed."

"Freddy—that all sounds good, but what do you mean by a seat at the table?"

I took a deep breath. "You serve any booze in this place?"

He jumped up and waved a waiter over. "I'm sorry Freddy—I got distracted. What would you like?"

"You got any champagne—any of the good stuff—to help us celebrate a new partnership?"

Now he was animated. "I don't know much about champagne. I'm a cognac guy, but one of my dealers—a white guy—gives me a bottle of Dom something for Christmas every year."

"Dom Perignon?"

"That sounds right."

"That'll work. Let's wait till it's served."

Sure enough—it was the real deal that had been wasted on a fool. The waiter only had cognac snifters, but they sufficed. We clinked glasses and savored our first taste. "Okay, Rick—here's what I propose and what Mr. Marcello has already agreed to. This is based upon a model that has worked up north, which is why I'm involved. The Italians turn over all of the distribution business to you—" his eyes bugged out, "—but you get your product from the Italians. They handle supply—you handle distribution."

"Freddy—Freddy—are you sayin that Marcello would agree to that?"

"No—I'm saying Mr. Marcello has already agreed to it."

"But, what if he jacks up the price and takes all the profit?"

"Rick—you gotta chill. Why would he do that? I'm from Chicago and you know what they say in Chicago? 'The pigs get fat and the hogs get slaughtered'."

"And you're telling me that the killing stops?"

"Nobody wins at war. It's an eye for an eye until everyone is blind."

"Freddy—what do you get out of this?"

"I go to bed tonight knowing that some of my people—some of our people—won't die a senseless death and that we finally got a seat at the table. Hopefully, we won't screw it up."

"Freddy—I was wrong about you. What do I have to do?"

"Mr. Marcello's right hand man, Dante Colangelo, will be picking me up in a few minutes. Just shake his hand and say we have a deal. Everything else can be worked out later."

"Freddy—will I see you again?"

"I don't know when, but I may have other plans for you."

"Just don't forget about me."

"No chance of that."

The car picked me up and Colangelo shook hands with a beaming Robin who begged us to stay and party, but we demurred. When they dropped me off on Royal Street, Dante got out and opened the trunk. "I've got a suitcase for you."

I was at a loss. "It's the files from the fuck up police chief. A gift from Mr. Marcello and the rest of the debt is cancelled."

"I don't know what to say?"

"You don't need to say nothing. You earned it and Mr. Marcello looks after his friends. I don't know where you learned about respect, but you learned well. Just don't forget it."

That added another hundred g's to the exit fund and I had what was left of the champagne. Dudley didn't have a taste for it.

CHAPTER 33

Money Talks and Bullshit Walks

Gary, Indiana

Big Judy was a legend in Gary's hood. The sobriquet came from a big rear end being called a back porch. Judy didn't have a big back porch—she had a frigging veranda! Her great grandmother had been a cook on a plantation owned by a Frenchman in Louisiana. He had imported a chef from France, as the ultimate status symbol among the plantation owners was who served the best food.

When her great grandmother's knowledge of herbs and spices was fused with classic French recipes the result was incredible. So much so that when her indentured servitude ended, the plantation owner agreed to put up the money for a restaurant in New Orleans that would feature their nouvelle cuisine. That dream evaporated when the Yankees—the damn Yankees (that term was coined before Babe, Lou and Joltin Joe were even born) came. They burned the plantation to the ground just for spite. The slaves were free, but left with just the shirts on their backs. Hallelujah! They were Black, poor and now homeless, but they were free now to be exploited by the abolitionist factory owners in the north.

Big Judy's family wound up in Gary where some of the men found work in the mills. Slave labor if there ever was. The women had trouble finding even menial jobs as it wasn't a prosperous area. Her great grandmother died of a broken heart, but before she passed—she imparted as much knowledge of the art of cooking as she could. The recipe books that had been patiently prepared, had been consumed by the fire that destroyed every other vestige of her previous life.

Big Judy was the first of her line to try to commercialize that knowledge. She had a job as a cook in a small local tavern and when the owner, who was the main cook, became ill—she took over the kitchen and started experimenting with some of the family recipes. In a more prosperous locale, she might have become a famous chef, but in Gary she was just a big fish in a small pond.

Speaking of fish—on Friday nights in the hood, Big Judy's was the place to be. She would whip up a mess of Lake Perch, Catfish or Walleye—whatever was fresh and deep fry it in her special batter. She first met Bobby Valentine when his entourage stopped in for one of her Friday night fish fries. Since that time, one table was always reserved for the Man, so to speak. She, like everybody else, kept hearing the name Cool Freddy and it was said that he was the real boss, but, like most everybody else, she'd never laid eyes on him.

One Friday Valentine and his men came in early with two huge boxes of fresh, jumbo shrimp on ice. They were delicious raw as a cocktail, but Valentine asked her if she could deep fry them in her special batter. The result was incredible and soon the word got out—even in the white community. Cars from Hammond and Michigan City would line up on Friday night for take-out. Problem was—Valentine only visited twice a month. On those occasions he brought as much shrimp as she could handle, as a favor, but he was also aware that the shrimp was attracting attention and attention wasn't a good thing in his business—which wasn't seafood.

Big Judy

"The best thing Bobby Valentine did for me was to loan me two thousand dollars so that I could buy food stamps for fifty cents on the dollar and we split the profit. On the weeks I don't get the shrimp—I make more money from the food stamps. Not to mention he leave at least a hundred dollar tip every time he eat here.

So tonight when that jive-ass, black Barney Fife, Otis, come back sniffin around, wantin to know if he could have one of the empty shrimp boxes— my antenna went up. He with the big-ass ego that got no connection to reality—that don't know the difference between Burger King and White Castle. I told him we threw 'em out, but I seen him out rummaging through the dumpster. Somethin told me I should let Bobby Valentine know. After all, money talk and bullshit walks. That's just the way it is."

Bobby Valentine was appreciative and reached out to Freddy following the phone protocol Freddy had adopted from David.

Bobby was contrite for the slip up, but Freddy was philosophical about it, "Shit happens." Bobby had been trying to help a sister and that was a good thing, according to Freddy.

"Bobby, this is a game we play and information is power in this game. It was good that you found out and told me—so we can stay a step ahead. When I sort things out I'll get back to you. In the meantime, we've got almost two weeks before the next shipment is due. That's plenty of time."

The element of time was more relevant to Freddy—another change and maybe a game changer. Or—maybe, it just moves up the timeline for my saying fuck you and goodbye to this game.

I knew that Tommy O'Brien would be plotting his next move on this chess board. I needed to counter that move—or, better yet, pre-empt it. It was time for me to call the master.

CHAPTER 34

The End Game

Tommy—Gary, Indiana

I was aware that the bureau was about to pull the plug on the mission. In their eyes one of the two primary objectives had been achieved and the co-opted local authorities were declaring victory and asking them to withdraw.

Me? I was torn. I desperately wanted to get back to Washington and Mary Kay, who was now pregnant with our first child—a gift from my Easter visit. And, I was eager to be assigned to a new mission where I was fighting just the bad guys, not the so-called "good guys", too. However, I knew the truth about the mission and it wasn't in my nature to walk away from a case that involved murder one—at least one murder one.

I called Butch McCarthy to apprise him of this significant break and get his advice on how to play it. It was with some trepidation, however, that I made the call. He was in a downward spiral, fueled by alcohol, due to the loss of his son and the breakup of his marriage. The remaining pillar in his life, the Bureau, was a shaky one at best. He was facing forced retirement at year-end for failing to play the game of protecting the rich and powerful—justice be damned. He would be exiting on a low note as Gary was coming up a cropper.

I was surprised, frankly, to hear a chipper and sober voice on the other end. He told me that his wife, who had been in therapy since their son's overdose, had been inspired in therapy to honor her son's life by funding a project in his name that might save others from a similar fate.

She had instinctively answered that she and her husband would love to do something like that. It forced her to call Butch for the first time in three years. He said it was a wonderful idea and that he would soon have the time to devote to it as he'd be leaving the bureau at year-end. His wife absolutely detested the Bureau—blaming it for all of their problems and Butch wasn't taking the other side of that argument any more.

The good news is that she was coming to visit—just for "the weekend" and just to discuss the project. Butch had a cleaning service scour the house and a gardener transform the grounds for her arrival. Most importantly of all—he was cleaning himself up.

I was almost hesitant to bring him down off of his cloud, even with supposed good news, for fear it might complicate his plans.

"Tommy, the truth is—they're pulling the plug on us at year-end regardless. At least you were victorious on half of the mission—the murder rate."

"Butch—you know I wasn't responsible for that."

"I know nothing of the sort. It happened on your watch—you get credit for it. That's the way this game is played. Maybe they were forced to make the truce because of your arrival. You ever think of that?"

I hadn't. I'd been too consumed with my pity party. "Are you saying we don't have time to follow this lead?"

"No. What I'm saying is we don't have time to go down a blind alley that will require warrants, which will never be granted—even if the judges aren't tainted. The connection—which I buy, by the way, is just way too thin."

"So—I should just walk away?"

"You wouldn't if I told you to and I'm not telling you to. You told me early on that the ex-police chief was the key to the case, but you needed to find out where the drugs were coming from to find him. Does that still hold true?"

"Yeah, and that might be doable given our time frame, but his files will only incriminate the conspirators while he was Police Chief. That was more than a year and a half ago. That won't cover the new mob boss and some of the new players."

"Tommy—the drug channel should still be the same. If you bust the ex-Police Chief for murder one and his co-conspirators, including the drug suppliers, in just two years with only one local assistant and very little other support—you'll be a hero!"

"What about Cool Freddy? He came after the chief."

"Tommy, I've never seen more John Doe warrants issued for one man. There is at least one local Judge that wants to make sure that if Cool Freddy is ever caught, he'll never see the light of day. An insurance policy if I ever saw one."

"I don't get it. Cool Freddy may be running things, and even that is open to doubt, but he's only been doing so for as long as I've been there."

"You can't see the forest for the trees. Don't you see what they've done? Cool Freddy is just a pawn in this game. A deception to make us think that Carlo Gambino all of a sudden decided to walk away from the drug trade and tens of millions of dollars. If and that's a big if—If the scheme ever blows up, the blame will be all on Cool Freddy. The Gambinos aren't just one of the most violent mob families—they're one of the smartest. Freddy is fucked. He just doesn't know it."

"Okay. The plan will to be to focus on finding the ex-Chief, but if he isn't in New Orleans I'm afraid we've run out of time."

CHAPTER 35

Leverage

Freddy—New Orleans

After I had spoken with Bobby Valentine and digested the new information, I realized I needed David's advice more than ever. We went through our phone protocol and made our connection. I explained to David what had happened and my fear of the potential consequences. As usual, David was the voice of reason and that was exactly what I needed.

"Let's take it from the top. Is it still your goal to get out of the game and hopefully disappear?"

"More than ever."

"And, you're convinced that this agent, O'Brien, is an obstacle to your plan?"

"The biggest obstacle."

"I don't know about that, but will get to that later. So, the big change is that the agent might know how and where the product comes from?"

"He'll be able to figure it out, now."

"Okay—relax. You got plenty of quarters?"

"I'm prepared."

"Okay. Let's start with who's who in the supply chain. Take each one at a time."

"All right. There's me, of course. There's Bobby Valentine—he's the head of the street gang."

"What's your relationship with him?"

"He's been a pleasant surprise. One of the victims of the Viet Nam War. He wanted to be an architect, but got drafted and learned to kill, instead. We've actually become friends."

"Would he disappear too, if needed?"

"I wouldn't be surprised if he came with me."

"Next."

"Next would be Louis (loo-ee). He drives the delivery truck."

"What's his story?"

"He's a victim too, but from other circumstances. He's driving long distance to be as far away from the crowd as possible. He's got enough money now to buy his own rig."

"Has he been careful with his money? I mean—are the feds gonna find a fortune in the bank account of a guy who makes maybe ten g's a year?"

"I imparted your advice in that regard in the beginning. Most, if not all, of his money is in untraceable bearer bonds."

"Good. Truth is, he'd be hard to convict anyway without something more than they got. What about the supplier?"

"It's actually suppliers, plural. The supplier of record, so to speak, are two brothers who are nothing more than middlemen who've been buying from the source and marking it up. I learned the identity of the source and I've been doing business with them, also, but that's known only to me and them."

"Are you telling me that Gary has been overpaying? If so, that means Marcello is getting shorted, too."

"That's what I'm telling you."

"How secure is the source?"

"They're natives, called Coon-asses who operate out of the Bayou."

"Say no more. So, theoretically—if the middlemen go down, Gary and Marcello could stay in business at an even better price?"

"Not just theoretically."

"And, you won't have any crocodile tears if the middlemen go down?"

"They're thieves, aren't they?"

"Agreed. Now, I seem to remember that the ex-Police Chief was still involved somehow."

"He's the connection to the middleman and provided the cover for the shipments for several years."

"Weren't you gonna try to get his files?"

"I got them. Marcello gave them to me."

"Wait a minute. Did I hear you say Carlos Marcello gave them to you?"

"I did him a favor, plus some serious tribute. He had an issue with a Black street gang in New Orleans. Same as happened in Gary."

"And you got it worked out?"

"Yeah. The guy was a total asshole."

"So, Marcello wouldn't mind seeing him go down?"

"If it didn't upset the apple cart—he'd love it."

"I asked for a reason. You think the agent is your biggest obstacle, but I'd be worried about Marcello and the Gary mob."

"Marcello isn't directly connected to Gary. The only connection to the new boss is through me and there's no way I'll give him up."

"Freddy. He's using you—don't you get it?"

"Yeah—I get it and I knew that from Jump Street. We all serve somebody. The only question is, do we get paid properly for our services? I got paid very, very well. Not to mention where we met, which would be very embarrassing for the government and whomever his sponsors were. Here's what's interesting—the ex-Chief's files are explosive. They were his insurance policy or so he thought. The thing is—they can bring down some big players, but only those who were involved during his time and that ended almost two years ago. Two years ago, the new mob boss was just a car dealer."

David was silent for an extended period—which I was used to. His mind was processing the data. "The way I see it, a warrant based upon a possible coincidence is far from a slam dunk. The agent would need a friendly Judge and that doesn't seem likely. It would take a long time and a lot of resources to put that case together. That doesn't sound like the guy you've described. My guess is that O'Brien will use this information to try to find the ex-Chief—his original target. What are his chances of finding him in New Orleans?"

"Let's put it this way. I wouldn't want to be the ex-Chief right now."

"If he gets his man—will the guy sing?"

"Like a fucking canary."

"This is not an easy call. Even if he gets the guy and he sings—you're still John Doe on the warrants and the John Doe warrants scare me. Let me tell you why. They're a message to you. If you get caught, at least one local Judge wants you to be the fall guy, but they still have to prove that you're Cool Freddy. So, if you think this O'Brien guy has a chance of getting the ex-Chief—who could implicate you—you would lose whatever leverage you have if he moves first. On the other hand, if you were to move first and contact O'Brien with an offer to deliver the ex-Chief and his files, in exchange for whatever conditions you seek, you'll make him a hero and save him a lot of time and frustration. It's called 'quid pro quo' and it's done all the time."

"What are the chances that they'll let me slide in exchange for the help—which will be huge?"

"Let me put it this way—if it was a horse, we wouldn't bet on it. Here's the rub—it won't be O'Brien's call at the end of the day. He'll have a voice, but if there are some people in high places that want to make you a scape-goat—you might still face some time."

"Any chance that the time could be done at Club Fed?"

"Nothing's impossible, but you're just a pawn in this game. The wild card would be the Appellate Judge. It's clear the local Judge is no friend. If this conspiracy extends into the Appellate Court—you're fucked, my friend. What the Brits call, royally fucked."

"What are the odds of that?"

"Can't say. I'd like to say slim, but someone in a very high place had to be responsible for the new mob boss being at Club Fed, too. It's possible that he isn't the one pulling the strings. That leaves you with your dick hanging out. I can't make this call for you. Can you do the time, if need be?"

"It all depends on how much and where."

"Why don't you do this first? Why don't you come up with a plan for how to get the mob boss and Marcello to sanction your move?"

"I've thought of that, but I have no move if Tommy doesn't go along with it."

"Tommy?"

"I didn't tell you. We have a history. I think it's worth a shot."

"You are an interesting young man Freddy. By the way—you haven't asked how the horse business is going?"

"David, you've been more than generous. I must have made over a hundred grand on a four g's gamble. I'll take that any day. You're okay, right?"

"Am I okay? I just helped syndicate a shopping center with a group of doctors. I made—get this—ten million, with an m, and it was legal! I'd retire if I wasn't having so much fun."

"How'd the doctors do?"

"They lost ten million, but got some tax write-offs and some experience."

I laughed. "Sounds like a fair trade to me."

"Let me know what happens. There's many ways to disappear, you know."

"I've got one, if I need it. I hope I don't need it."

CHAPTER 36

Reach Out and Touch Someone

Tommy & Freddy—Gary, Indiana

Since I was a young lad, whenever I was confronted with some type of crisis, or needed to make a big decision, I would get out pen and paper and try to list the pros and cons. It served me well over the years. When I took Accounting 101 in college, I learned there was a name for it—a balance sheet. The pros and cons had names, as well—assets and liabilities. As I made a line down the middle of the page, with assets on the left and liabilities on the right, I had to smile. This was indeed a business decision I needed to ponder. Crime was a business and business was good.

I started with the assets. The bad guys didn't know—at least I didn't think they knew—that the clock was ticking on this mission. On the right side of my ledger, I had to note that I had approximately four months to nab the ex-Chief or the plug would be pulled.

Back to the assets: I had a good idea where the ex-Chief could be found. NOLA, as the natives called it. On the right side, I noted that it would be a one-man show, as Otis would be way out of his element in the Big Easy. Violence wasn't just a possibility—it was a certainty.

Asset: They didn't know what I knew. Liability: I didn't know much.

Asset: I had a bottle of Jameson. Liability: It was half-empty.

So much for the balance sheet. This business would be lucky to keep the doors open till year-end.

I was headed for the nectar of the Gods when my phone rang. I looked at the clock. It was just after one A.M. I answered, "Who is it?"

The voice on the other end replied, "I hear you've been looking for me."

"You just narrowed it down to about fifty people. Let me ask again, who the fuck is it?"

I was surprised and a little irritated to hear a soft chuckle. "In Gary they refer to me as Cool Freddy. Is this a good time to talk?"

"Cool Freddy—if you are Cool Freddy, your timing sucks. You should have asked that in the beginning."

That elicited a laugh. "Tommy O'Brien—you're still a hard ass."

I was trying to decipher the conversation. "In Gary they refer to me as Cool Freddy" and "you're still a hard ass."

"Listen, Cool Freddy, or whoever you are—do I know you?"

"Several years ago, in the old neighborhood you knew me as Fat Freddy."

My head was now spinning. "What old neighborhood would that be?"

Another laugh. "Ninety-Second and Wallace, where else?"

"The Fat Freddy I knew got sent away on some trumped up charges. Nobody knew where he was sent. They must have had a gym."

Still laughing, "A running track. This is good—I haven't had a good laugh for a long time."

"I'm happy I amuse you, but did you notice that I'm not laughing with you?"

"Sorry—it's just—it's just I've thought about you a lot over the years. You saved my Black ass and I haven't forgotten that."

"If I'd known you were gonna wind up dealing drugs, I wouldn't have bothered."

"Yeah you would have. I've had quite a journey in my young life, but I've never met anyone as straight arrow as you."

"Freddy—I mean Cool Freddy—is there a purpose to this call besides reminiscing about the old hood?"

"Tommy, everything isn't as it seems. I'm still Fat Freddy. I haven't changed, but circumstances sure have. I hear you're looking for someone and I can help you find him."

"And—why would you do that?"

"That I owe you my life is a good place to start, but you're also looking for me—you and others."

"You help me and maybe I help you? Is that it?"

"I help you and you help me—no maybes. Isn't that the way it's done?"

"That'd require a lot of help and soon."

"I got everything you need and the sooner the better for me."

"You know there are multiple warrants out for you?"

"Those warrants are for some dude named John Doe and I don't know any colored guys named John Doe—although I did meet one named Dudley recently."

"How do you want to play this?"

"How about we go back to the beginning? You remember where I beat up the Police Captain's son that started all this?"

"The colored beach."

"That's one name for it. How about you meet me there at four P.M. today. It should be less crowded then. And, Tommy—I'm trusting you. This is just you and me. If you're not satisfied with what I tell you—we walk away. Do I have your word on that?"

I hesitated before answering. "I'll see you at four."

The Proposal

Tommy & Freddy—Chicago

Tommy consulted with Butch before deciding to follow through with the meeting. Both agreed that there was no incentive for Cool Freddy to set Tommy up. Until now, Tommy didn't know who he was. Both were also extremely anxious to hear what Freddy's proposal would be. Butch cautioned, however, that it was highly unlikely that the District Judge, who signed the warrants, would agree to any type of deal. That would leave the Court of Appeals as Freddy's last hope and that was a wild card.

The beach was still pretty crowded on this late summer afternoon when Tommy arrived. He immediately realized the wisdom, Freddy's wisdom, in choosing this location. Tommy was the only white face in the crowd and it was highly likely that some of the "bathers" were Freddy's guys. Truth is, Tommy was hoping for, in fact relying on, Freddy's discretion.

One of the more buff Black beach-goers emerged from the crowd with a towel over his shoulder. "It's been a long time, Tommy."

"Freddy—it's not like you and I were buddies. I barely knew you."

"Yeah, but you were there for me when I needed it and I've never forgotten that."

"No offense, Freddy, but that was just a case of right and wrong in my neighborhood. It wasn't about you."

"So, I can forget about the man hug?"

Tommy had to smile. "Look Freddy—why don't you put your shirt on and we'll sit down on one of the benches."

"Is that a better angle for your snipers?"

"I gave you my word that I'd come alone."

"Your word is good enough for me."

They found an empty bench out of ear shot of the crowd. There was a pregnant pause before Freddy broke the ice. "So—you're wondering how I got from the hood to here?"

"It crossed my mind."

"It wasn't by design."

"Life rarely is."

"While I was doing my time.."

"Where was that, by the way?"

"That's not part of this discussion. Anyway, I did my time and got an Associate's Degree from a Community College. I'd gotten myself in shape and was looking forward to a new lease on life—one with unlimited potential. That's when I ran smack into that fickle thing called reality. Every application I completed asked for race and criminal history. Good luck with the new lease. It was there, however, that I was recruited for the role of Cool Freddy. The mob was forced to make deals with the emerging Black street gangs in order to stop the bloodshed that was attracting the wrong kind of attention. They needed a Black man to be the liaison. I had nowhere to go and no prospects. I couldn't go home as long as Captain Murphy was still around. I was told that I'd be saving lives—Black lives, by helping to end the bloodshed."

"So you're not the boss. You're just the liaison—which means the mob is still involved and the mob, now, means Richie Vecchio."

"You're moving way too fast. I can't help you with Richie Vecchio."

"Can't or won't?"

"The result is the same."

"Okay, so what can you help me with?"

"I've gotta have some assurances from you first. It's called 'quid pro quo'."

"Look Freddy. I'm not gonna lie to you. This situation is really fucked up. There are some very powerful people who don't seem to want to see me succeed. That may include members of the Judiciary."

"That does include Judges."

"That's not good news for you."

"Are you saying there's no reason for us to try to make a deal?"

Tommy was pensive and blew out a big breath before responding. "When you called, you said that you knew I was looking for someone and that you could help me find him. Let's make sure we're talking about the same guy. The guy I want is the ex-Police Chief. We on the same page?"

"What about a deal?"

"If you can tell me where I can find the ex-Police Chief—I can't make promises that are out of my control, but I give you my word that I will fight for you."

"I don't recall you ever losing a fight. I can do better than tell you where you can find him. You agree to my other conditions and I'll deliver him to you on a silver platter."

"Like a sting?"

"Call it anything you want. I'll set up a buy and you can have him redhanded."

"What are these other conditions you mentioned?"

"Let me tell you what I'm going to give you first. That should put you in a proper frame of mind."

Tommy motioned for him to continue.

"You're right that he didn't die in the fire. I don't know the identity of the person who did. I just know the ex-Chief's a sick fuck and he belongs to a cult that gets their jollies off torturing and killing migrant workers in New Orleans."

"Let me worry about the victim."

"I'm just saying. There was something else that didn't go up in flames that night. It seems like our Mr. Hyde was also paranoid and didn't trust his co-conspirators. He kept detailed notes and even taped some conversations."

Tommy's eyes lit up. "And you know that he has this information?"

"He doesn't. I do."

Tommy jumped up. "Does he know you have it?"

"Nope."

185

"How'd you get it?"

"We can talk about that later. That is—if we have a deal."

"Are you telling me that you can not only set up the ex-Chief, but you can also hand over evidence that can incriminate the other parties?"

"That's what I'm telling you."

Tommy was now animated. "Whew! Let me tell you this—and this is based upon everything you told me being true. If you can deliver the ex-Chief and the incriminating evidence—and in a timely manner ...."

"How about ten days from now?"

"If you can do that—no promises, but you have my word that I will use everything in my power to help you. What about Richie Vecchio and the others?"

"That's a no go. The ex-Chief's files are explosive. I've read them. The only problem is that they end with his faked death. Anything after that is off the table. I can't—I won't go there."

"What about the drug supplier?"

"That hasn't changed."

"Is he, or they, in play?"

"Part of the deal."

"Let me ask you this. Is the New Orleans mob involved at all?"

"Only with street tax. I don't want to go there."

"So let me get this straight. In exchange for the ex-Chief and his incriminating evidence—you want to walk away, but you refuse to help with anything that happened on your watch—so to speak?"

"That's about it. Can you do it?"

"What did you mean about the ten days?"

"Just what I said. If you're ready to travel, we have ten days to set the trap before the next shipment."

"You know that if we travel—it's got to be together. I didn't just fall off the fucking banana boat."

"I hope you don't snore."

"That's the least of your problems if you fuck with me."

"My ass may be dumb, but I'm not a dumb ass. Check your schedule. I'll call you tomorrow."

"Before one A.M. I hope."

CHAPTER 38

The Commission

Gary, Indiana

While the gist of the proposal appeared viable to both Tommy and Freddy, each had some issues to resolve prior to moving forward. It was called housecleaning.

Tommy

Tommy's dilemma was whether, or not, he should seek approval from the District Judge Robert Wilson before he proceeded. It was Wilson who issued the John Doe warrants.

There was a distinct possibility that Wilson was compromised, as the multiple warrants appeared to be as threatening as punitive.

Alerting him, which in any other circumstance would be SOP, could doom the project before it was even launched.

The sensitivity and need for secrecy begged for winging it without the presiding Judge's knowledge and there was some logic to doing so. Freddy, regardless of "Fat" or "Cool" was still a leap of faith. The success of the mission remained in doubt.

On the other hand, if Freddy delivered as promised, the Judge should welcome the results. Should, was the key word. He would alert Butch McCarthy in the event they needed to go over Wilson's head, but that was getting into rarefied air with only the Appellate and Supreme Courts above.

Cool Freddy

Freddy's problem was more complex because it involved two parties, Richie Vecchio and Carlos Marcello, and the mob operated by a different set of rules. You fucked up with either party and there was no appellate process.

His hold cards were the ex-Police Chief's files, which could convict the other conspirators, and the contact with the Coon-asses, the real source of the product. Theoretically, he could protect the new players and save them money, while severing the ties to the old regime. It would be like a controlled burn of the underbrush in a forest, which allowed for new growth and assured the forest's survival.

More often than not, pure, unadulterated greed would have intervened, but if there was one of David's messages that Freddy took to heart it was, "make a plan and stick to it."

He and Jasmine had worked the numbers over and over and their number was two million dollars, which they budgeted five years to get. Merely two years later and they could exceed that goal. It was no time to get greedy, with Jasmine with child and Tommy O'Brien in the picture.

The Commission

When the Vecchios took over, Anthony Vecchio conceived of a plan for a micro version of the Mafia Commission, whereby all of the power players in Gary could not just share in the rewards, but also have a say in shaping policy.

It was decided that the Commission would have five seats. Two would be held by Anthony and Angelo Vecchio; one by the Mayor; one by the Chief of Police; and one by a District Judge.

It was a worthy idea, but "that was then and now is now."

Anthony Vecchio was dead. The ex-Police Chief had faked his own death. Judge McMahon had been promoted to the Seventh U.S. District Court of Appeals and Angelo Vecchio was in federal custody and never coming back.

Richie Vecchio now occupied the "Vecchio" seat. Honorable Robert Wilson, McMahon's protégé, inherited his seat as the new Presiding District Judge and the Fire Chief, McNally, was given a seat due to his patronage army. The ex-Police Chief's seat was vacant and likely to remain so until the next election, which was two years away.

During Angelo Vecchio's tenure, he ruled by fiat and no one dared to oppose him. Autocratic commission was like jumbo shrimp, military intelligence and civil war—an oxymoron.

Now, however, with a Federal investigation hanging over their heads, albeit with only one investigator, there was a sense of Benjamin Franklin's advice to his fellow patriots, "We either all hang together or we will all hang separately!"

The Honorable Judge Wilson didn't have a vendetta, or even ill will, for Cool Freddy. In fact, he had only met him once and briefly when introduced by Richie.

Rather, Wilson understood that he was the first line of defense for the commission if Cool Freddy ever flipped. He, alone, could decide which testimony and evidence could be admitted at trial.

Abuse of that power almost always guaranteed an appeal, but Wilson was confident that his mentor, Honorable Francis Xavier McMahon, would be the last line of defense and would dismiss with prejudice any such appeal.

All of that should have been implicit to a smart guy like Cool Freddy and likely was, but he could not even go there with Tommy for fear of opening "Pandora's Box" and incriminating Richie. If that was his final option—Freddy would do the time.

If Freddy could sell his plan to Richie and Carlos Marcello, maybe all of that could be avoided. He would start with Richie.

CHAPTER 39

Marketing 101

Freddy—Gary, Indiana & New Orleans

had taken several basic business courses as part of my college curriculum. I strived to recall the lessons from my marketing course as if my life depended on it—which it did.

1. Have a viable plan that is easy to understand and implement;

2. The plan has to have meaningful benefits, the more, the better; and

3. It needs to be devoid of as much liability as possible. In short: It needs to be a "Win-Win" for both parties.

The three pillars of my plan were Bobby Valentine, the "Coon-asses" and Tommy O'Brien.

I had gotten to know Bobby Valentine over the course of our relationship and was actually embarrassed by labeling him as a gang-banger in the beginning. It was also hypocritical, as I hated being labeled by potential employers as a felon.

That's the problem with labels. We are complex, rather than simple, people. It is possible, if not likely, that we have more in common than which sets us apart. By labeling people, because of a single issue, we're prevented from getting to know the real person. When society accepts labeling as such—it affects us all and diminishes society.

Bobby Valentine was a gang-banger by circumstance. It was "Uncle Sam" who interrupted his education to teach him how to kill and, now, the same "Uncle" who labeled him a killer.

When I realized that he was a bright and ambitious young man, I knew I had the missing link to my plan. I had patiently and cautiously introduced him into the nuances of the trade. He was a star pupil. By elevating him to my position, it would create a seamless transition and allow me to exit the game. He would make "fuck you" money and be a step removed from gang life. By selecting a replacement within the gang, he could create a loyal associate. Everybody moved up a notch.

When the Garcia's went down with the ex-Police Chief, Bobby could deal directly with the "Coon-asses", eliminating middlemen and assuring a better price for all. The channel was already open. There would be no disruption of supply.

Finally, if Tommy accepted the deal, Richie and Marcello were off-limits.

Richie was suspect at first, but, as a businessman first and mobster second, he understood the concept and appreciated the KISS format.

Ultimately, though, he told me that I would be guaranteeing the deal with my life. "That's just the way it is."

I confirmed that was implicit.

Carlos Marcello was even more suspect as I expected, but I was offering further tribute. His fifty g's a month would double and that was meaningful tribute.

I explained that I had to exit as a condition of the plan and that I was willing to do so. He mused that, as an outsider, not a member, of "Our Thing" I wasn't bound by the same rules and it could possibly work. Then he surprised me.

"Freddy, I'm going to miss you. I never thought I'd say that to a—to a

"To a mouli?"

We both laughed.

"Freddy—are you gonna be okay? I mean moneywise. You're giving up a lot."

"Mr. Marcello, I had a great mentor when I was doing my time. You remind me of him and that's a compliment. One thing he ingrained in me was to make a plan and stick with it. I'll be okay."

He was then pensive. I knew he had something else on his mind. "Freddy, with this change of plans, so to speak, is there any way possible to get rid of that fucking bird man (Robin)?"

I thought a minute before replying. "I told the agent you were off-limits as the only connection between you and the Garcia's is street tax. Small potatoes. If we throw Robin into the mix that creates a more direct relationship. I've got a better idea. You're gonna like Bobby Valentine, if you like me. Let the dust settle a bit after the indictments and trials, if any, then let Bobby Valentine handle it. You need the bird man, as you say, to disappear. Bobby's guys can make that happen with no reprisals. Robin's men may be killers, but Bobby's men are stone-cold killers. There's a difference."

I told him of Richie's condition and he echoed it, reluctantly.

Freddy—if you ever need anything, you know how to reach me. I'm sorry to see you go, but—and don't tell anyone—I envy you. Capiche?"

"Capiche."

Now, it was all up to Tommy O'Brien and the Honorable Robert Wilson.

CHAPTER 40

Southern Comfort

Tommy & Freddy—Heading South

The next opportunity for the bust was ten days after the meeting at 79th Street beach. After sleeping on the proposal and re-confirming their interest the next day, they still had to hustle to meet that deadline. Freddy's prep was more involved because he had to get Marcello's blessing even if Richie gave the green light. Things went well with Richie, but Marcello required Freddy to take a morning flight to New Orleans for the face-to-face meeting and do a turn-around in the evening.

On the morning of day number three, Freddy called Tommy to make plans for their trip to New Orleans. Tommy thought Freddy was nuts. "I'm starting to wonder if I'm partnering with an idiot. You were in New Orleans yesterday, why didn't you just stay? I could have flown down today."

"Because there's something I want to do. Something I feel like I have to do. We can drive down in two days easy. I need to stop by my family's homestead in Mississippi and say hello and goodbye to my relatives. It may be my last chance. Trust me on this one. It will be good for your soul."

"Freddy—I'm warning you. Don't make this complicated. Not to mention I'm not crazy about spending several hours in this government-issue car."

"Not to worry, I've got that covered. I've got a loaner. You're gonna like it."

"What do you mean, a loaner? From who?"

"Chill out, my man. Trust me on this one."

"You keep saying trust me. Do you know how to say 'Fuck you' in Yiddish? 'Trust me'."

Freddy laughed. "Give me directions and I'll pick you up in thirty minutes."

Tommy was waiting outside his rental house in Hammond with a duffel bag for his clothes. He was wearing khaki slacks, a knit shirt and a light sport coat that covered up his shoulder holsters that held twin Colt 357 Magnums, grips facing forward. Oh—and a Bears baseball cap. He literally dropped the duffel bag when he saw Freddy tool up in a brand new "Goodwood" green 1967 Corvette Stingray convertible with the top down.

Freddy exited with a big smile on his face. "What do you think? I was told you'd like it."

"Now I know you're a fucking idiot and I want out of this. There is no way I'm gonna ride in one of Richie Vecchio's cars."

"Tommy, get a grip. Do we have a deal or not? Is your word good? The deal was that Richie Vecchio was off-limits. If he's off-limits, he's not a target. If he's not a target—what's the problem? By the way, and I don't want to bust your bubble, but I know for a fact that Richie has friends in very high places that don't want to see him indicted. If you can't get over your obsession with Richie Vecchio—go see a shrink."

That was the first real dust up between them and Tommy knew that Freddy had a point. Truth is, there was another side of Tommy that wanted to be Br'er Rabbit—forced into the briar patch. He breathed out, "It's not an obsession. I actually like Richie, but what I don't like is being played."

"Well, he sure likes you and I got news for you. We're all being played by somebody higher up the food chain. Get used to it. Now, do you want to take the first turn as driver?"

Tommy removed his sport coat and shoulder holsters with the twin magnums and stowed them with his duffel bag behind the seats next to Freddy's bag and a steel briefcase. Freddy's eyes got big when he saw the Colts. "What—you didn't want to bring a howitzer?"

Tommy smiled. "Freddy, I don't like to waste ammunition. I rarely need a second shot with these. What's in the briefcase?"

"That's need-to-know, but I'm gonna be transparent with you. There are three thousand Benjamin Franklins in there. One thousand we need for the bust. The other two thousand I have personal needs for. Trust me."

"Do me a favor. I like 'fuck you' better."

Freddy smiled. "Okay—fuck you."

They both laughed as Tommy put the Vette in gear. "Where to?"

"South. I'll navigate."

The Trip

It was a beautiful day and Tommy was having trouble keeping under eighty when they had some open road. He was stopped once for speeding, but after showing his badge, an Illinois State Trooper named Leming waved them on their way.

They were stopped once in Missouri and once just south of Memphis, both times with Freddy at the wheel. He had been careful not to speed, but the coppers saw a Black man driving a new Vette with dealer's plates and that was an anomaly to them. Tommy's credentials once again came to the rescue. Tommy told them that Freddy was helping with a sting to set up some of those trouble-making Yankee Jews, and Papists who are trying to register colored voters. That got them quickly on their way. They declined an escort.

The only other "situation" they encountered was also with Freddy driving when he pulled into a gas station after we crossed into Mississippi. When he pulled up to the pump, it looked like a joint meeting of the Future Klansmen of America and Hitler Youth Club had just broken up. The attendant smirked as he said that they didn't pump gas for n****rs in stolen cars, as a group of the in-breds headed toward our car.

Tommy, all six-five of him, calmly exited and then reached back in to put on his shoulder holsters with the twin magnums. If there is a sound made when people stop quickly on gravel—they collectively made it. Tommy pumped the gas, eight dollars, worth (gas was thirty-three cents per gallon). Then, looking straight at the crowd, he threw a five and three ones on the gravel before getting back in the car. Freddy purposefully spun out throwing gravel all over the crowd. Almost too much fun.

The Destination

The destination was a restored plantation named Marseille bordering the Mississippi River in southernmost Warren County between Vicksburg and Natchez. On the trip down Freddy had given Tommy a history lesson about the area. It was a troubled history. Marseille was named after the French city where the original settlers had emigrated from in the early part of the eighteenth century. It had remained the property of the same family over the years, but had been forced to rise from the ashes, on more than one occasion, after conflicts with the indigenous tribes; the Yazoo, Natchez and Choctaw; the British; the French and remnants of Grant's Union Army that besieged and forced the surrender of Vicksburg on July 4, 1863, the day after Lee was defeated at Gettysburg.

Some of the antebellum mansions near Natchez survived in better condition, but Marseille, being closer to Vicksburg, was almost totally destroyed by the rabble that pretended to be loyal to a higher cause. An even worse scourge emerged during so-called Reconstruction when many of the plantations were subdivided among the slaves and the worst riff-raff imaginable, in the form of Carpetbaggers.

Freddy was a descendant of a tribe of Jesuit-educated and respected traders in West Africa. The family was multi-lingual as they traded timber and food stuffs with several of the European consortiums. When slaves became an even more valuable commodity, his family wanted no part of it. They were taken hostage and sold by a rival tribe jealous of their success and culture.

They wound up at Marseille and when the owner learned that Freddy's great grandmother was fluent in French, classic French, not the patois spoken by the settlers, she was made a tutor for his children. When word got out, the school was expanded to include the children of nearby plantations, as well. Thus the family had a small, but tidy residence within view of the manor house.

When Freddy was just a baby, one of the heirs to the original title, his wife and son Patrick III, also a baby, arrived at Marseille with plans to restore it to its former glory. The father had graduated from Tulane and made a small fortune trading commodities. He would need every bit of it and more. Even the subdivided plots were barren for lack of money for tools, seeds, equipment and livestock.

The only solution was to divert precious funds needed for the restoration into re-purchasing the subdivided parcels. The former slaves were promised that they could remain on the property rent free for as long as they like, provided they used the funds to restore their homes, plant gardens and purchase livestock. With a garden, chickens, a milk cow and a few pigs, the tenants could be self-sufficient and restore a sense of life to the property.

As they grew, Freddy and young Patrick were almost inseparable. They were tutored by Freddy's grandmother and had some chores to do in the mornings—fetch the eggs from the hen house, weed the garden and such, but the afternoons were theirs. That generally meant swimming and fishing at their favorite pond, or watching the river traffic from the bluffs of the Mississippi. At night it wasn't uncommon for Patrick to sleepover at Freddy's or vice versa.

When they grew a little older, their favorite time was canning season. In late summer, with the most oppressive heat and humidity, the womenfolk would prepare fresh fruits and vegetables to be stored in Mason jars for the fall, winter and spring. To bear the heat, the women and girls, like Freddy's cousin Sissy, would strip down to their bras and panties. On more than one occasion, the young voyeurs were caught and given a lecture—which was futile. Ask the wind not to blow!

The night times were the best. After his favorite dinner of fried chicken (plucked that afternoon), mashed potatoes and gravy, green beans fresh from the garden, fresh-baked cornbread and sweet iced-tea or lemonade—they would make home-made ice cream while they played their instruments and sang gospel songs. Many times, Patrick and his parents would join in. It was magical.

But, like they say, "all good things must end". The end for Freddy and his dad came when Freddy's beautiful, but sickly, mother finally succumbed to a congenital heart defect. They followed others in their great migration to Chicago to escape the heartache of her loss. There were few nights subsequently that Freddy didn't dream about "home" and Patrick and Sissy. They left in 1953 when Freddy was twelve and only returned once for his grandmother's funeral in 1955. It had been twelve years since Freddy had been away and this might be his last visit.

The Homecoming

They made great time and pulled into the little driveway around four in the afternoon. It was a familiar tableau to Freddy. The little white house was not too much the worse for wear—a shingle missing here, an eave sagging there and in need of a coat of paint, but it exuded life. Save for the ubiquitous chickens, the other life, two young girls skipping rope and a teen aged boy shooting hoops at a rim nailed askew to the garage, halted as Freddy pulled up in the new Vette and exited the car.

The first one to come out of the house to investigate was Sissy and she let out a scream that was likely heard at the manor house a quarter mile away. "Freddy!!"

She ran to him and he picked her up and twirled her around while others emerged from the house.

Sissy was Freddy's age and an absolute knockout. Everything was in the right place. Freddy held her at arm's length to inspect her. "Ooeee, would you look at you girl. You make me have evil thoughts."

Sissy laughed. "Freddy you'll never change, but look at you! Tweedle Dum has turned into Prince Charming."

"I was Tweedle Dee. Patrick was Tweedle Dum."

"Have you seen him yet?"

"Would I not stop and see you first?"

"He gonna go crazy. He drives me crazy—askin about you every time I see him."

Sissy's husband Thomas and her mother Aunty Mae approached. Aunty Mae hugged him and was crying. "Freddy, I swear I was afraid I'd never see you again. Your daddy writes every week and always includes some money—even when I tell him not to. He said you was going to college and look at you and is that your car? Oh Lordy, where are my manners? Who's your friend, Freddy?"

Freddy called Tommy over and introduced him all around.

Freddy gave a man hug to Sissy's husband Thomas and, turning to Sissy said, "Thomas—you're one lucky guy. I wanted to marry Sissy."

Sissy screamed, "You still crazy. You're my cousin and we ain't rednecks."

Freddy just grinned. "There is that."

Aunty Mae said, "Freddy—you and you're friend gonna stay for dinner. I remember your favorite. I hope you're gonna stay the night."

The teen aged boy Lucas had wandered over and sat in the driver's seat of the Vette. When he saw Tommy's pistols he jumped as if he saw a rattlesnake.

Freddy realized what happened. "Tommy's a federal agent. That's why he has the guns." Tommy showed them his badge.

Aunty Mae seemed impressed. "Freddy—are you workin for the government?"

"Helping out, Aunty. Just helpin out."

They could hear the phone ringing inside and Sissy went to answer. She came back grinning. "That was Patrick. They saw the commotion over here. You best get over there before that poor boy has a heart attack. Oh, and Patrick said we're cooking and eating in the big house tonight, so we'll see you later. That is if you come back and get me in your car."

"Sissy, if I get you in that car, I may kidnap you and never come back."

"You so crazy!!"

CHAPTER 41

Marseille

Tommy & Freddy—Warren County, Mississippi

As they cruised down the tree-lined drive to the manor house, Freddy could sense that Tommy was drinking it all in and it was good. As they pulled into the circular drive and parked before the massive veranda, Patrick, his wife Jenna and their son, Patrick the fourth, came rushing down the steps. Freddy and Patrick embraced.

Patrick turned to Tommy. "Tommy welcome to Marseille. News travels fast around here and any friend of Freddy's is a friend of ours. The house is still a work in progress, but we insist that you spend the night with us. Now, I don't know what you Yankees do at five o'clock, but that's a sacred hour down here and I've got everything we need on the veranda."

They all adjourned to the veranda where Jenna and young Patrick excused themselves. Tommy had a scotch on the rocks while Freddy joined Patrick in a hand-rubbed Mint Julep. Freddy turned to Patrick. "This is going to be a short visit, but I wanted to see you as I don't know when I'll get back this way. Tommy can stay here, thank you, but I'm gonna sleep in my room—our old room tonight," They laughed. "I do have a favor to ask of you."

"Anything Freddy, you know that. That will never change."

"Patrick, how big is the parcel that was subdivided for my family?"

Patrick furrowed his brow—puzzled at the question. "The tillable portion in about seventy-five acres. The timber and our swimming hole is about twenty-five acres. Why do you ask?"

"Patrick, I want to buy that property back, if I can."

"Freddy—why would you do that? They can live there rent free for as long as they want."

"I have two reasons. Number one—it would make them proud. Number two—your dad gave them money that he had earmarked for restoring Marseille and you still have work to do. What does land around here go for these days?"

Patrick gave a short laugh. 'There's not much demand for land around here. Some land north of here sold for two hundred an acre last year, but that was all tillable."

"How about I give you twenty-five thousand for the hundred acres?"

"That would be very generous, but totally unnecessary."

"Let me ask you this, can you find a use for the money?"

Patrick waved his hand around. "You know I can."

"Then it's a deal. I'll go get the money." As Freddy went to the car to fetch the money, Patrick turned to Tommy. "Tommy, is our friend crazy?"

Tommy laughed as he replied, "Idiot is the word I used this morning, but now I realize he may be the sanest one of all."

Freddy returned with two bundles of hundred dollar bills. Patrick's eyes almost popped out.

"Here's twenty-five for the property and another twenty-five thousand for a rainy day fund for both you and them. You can take money out for a lawyer to do the paperwork."

"Freddy—I don't know what to say. I can't tell you I love you any more than I already have. Tell me you guys didn't rob a bank and are on the lam."

"Tommy's a federal agent." Tommy showed Patrick his badge. "I'm helping him on a project. The money's all mine and all legit."

Tommy choked on a piece of ice as Freddy said that and they all laughed.

Patrick gave Tommy a tour as Freddy went to get Sissy.

Dinner was incredible. Freddy's favorite served at a mahogany table that seated fourteen. It was set with Irish linen, Waterford crystal glassware and silver service. Patrick sat at one end and Freddy at the other. In between were Aunty Mae, Sissy, Thomas and their three children; Jenna and young Patrick; and Tommy.

It turns out that Thomas was a deacon at the local Baptist church and he led them all in a prayer of thanksgiving. Then Patrick poured a vintage French champagne for himself, Jenna, Freddy, Tommy and Sissy, over Thomas's weak protestations. After all, this was a time for celebration. Patrick disclosed Freddy's generosity and then proposed a toast. When Aunty Mae learned of the offer, it was feared she was having a heart attack. Patrick rushed to the sideboard for a bottle of bourbon and poured some in a glass. "Here, just swallow this. It will help." Aunty Mae appeared to recover, but suggested that Patrick fill up her glass, as she wasn't out of the woods yet.

After dinner, Patrick, Freddy and Tommy retired to the gazebo on the great lawn that sloped down to the river bluffs. Patrick served Cuban cigars and a vintage Port—surprised that Freddy was familiar with and partial to both. Freddy excused himself after his cigar and drove Sissy, who had stayed to help Jenna with the dishes, back home.

Patrick and Tommy had a chance to fraternize—a lot of it about their mutual friend. Patrick sensed that there was some danger lurking as all of Freddy's actions seemed to be some type of final preparation. "Tommy, is Freddy—I mean you and Freddy—are you going to be okay?"

Tommy chose his words carefully before replying. "Patrick—as you know, I'm a federal agent. Freddy is helping the government on a case against some bad people. That's all I can say about that. I will say this, Freddy and I are both survivors."

Patrick smiled a sad smile. "Tommy, it's a strange world. We sit here tonight, serenaded by the crickets and the owls, but there's been a lot of blood spilled on this very spot over the years. You just never know. When we were kids we dreamed of being pirates and living on an island somewhere in the Caribbean. Freddy was Henry Morgan and I was Jean Lafitte.

Tommy, promise me one thing. Someday, God willing, bring your wife and family for a visit. Come stay for a while. Who knows—Marseille may be finished by then? Then maybe you can tell me what happened and maybe, God willing, the story will have a happy ending."

"Patrick, this is my first taste of Southern hospitality. It's not a myth and Mary Kay would love it. We're both history buffs and this place is loaded with history. Like you say, God willing, Freddy and I will both return someday."

As Tommy went to his room, which was like a museum, he was curious about the contents of a letter he saw Freddy hand to Patrick as he was leaving. Before he retired he walked out on the upper veranda to take another breath of the bougainvillea-scented night air. Glancing down on the lower veranda, he saw Patrick reading the letter and deep in thought. As he turned to go back inside, Patrick lit the edge of the letter with his cigar and watched it burn.

CHAPTER 42

The Files

Tommy & Freddy—New Orleans

Neither spoke much on the drive to New Orleans. Tommy knew the letter was somehow important, but also knew it would be futile to bring up. He thought to himself, "Keep your eyes on the prize" and the prize was just six days away. He had a lot yet to do to make it happen—particularly getting the warrants. That should go fairly smoothly with the cooperation of the local FBN, but how smoothly might be a function of the content of the ex-Chief's files, which Freddy promised to hand over in New Orleans. He told Tommy they were at his apartment on Royal Street, where they would be staying.

Freddy's mind was occupied with tying up the loose ends. There was an ulterior motive for him staying at the homestead, instead of the big house. He used the telephone to call Louis and make final arrangements.

After meeting with Marcello, which was only two days ago, Freddy had Louis drive him to the airport where they had ample time to talk.

He told Louis that the route may have been compromised and that this was a good time to give notice to Blue Bayou. Bobby Valentine would be making new arrangements. It so happened, Bobby's father had been a conductor for Illinois Central RR for almost thirty years, but could barely afford to retire. That was about to change.

Louis seemed relieved at the news. "Freddy, I been meaning to tell you that I've got enough money and the trip was wearing me out."

"Louis, what do you know about boats?"

"Motor or sailing?"

"Let's say motor, to start with."

"Well—I love the water, which is why I thought the off-shore rig might be a good place for me and I've always been good with any kind of motor. Why?"

"Louis, Jasmine has found a place for us in the Bahamas. It has its own natural harbor. I'd like to have a nice sport fisherman charter, but I don't know anything about boats. How would you like to join us and be in charge of the boat?"

Louis beamed at first, but then grew pensive. "Freddy, I'd like nothing more, but I have a couple of issues."

"Which are?"

"For instance—what do I do about my money? It's mostly in bearer bonds, like you advised. Over four-hundred grand plus interest. But that's actually the least of my problems."

"The money is easy to handle. I'll give you the name of a banker here in town. Tell him I sent you. He'll transfer the money in cash to a numbered account in the Cayman Islands. The same bank I use. He'll charge a fee for doing so, but it shouldn't be as much, because he can use the bearer bonds immediately. I'll call him and negotiate the fee. Also, there's an attorney in Nassau who specializes in new identities—birth certificates and Bahamian passports. I'll cover the expense. Now what's the big problem?"

"Freddy, you know my history of sexual abuse. I'm coping with it and likely will be the rest of my life—so the island sounds perfect, but I met someone. She came in the Seven Seas one night. Her name, what she calls herself, is Sam. She was a mess—is a mess. She might be eighteen, but going on forty. I could tell she had been very attractive—still is—and by her speech and manners I knew she had come from a privileged environment. I sensed what had gone wrong and how she wound up as a dancer on Bourbon Street. I guess it's an instinct after experiencing it myself. She had a hard shell to penetrate, but I'm the least threatening guy in the world. Long story/short—she was raped by her father's best friend and, get this, on his grave the day after his funeral! She had some money saved up from baby sitting and caught a Greyhound to New Orleans. What I'm saying—I mean asking, is—could I bring her with?"

"Find out if anyone would object. If so, I'll get it taken care of, but Louis—she can't ever know about what we did or—who I am. Deal?"

"Deal."

Freddy called Louis from Sissy's and told him to meet them at the apartment and take the car. Wait for us on the balcony. You'll see us—it's a green Corvette convertible.

Royal Street

When they arrived, Louis ran down to greet them. Freddy and Tommy removed their bags and Freddy motioned for Louis to take the car. Tommy watched him pull away as Freddy opened the gate. "Don't tell me—you have valet parking."

Freddy laughed. "That's Louis, he does odd jobs for me."

"What type of odd jobs?"

"Don't go there. Does he look like a body guard to you?"

"You know what they say, 'God made men. Samuel Colt made them equal.'"

Tommy was blown away by the courtyard and fountain with the Koi fish. The apartment left him speechless. "Freddy, this is a lot to walk away from."

Freddy looked at him. "It's not too late. You want to cross over to the other side of the street?"

"You know I won't do that."

"Then let's put something to bed. I wouldn't either, if I didn't have to. I wound up doing time and being labeled a felon because I defended myself against a copper's son who came looking for trouble. All society's doors are now closed to me. I did what I had to do and only until I could get enough money to get out. I saved some lives and am helping a government that doesn't give a fuck about me. So please—no more, high moral dudgeon, if you know what that means. I wanted you to see where I came from. That's me. Cool Freddy is an act—a role that was invented for me. They were using me, but I was using them, too."

Tommy sat down in one of the leather chairs and buried his face in his hands before standing again and facing Freddy. "Freddy—I deserved that. It's just—it's just that this particular job has me all fucked up. It's like *Alice in Wonderland*, up is down and down is up. The good guys are bad and the bad guys are good. Things can't get any stranger."

Freddy laughed. "Hold that thought. You haven't met Tinkerbell yet. So, Tommy—are we a team?"

Tommy walked over and gave Freddy a man hug, but then looked sad. "Freddy, I'm gonna keep my word and fight as hard as I can to wipe your slate clean, but I was being honest when I said the final decision won't be mine."

"I just ask that you do what you can do. Now, you ready to look at the files? I'll have Louis and Tinkerbell bring us dinner from The Court of Two Sisters. It's not a good idea for us to be seen together. Everything else you need is here. You can find it. I'm gonna stretch my legs while you read."

I'd told Freddy that I wouldn't cross the proverbial street, but as I wandered out on the balcony with the files and a glass of scotch I looked upward and muttered, "Lord, you are really testing me."

Freddy was right. The files were explosive and incriminating. Go figure—the guy had been anal about keeping records. Maybe paranoid was more appropriate. Having said that, there were several redactions—particularly when describing the business of the so-called commission. There were five seats apparently: Angelo Vecchio, who clearly ran things; the Mayor; the Fire Chief (which made Tommy smile); the ex-Chief, of course, and one name that was redacted in all documents relating to the commission.

That begged two questions: who was the mystery member and who made the redactions, the ex-Chief or Freddy?

Regardless, even with the redactions, there was enough evidence here to convict the four others, albeit that the leader, Angelo Vecchio, was already up the river.

Usually in a bust of this scope and nature, we would orchestrate a minimum of two buys. The incredible detail of the files and some tapes—which

I hadn't even listened to yet, were enough to obviate the need for a second or third buy. That was good.

I went to the phone and called the local FBN office. We decided the less I was seen on the street, the better. Two agents would meet me at the apartment tomorrow morning.

I relaxed on a chaise lounge on the balcony and took stock of the situation. The warrants would be no trouble with the files as evidence. I wasn't worried about the bust as they had no reason to expect anything different from their bi-weekly transactions of the past several years. They'd be locked up in New Orleans until extradition to Indiana—which could delay things a bit. Particularly if they fought it.

Then the picture got murkier. I had chosen not to advise the district judge about using Cool Freddy in the operation, despite the outstanding warrants. At minimum it was a breach of protocol. He wouldn't be a happy camper and that wouldn't be good for Freddy's desire to avoid jail time. I would reach out to Butch McCarthy after that meeting.

My thoughts then drifted back to the road trip and the visit to Marseille. I can't remember when I had a better time. Even the dust up with the Hitler Youth was fun. I was naturally curious and the mysterious letter gnawed at me, but Freddy would have been foolish to disclose his innermost thoughts to me—a least at this time. We were definitely bonding, but it was early and, truth is, I wouldn't have respected him if he were a fool. It was obvious that Freddy trusted Patrick. I mean, how many guys do you hand fifty grand to and tell them to handle the paper work?

I decided it was best for me to stay in my lane for a while and tread lightly in re the redactions. Freddy would tell me what I needed to know and I already had a good idea who the fifth party was. One of my favorite lines from my Shakespeare course in college was from "Hamlet", "The lady doth protest too much, methinks."

Judge Wilson was a little too strident—methinks.

CHAPTER 43

The End of the Beginning

Tommy & Freddy—New Orleans

While I was meeting with the local FBN agents, both of whom were impressed by the digs and neither of whom, I inferred, were as "straight arrow" (Freddy's phrase) as I was—Freddy was rallying with the ex-Chief to make the arrangements for the buy.

Freddy had prepped Richie Vecchio on his plans. Richie was not to accept a call from the ex-Chief under any circumstances. That wasn't a hard sell. Freddy met the ex-Chief for coffee and beignets. He handed him an envelope with an extra ten g's in it—explaining that "the boss" wanted the ex-Chief to take a more active role in the transactions, starting with the next buy. That additional responsibility meant additional cabbage. The news and the gesture were received very well.

"So—let me get this straight. Richie...."

Freddy held up his hand. "I mean, the boss, wants me to get more involved. What'd you do? Fuck up a little bit?" Said with a grin.

"Maybe. He just said that the Garcias were your contact and it was best for you to handle the buys."

"Fucking A. Mind you—I didn't make a big fuss when you got involved. No offense, but I knew the time would come when Rich—when the boss came to his senses."

"None taken. I'll bring you the money. If you want me there, I'll be there. If you don't—I won't."

The ex-Chief thought for a moment, "No—you should be there. Maybe you'll learn something."

"You never know. Oh, by the way—I've already rented a motel room out by the airport. That's been the usual protocol."

"No reason to change."

Freddy gave him the name of the motel and the room number. It was Monday today. Freddy was to check in on Friday and the deal would go down Saturday between ten A.M. and noon. Pretty much SOP.

Tommy called Father Thul to tell him what was happening. After re-affirming his promise that no harm would come to the widow or children, Father Thul gave Tommy the victim's name, Serafin Gonzalez, for the added charge of murder-one on the warrant. Father Thul then confided that at least four other migrants, all family men, had disappeared and were feared dead over the past year. All had been picked up by a fiftyish, white male for odd-job labor.

Tommy spent the better part of the day with the N.O. agents doing the necessary paperwork and making the plans for the bust. Freddy had called to confirm the venue and the time. Tommy and the agents would meet there on Friday afternoon and install hidden cameras and mics. Tommy would then spend the night in the adjoining "control room" where he would be during the transaction. A SWAT team of four N.O. police officers would back up the agents on the bust.

That was, provided that the warrants were approved and signed, but they had three days to accomplish that without creating undue anxiety. In the meantime, Tommy would wear a ball cap (LSU, not Bears) and dark glasses and frequent the tourist destinations that the locals tended to avoid. That was no problem as Tommy could spend most nights happily at Preservation Hall or Your Father's Mustache after cold beer and oysters at Felix's. He did have to learn the nuances of the French Quarter. He liked Lafitte's, but wondered why he never saw any women there. He found out soon enough when a six-four, two hundred-forty pound off-shore oil worker proposed to him after only brief conversation. His suitor admitted he was rushing things a bit, but he was due back on the rig in two days—not to return for the next sixty. Tommy explained that he would wait and, hopefully, his venereal disease would be better by then. By the time he finished the sentence, he was talking to a half-empty bottle of Jax beer and an empty stool. Romance sucks sometimes.

Friday

The technicians worked into the evening getting things just right as this was a "one and done" deal. They would return around eight the next morning, "Bust-day", to do a final audio-video check. Louis had dropped off shrimp and oyster po' boy sandwiches and a six-pack of Jax beer to complement Tommy's bottle of Dewars.

They were in a good mood, fueled by the adrenalin that always accompanies danger. Tommy thrived on it, but Freddy was naturally apprehensive—this being his first barbeque, so to speak. They had just killed the last bottle of beer when there was a knock on the door. Without responding, Freddy peeked through the eye hole and saw the ex-Chief and the Garcias. He freaked. Tommy went to escape through the adjoining door, only to find it locked from the other side.

There was only one thing to do. They knocked again, but this time Freddy called out, "Hold your fucking horses." Fortunately, only one light was on. Freddy quickly disrobed and wrapped a sheet around him. Tommy, all six-five and dressed, crawled under the covers in the other twin bed. Freddy cracked the door, but didn't remove the chain.

"What the fuck are you guys doing here? We said Saturday morning."

The ex-Chief tried to push his way in, but Freddy resisted.

"We were having dinner and decided to move it up to tonight."

"Look—in case you can't see—" they were straining to see through the crack in the door, "—I have company, but more importantly—the money doesn't come until tomorrow morning. There was a little delay. So you got two options. One—leave the product and come get your money tomorrow, or two—come back tomorrow as planned."

The ex-Chief looked confused. "I thought I was supposed to be in charge of this one."

"You are and you will be, but until the money comes—there isn't going to be any this one."

"You know I'm going to speak to the boss about this."

"Be my guest. Now—if you don't mind, I'll see you in the morning."

Freddy closed the door and leaned on it as he exhaled. Tommy emerged with a magnum in his hand. They listened by the door. They had to stifle a laugh when one of the Garcias said, "Did you see the fucking lump in that bed? That was a big-ass girl. Freddy must be into Amazon pussy." They all laughed as they walked away.

The Bust

Hollywood directors and producers would have been envious. The transaction went off without a hitch and the audio/video was perfect. When Tommy entered with guns drawn from the adjoining room, as the SWAT team knocked in the door, he felt like saying "That's a wrap."

They were careful to give no indication that Freddy was involved, although the ex-Chief's mind was working overtime trying to process what just happened. Tommy took the opportunity to prank Freddy a bit. "You guys cuff them—I'll cuff the shine." He even gave him a good shove as Freddy shot daggers at him.

The ex-Chief finally had a revelation. "Hey—I know you. You're that federal agent, O'Brien."

"Sorry I missed your funeral. I hope this makes up for it."

They read them their rights. Told them they had the right to remain silent. The ex-Chief had the right to remain silent. He just didn't have the ability. He was swearing up a storm as Tommy took him in the adjoining room and told the others to clear out.

The ex-Chief knew what was coming when Tommy put down his guns, donned a pair of gloves and un-cuffed the prisoner. "Hey, you can't do that." The last word uttered as Tommy proceeded to beat the living shit out of him as the agents were pounding on the door. Tommy then leaned down and said, "That was for Serafin Gonzalez you fucking piece of shit."

He put the gloves away and opened the door. "Put the cuffs back on him. He tried to escape."

The two local agents took the Garcias downstairs to their car. They nodded to Freddy, "What do you want to do with him?"

"You mean Sambo? I'll bring him in." Freddy just seethed.

"We may have to get an ambulance for the other guy. He's still out."

"Yeah, he tripped and fell trying to escape. He'll be okay."

One of the agents turned to Tommy and smiled. "Tommy, we heard a little bit about your reputation when we checked you out, but this is the most fun I've had since my mother-in-law died. Remind me to never piss you off."

Freddy and Tommy were left in the room alone after the others departed. Freddy was still cuffed. "Tommy when you take these cuffs off—I swear I'm going to kick your ass. I don't know how, but I am."

Tommy sat down and smiled at him. "I guess I better leave you cuffed, then. I mean—I know how you people are."

"I'm warning you, Tommy! Let me out of these fucking cuffs—now!"

Tommy waited until Freddy stopped hyperventilating. "Now—are you gonna be nice? Can I trust you?"

Tommy took the cuffs off and first Freddy, then Tommy began laughing out of control. "We did it. We fucking did it!"

Tommy thought later, yeah we did it and according to script. Unfortunately, this is just the end of the beginning, not the beginning of the end.

CHAPTER 44

Man Plans and God Laughs

Tommy & Freddy—New Orleans & Gary, Indiana

The Garcias and the ex-Chief were processed and booked into Orleans Parish Prison to be held for extradition to Indiana. Cool Freddy was listed as being in Federal custody. Just the thought of Orleans Parish, like Angola upstate, and Parchman in Mississippi, could strike fear in the hearts of the most hardened criminals. They said that Hell would be like Palm Beach in comparison.

The Garcias were kept in one cell and the ex-Chief, after a couple of days in the infirmary (not St. James, by the way), was kept isolated in a cell by himself. Tommy did what he could to expedite the paperwork, but, and like David was fond of saying, "Man plans and God laughs." On the third day, while the ex-Chief was being escorted to the shower, a fight broke out—a diversion. When order was restored the ex-Chief had bled out in the shower. The victim of at least fifty stab wounds from a prison shank.

There was no lack of plausible suspects, but Dante Colangelo told Freddy that if Marcello wanted him dead—he would have been dead long ago. Some claimed that he was recognized by one of the victims of his sadistic torture cabal, but few had survived to talk about it. It was more probable that some fellow enthusiasts, who were otherwise pillars of local society, feared exposure of their involvement in the dark arts. His death was classified a suicide. The south had their own definitions of causes of death. Suicide by fifty stab wounds didn't quite trump drowning while trying to swim with eighty pounds of stolen log chains, but it was right up there.

Upon reflection, it created a mixed bag for Tommy. There wouldn't be a long, drawn out show trial and justice had been swift—as guaranteed by the Constitution, but it cast a shadow on the efficacy of the files—particularly the redactions. He could argue the effect on Freddy both ways. With the ex-Chief dead and the redactions, the mystery member might feel they had dodged the bullet. On the other hand, they might regard Freddy as the only living threat to their exposure. He'd know the answer very soon.

Freddy's lease expired at the end of October, so it was decided that he would stay on Royal Street while Tommy returned to Gary, with the provision that Freddy not leave the premises. The Garcias weren't the cartel they pretended to be, but they were a large family and a much poorer family because of Freddy. Louis and Tink would look after Freddy.

Deciding that discretion was the better part of more than just valor, Tommy took the City of New Orleans back to Chicago and left the Vette for the ever-helpful Louis to return. Freddy said Louis knew the route.

He wasn't surprised to receive a message that District Judge Wilson wanted to see him immediately upon his return. He just wasn't looking forward to the meeting and thought it best to touch base with Butch McCarthy first. He found Butch in a chipper mood.

"Tommy, the powers that be were happy to wrap this up and declare victory because of the drop in the murder rate, but they're absolutely ecstatic with the news of the bust. Privately, I think what they're most happy about is that the ex-Chief is dead. Really dead this time."

"Butch—you don't think they had anything to do with it, do you?"

Butch laughed, "I don't think they could act that fast."

"The main reason for my call is that the District Judge, Wilson, wants to meet with me immediately. You know my concerns in that regard."

"You have to meet with him. Hear what he has to say, but don't give anything away."

"Butch—I don't want to see Freddy do any time. He's as much a victim as anyone."

"Tommy, I infer that you two have bonded, but he isn't innocent. He may be a victim, but, if so, he's likely the richest victim. Where is he now?"

"At his apartment in New Orleans."

"So he could just disappear if he wanted to?"

"Off the record—one side of me hopes he does."

"That wouldn't look good for you."

"Butch—I don't know if I give a shit after what I've learned these past couple of years."

"I may be able to help."

"I'm all ears."

"I'll try to make a long story short. This is a case of 'God working in strange ways'. I grew up on Long Island."

"I thought you grew up in Chicago. How'd you get to be a Bears fan?"

"I was a Giants fan growing up in New York. I was posted to Chicago for my first ten years. Being an NFL fan, I adopted the Bears. Anyway, the current Cardinal in D.C. grew up right down the block and he and my older brother were inseparable. They were four years older than me. We went to Chaminade High School where they excelled at athletics and both received football scholarships to Boston College. After graduation they entered the seminary, but that's where their paths finally diverged. My brother wanted to be a Jesuit missionary, while the future Cardinal was more politically inclined."

"Where's your brother now?"

"In heaven. He was teaching at a Jesuit school in Angola during the civil war. His village was overrun and all of the priests were massacred. Martyred, I should say."

"Whew—I'm sorry."

"Don't be. It was the life he chose and he died doing what he loved to do. We should all be so lucky. Back to the story. Fast forward to a few years ago, and guess who was appointed Cardinal for D.C.? It was a blessing for me as he has been my rock throughout my personal turmoil. We have dinner at least once a week as he still regards me as his little brother. It turns out that he has a charity that benefits the less fortunate members of society and I sit on the board with a lawyer named Carlton Anthony. Does that name mean anything to you?"

"Zip."

"I'm not surprised, but if you controlled one of the levers of power you would know who he is. Many people regard him as the most powerful man in D.C. "

"You mean after the President."

"I mean—including the President."

"Wow."

"Wow is right. It turns out that he's the Cardinal's leading benefactor. Rumor also has it that he's also the sole voice in Washington for the Mafia Commission."

"Wow again."

"That may not be your last wow. Anthony is known for having perhaps the top staff in Washington. He hires the best ex-legislative aides and a few ex-Congressmen. Well—last summer, one of his favorite young aides was returning from a late night party and passed out at the wheel. When the D.C. police arrived they found his BMW wrapped around a light pole and the driver pretty banged up. They also found open liquor in the car."

"That's not good."

"That's nothing compared to what else they found. Enough cocaine to qualify as possession with the intent to distribute. Now say it."

"Wow!"

"He hadn't been charged yet because he was still being attended to. Police were waiting outside his room at the hospital, when I got a late night call from the Cardinal. Carlton Anthony had called him to ask if I might do him a favor, a big favor. Help get his aide out of this jam and avoid the publicity. I jumped at the opportunity, as favors are the most valuable currency in this town and no one is more powerful than Anthony. I got dressed quickly and raced to the hospital where the aide was still being attended to. Probably no coincidence. Anyway, I showed the police my credentials and told them that the aide was working as an asset for me in a drug sting which accounted for the cocaine. They bowed out gracefully. At the next foundation board meeting, Anthony thanked me and said he looked forward to returning the favor someday."

"I'm still a bit confused."

"As you would be. Here's the connection. If, and I say if, the District Judge is compromised and refuses your plea for leniency for Freddy—any appeal would be heard by the Seventh U.S. District Court of Appeals. If they don't overturn the District Judge's ruling, then Freddy is fucked."

"Do you know anyone on the Appellate Court?"

"I don't, but Anthony does. The Cardinal's annual dinner was two weeks ago and I sat at the Director's table with Anthony and his guest. You ready? The Honorable Frances Xavier McMahon of the Seventh U.S. District Court of Appeals."

"Do you think Anthony would return the favor?"

"Favors are sacred things in this town and the one I did for him was significant. Just hold that thought as we are a long way away from that point."

"At least there may be some hope. I'll meet with Wilson and report back to you."

CHAPTER 45

The Mystery Member

Tommy—Gary, Indiana

I touched base with Freddy just before I left to meet with Judge Wilson. I was half-hoping that Louis or Tink would answer and say that he took off for parts unknown, but it was Freddy who answered the phone. He re-iterated that he couldn't do either long or hard time. I promised to brief him after my meeting.

Judge Wilson's Chambers

The Judge was seated behind his desk. He didn't rise as I was escorted in. A District Attorney, Elliot something, was present and he rose to shake hands after the Judge made the introduction. Wilson never offered his own hand. No problem.

"Agent O'Brien."

"You can call me Tommy."

"Agent O'Brien. You've been a busy boy. Let's see—we have a dead ex-Police Chief who was alleged to be involved in the drug trade."

"That dead ex-Police Chief was arrested in a sting operation that has audio and video confirmation and he left detailed files regarding his—his and other's—" Tommy paused, "—criminal activities. I sent over a copy of those files."

"You did indeed and we—" pointing to the D.A., "—have gone over them carefully. How did they come into your possession?"

"They were given to me by Cool Freddy, who has been cooperating with the Bureau."

"Is this the same Cool Freddy who I signed warrants for?"

"You mean the John Doe warrants? I guess it is."

"And where might this Cool Freddy be at present?"

"In Federal custody in New Orleans."

The Judge smirked, "Too bad for the ex-Chief that he wasn't in Federal custody, also."

I ignored the snide comment.

"Okay—let's talk about the so-called files. I don't know where to start." Turning to the D.A. he said, "Elliot, why don't you go through your list of concerns?"

The D.A. stood up and read from a legal tablet. "Agent O'Brien, How can you prove those files were created by the ex-Chief and not your informant?"

"Cool Freddy told me."

The D.A. scoffed, "That's pretty convenient isn't it? I mean—the ex-Chief is dead and he's trying to use the files as leverage to reduce his sentence."

"He gave me the files before the bust."

"You still haven't answered my question, but let's move on. Let's talk about the numerous redactions in the files. Same question. Who made the redactions?"

"I don't know."

"Of course you don't. It appears that whomever made the redactions, did so to protect the identity of a member of the so-called commission."

"That's the way it appears."

"Well, the way it appears to me is that Cool Freddy might have redacted his own name to protect himself."

"That would be impossible."

The D.A. raised his eyebrows. "Please enlighten me."

"You see, the files end contemporaneously with the ex-Chief's faked death and we do agree that he faked his own death, don't we?"

The Judge and the D.A. both averted my gaze.

"And—Cool Freddy didn't arrive on the scene until afterwards. He wouldn't have had any knowledge of what happened previously."

"Unless he made it all up. I mean, the redacted name could be anyone he claimed. He could use that to try to extort someone, but the problem, Agent O'Brien, is—it's only his word that we have to go on and that's just not good enough."

The Judge looked directly at me. "Let's cut to the chase. You made a mockery of this court by using an informant—an informant whom you know has outstanding warrants from this court—without any advance notice, let alone advice or consent. And now, I presume you are seeking some type of leniency from the court you abused, based upon some files of questionable origin with numerous redactions."

"I was sent here by the DOJ to do a job and I did it, but I couldn't have succeeded without the informant's help. I acknowledge that I breached protocol."

The Judge stood and roared. "Breached protocol? You fucking blew it up as you've done with everything in your path since you arrived. Frankly, I'm not certain that the files have any value whatsoever."

"Are you serious? They implicate a criminal conspiracy between the mob and prominent city officials. Plus, of course, the mystery member." He said, staring at the Judge.

"Elliot—what about the files?"

"Well, assuming they are real, and were created by the ex-Chief, they do clearly implicate him, but he's dead. They clearly implicate Angelo Vecchio, the former leader of the local mafia, but he's already in prison for the rest of his life. So that leaves us with the Mayor and the Fire Chief—two very popular elected officials. Now—I'm not their attorney, but the files are essentially their word against that of a dead man—a dead criminal. They're almost certain to plead not guilty while—and get this—your informant, Cool Freddy, admits to being involved in the drug trade. He was John Doe to us until you went on your witch hunt, which makes us wonder what his game is."

"Look—and with all due respect. I've been patiently listening to you twist the evidence into a pretzel. You seem to have forgotten about the Garcia brothers, who were the suppliers of the drugs to Gary and they're in custody in New Orleans."

The Judge made a little smirk. "Interesting that you would bring that up. You busted the supplier, but the feedback we get from our sources tell us that there has been no disruption in supply—none. How do you explain that Agent O'Brien?"

"You guys know what a whack-a-mole is?"

They looked at each other—puzzled.

"A whack-a-mole is that game where you whack the mole with a mallet only to see another one come up in its place and so on. I guarantee you that the moles, so to speak, on the commission will be replaced as will the suppliers. Maybe already have been."

The Judge scowled, "I'm going to ignore your insolence. In fact, I'm going to ignore just about everything you've said. Cool Freddy is a criminal and I've heard nothing to even consider leniency in this case. Do you disagree, Elliot?"

"I couldn't agree more."

"So here's how we're going to play this in MY court. I'm putting a gag order on any further discussion of the case and I'm setting an expedited hearing date for Cool Freddy one week from today. If you fail to produce the defendant on that date, you will be held in contempt. I think we're through here. Elliot show Agent O'Brien out."

CHAPTER 46

The Star Chamber

Michigan City

Judge Wilson and Elliot, the D.A. stayed in his chambers to "chop up" their meeting with Agent O'Brien even though Elliot was just a sycophant and was oblivious to Wilson's role in this drama. That actually suited Wilson's purposes, as Elliot was as much of a Devil's advocate as he was likely to find.

Wilson was no dummy. He knew that O'Brien was tough as nails and impossible to bully. That was the reason for having Elliot—an apparent second professional opinion. That might work with Farmer McDonald or Joe Bag-o-Donuts, but O'Brien would see through it. Having said that, Elliot's arguments even swayed Wilson a bit. It's funny how that works. You hear what you want to hear.

Even Elliot, though, conceded that O'Brien's head was "bloodied, but unbowed". That begged the questions. What was Freddy's game? And, how much did O'Brien know?

The conclusion was that no blood had been drawn by either side. In a championship boxing match, a tie is a win for the holder of the title, but there was no clear champion at this time. Just two worthy opponents who were destined to resolve that issue in seven days.

Wilson needed the advice and counsel of his mentor, the Honorable Frances Xavier McMahon. He arranged to meet McMahon at his lakeside estate the following day.

The impressive estate was named simply "Clare", for the county in Ireland his grandparents had emigrated from. The fifty acres of land were a reward to his father, the original Frances Xavier aka "The Hammer", for his valuable services to Gambino in the early days of his takeover. The massive manor, pool, tennis courts, gardens and guest quarters had been made possible by dividends from the "Commission". The Judge had dropped the Jr. and II long ago in an effort to escape an uncomfortable past.

Wilson's car had been waved through the gated entrance and the butler escorted him into McMahon's den which appeared to be a shrine to Notre Dame football. Not unusual for the area.

After greeting each other, Wilson said, "I want to brief you on my meeting with the agent—O'Brien."

McMahon replied, "I was just getting ready to take a sauna, why don't you join me?"

Wilson appeared stunned. "Wait a minute. You don't think I'm wearing a wire do you?"

"Of course not. Will you join me?"

Wilson followed him downstairs to the sauna, where they disrobed and wrapped themselves in towels before entering.

McMahon took a deep breath and exhaled. "You have the floor."

It took Wilson a little time to collect his wits. "I met with O'Brien as you suggested."

"How did it go?"

"Honestly, I don't know. He'd be a good poker player, but I had a D.A. with me and he did a good job playing Devil's advocate in re the evidence."

"We were fortunate that the Chief got his just desserts. Should've happened sooner."

"I hear you. That's undercut O'Brien's case. It's built on the supposed files of a dead man. A dead, bad man."

"Certainly enough reasonable doubt. What's he want?"

"We kept him on the defensive, so I'm not exactly sure, but it involves leniency for his informant."

"You mean Cool Freddy?"

"Yeah."

"How much leniency?"

"We didn't get into that. I set an expedited hearing for next week."

"Whew—they could contest that."

"He didn't object."

"Let's de-construct this. What is it you fear?"

"The only thing I fear is what I don't know. If Freddy redacted the name, he knows it's me. In that event, he's the only person who can possibly harm me, with the Chief dead. Is that a risk worth taking?"

"Don't you feel you're a little paranoid?"

"With all due respect—you're the one who suggested the sauna and I'm close to well done now."

"Touché. Let's adjourn to the library for a cocktail."

Now seated in deep leather chairs in the museum-quality, mahogany library, McMahon appeared to study his martini before speaking. "Here's the way I see it. Cool Freddy is a wild card. You met him didn't you?"

"Just once and briefly, but he understood what he was getting into and he was paid well for his services. No one told him he could unilaterally decide to retire. I mean—it would be different if he just disappeared. How hard is that for a Black guy?"

"I agree. We're missing something. I can only think of two possibilities. Either he made the redactions as an insurance policy, or as a tool to extort us later."

"Why didn't he reach out to somebody?"

"You mean why didn't he commit suicide?"

"Yeah—I get it."

"Think about this. Look what happened to the Chief. How long will a snitch last in prison?"

"Not long, but how will they know he's a snitch?"

"That's easy and that means even six months is a death sentence."

"I'm not saying I want to kill him."

"You aren't killing him. You're just sentencing him and didn't he admit to being Cool Freddy?"

"So—you're saying I could agree to be lenient. Cut the sentence in half, or more, and it wouldn't make a difference?"

"Or—just let it be. Give him a suspended sentence on the advice of the DOJ—total coverage, and take your chances."

"You know this may affect you, as well. We don't know what else may have been removed from the files."

"If you want my opinion—I'm inclined to let him go. What's his incentive to come after us? We didn't put a gun to his head. He made a fortune that must be stashed somewhere. So it isn't money. Maybe he just wants out. I can't blame him for that."

"Is it guaranteed that he'd be killed in prison?"

"I wouldn't say that. It's like this—if the DOJ wants to protect him, they will, but I don't see them getting involved if it's a minimum sentence. Who can argue with that?"

"But, there is a possibility that word gets out and he winds up like the Chief?"

McMahon laughed. "I heard he was stabbed fifty times. That was passion, my friend. Even snitches don't get that much."

"What if I let O'Brien know …."

McMahon jumped in, "As a gesture of goodwill."

"What if I let him know, as a gesture of goodwill, I'm willing to reduce the sentence to ten years with time off—be out in five?"

"I'd say that's a reasonable sentence, if not a generous one. Yet still achieving your objective. If he lasts five years, bully for him."

"It just might also create some friction between O'Brien and Cool Freddy. O'Brien knows that's a good deal."

"Question is—does O'Brien know it's a death sentence?"

CHAPTER 47

Time to Fish or Cut Bait

Tommy—Gary, Indiana

A fter the meeting, I spent the rest of the day trying to sort out my thoughts. Wilson was no pushover. I shouldn't have been surprised. You don't climb the layer cake in life without having something on the ball. Not to mention, the best lawyers can piss on you and make you believe it's raining. It must be taught in law school.

I wasn't ready to brief Freddy. I knew that Wilson and Elliot, were posturing and Freddy might not understand that. Having said that, they betrayed no inclination to be lenient. On the other hand, I thought, maybe it would cause him to freak out and bolt. That might be his best option. I asked Otis how long a snitch might last in prison.

"It depends on the joint. Minimum security—who knows? Terre Haute or Jackson—he might not make it through the first night. Too many inmates there because they were ratted out. Snitches and child molesters don't have a long shelf life."

"So you're saying—it's not just how long, but where?"

"It's all about where."

That conversation became relevant when I received a surprise call from my new best friend, Elliot, the following day. "Agent O'Brien, Elliot here—the D.A."

"What can I do for you?"

"Judge Wilson and I reviewed yesterday's meeting and concluded that both sides may have let emotions take over a bit. That's not unusual. While,

235

it's fair to say, the Judge has issues with the way you've proceeded, he wants you to know that he acknowledges the difficult spot you're in. Accordingly, and as a gesture of goodwill, Judge Wilson is willing to consider ten years with time-off. With good behavior—he could be out in five or less."

My head was spinning. If they had offered this in the first place I would have jumped at it. Freddy could have made his decision accordingly, but why now? Why such an about face?

"Elliot, I appreciate the gesture and will convey that to the informant. One question. Where would the time be served?"

I noticed a too-pregnant pause on the other end, inferring that Wilson was listening in. Elliot finally answered. "Well, um, I'm not sure that has been determined, but it would be in the area."

"Maximum or minimum security?"

Another long pause. "That would, um, be up to the discretion of the Judge. Please keep in mind, he's the one exhibiting good faith. If you deliver the informant next week, as planned, and he seeks the mercy of the court, those things will be taken into consideration."

The battle lines were now drawn, but I harkened back to Otis's comments. Wilson's goal was to get Freddy into a system that wouldn't protect him, while appearing to have no blood on his hands. A modern day Pontius Pilate. Regardless, it was time to fish or cut bait. I put together a to-do list. Calls that I needed to make prior to giving Freddy the news.

My first call was to Butch, who wasn't surprised at my recap of the meeting, but did find the subsequent offer curious and reasonable. I told him to reach out to Carlton Anthony in re getting Judge McMahon to possibly grant an appeal, if needed. Butch knew the details and would vouch that Freddy had no hidden agenda. He just wanted out.

My next call was a personal one. A very personal one. I needed some serious spiritual guidance as Man's Law and God's Law were colliding big time in my brain. Father Thul would be the perfect person to offer guidance and I owed him a call about the ex-Chief's fate. He was very gracious to accept my call and betrayed no emotion at the news of the ex-Chief other than "May God have mercy on his soul." I wish I could be that good.

"Father, I need some guidance. Do you have a little time for me? It's been a long time since my last confession."

"Tommy, I didn't ask and I always have time for you."

I bared my soul as I told him of my trials and tribulations in re Freddy's fate. "Father, I know Freddy did wrong, but I also know why. He's a victim and was left few options in life. To his credit, he wants out and helped the government that now wants him dead, apparently. And, shame on me, perhaps, but I don't like losing to someone in a rigged fight."

I was surprised to hear the good Father chuckle. "Let's take things in order. The government, a government of men with feet of clay, likes to say, "In God we trust" and invoke God's name whenever possible, but our God, the New Testament God, is a God of second chances. That was memorialized when Moses returned with the broken tablets of the Ten Commandments. What was God's response? He replaced the tablets without changing a letter. Even then, when they hadn't been obeyed, he sent His son, Our Lord and Savior Jesus Christ, to spread the Gospel based upon those Ten Commandments. He didn't change the message, rather He admonished the Priests for knowing the letter, but not the spirit of the law.

"According to God's Law, Freddy is entitled to the same second chance that Moses was given. You're on solid ground, there. Now—" chuckling again, "—in your concern about losing a rigged fight—part of that is pride and pride is one of the seven deadly sins. I would rather go back to the Leo gymnasium and use that heavyweight title wrestling match as a metaphor. You lost that match, according to the rules, but the outcome was rigged. However, you left that gym with head held high, because you won the battle fair and square and that was plain to everyone. Keep score according to God's rules, not those of men."

"Father, if you were in my shoes, what would you advise Freddy to do?"

"Tommy, when you talk about Freddy, I hear the emotion in your voice. I hear your heart. You wouldn't feel that way unless you cared for him. I'll pray for him, but I have a feeling he'll make the right decision when the time comes. One of my students once told me that he read, fear was an acronym for, False Expectations Appearing Real. Trust in the Lord."

"Father, is there anything I can do for you?"

Laughing, "Tommy, all I need are a couple of new golf balls, but Serafin Gonzalez's wife and family want to return to Mexico. They don't have the money to do so. Any contribution to them will be greatly appreciated."

Tommy thought for a moment. "Father, I have an idea. Can I get back to you on that?"

"Of course and, Tommy, I'm always just a phone call away."

My spirits were buoyed by my conversation with Father Thul and helped me to frame things better for my next call. The one I'd been avoiding.

Freddy answered, "I've been wondering how things went with Judge Wilson."

"Freddy—have you ever met the Judge?"

Silence—which was an answer. That had just been a hunch on my part.

"Next question. Who made the redactions, you or the ex-Chief?"

More silence.

"Okay. Well—here's the deal. The meeting was contentious, as I expected, and now we all know why. He fears you."

"He has nothing to fear. I just want out."

"Yeah, well—he needs a little more meat on that bone. It's possible he fears something that you know nothing about, but I don't know how to convince him in that regard. Anyway, I received a call this morning in which his D.A. was quite conciliatory and offered to seek just ten years with time off for good behavior. Maybe out in four or five years. That's quite a reduction from a possible forty years or more. In five years you'd be, what, thirty-one, thirty-two?"

Freddy paused for a minute.

"You there?"

"I'm thinking. Where would I do the time?"

"To be determined."

"Uh huh. What about your friend in Washington—your boss?"

"I called him and he's on it."

"What are the chances of getting some help?"

I paused, "Freddy—I'm not gonna lie to you. I think they're pretty good, but I'm not sure."

"Tommy, I know I've put you in a tough spot, but I need to know who my friends are. Fact is, I haven't had many close friends in my life. I'm very grateful for everything you've done for me. I know it hasn't been easy."

"What're you gonna do? I'll understand either way?"

"It's important to me to get closure on this. I'll be there Monday morning."

"You know what you're doing, right? I can get us more time."

"Let's get this over with. I have just two conditions."

"Which are?"

"I'll surrender to you in the hallway outside the court room. Just you. Second, I want a meeting with all parties in the Judge's chambers before the hearing to hear a special request regarding a health issue."

"I don't think that'll be a problem. Freddy, are you okay?"

"I'll see you Monday."

"Ten o'clock sharp?"

"Ten o'clock sharp."

"Oh, Freddy—can we switch subjects for a minute."

"Only too happy to."

"Has Louis headed north yet to return the Vette?"

"He's sitting here with me, getting ready to leave. Why?"

I told him about Father Thul and the Gonzalez family. "You asked if I needed money. I don't, but they do. Can you help?"

"How much help do they need?"

"Five thousand would be very generous."

"How would ten, be?"

"Even better."

"I'll give it to Louis and he'll call you when he gets to Gary. Probably tomorrow afternoon some time."

Bob

Tommy—Gary, Indiana

L ouis didn't arrive with the Vette and the cash for Father Thul, until late afternoon on Thursday. A day later than planned. I told him he could crash at my place and we'd drive over to Michigan to see the good Father in the morning. He was a wee bit apprehensive at first, but we went to Phil Schmidt's in Hammond for dinner and talked about everything but the matter at hand. He was a gentle soul and great company, as it turned out. It was the first direct contact I'd ever had with him.

He said that Freddy was okay and appeared to be in good spirits, but that he'd been keeping to himself, mostly, the past few days.

"So Louis, what happens to you now?"

"I'm going to get away for a while. Maybe a long while."

"You know where you're going?"

"Somewhere I've never been before. I met someone who is also a victim of sexual abuse—maybe more than me. I'm going to try to help her. Just like Freddy helped me." He teared up a bit. "Paying it forward, I think it's called. In that regard, I'd also like to kick in a couple of thousand dollars for the Priest, if I may."

"Louis, that will be most appreciated. You're in for a treat when you meet Father Thul and we'll be sure to get you his blessing."

The following day we drove over to Berrien Springs. I was thinking that was likely my last ride in the Vette and Louis was happy to let me drive. Father Thul was absolutely blown away to receive twelve-thousand dollars in cash. He was animated in re how he was going to be able to use the bulk of it for emergencies within the migrant community.

He didn't just give Louis his blessing, but heard Louis' confession. When they re-emerged, Louis had tears in his eyes and Father Thul had his arm around his shoulder. I admit that I misted up a bit at the sight.

Louis dropped me off before returning the car. He said he'd made arrangements from there and I didn't probe. I just wished him well and truly meant it.

The only contact I had with Freddy between that day and the hearing on Monday, was a brief chat I initiated on Saturday. Once more, I half expected/wished to find that he had flown the coop, but he was still intent on having the hearing. I knew from training and common sense that he would need some space with which to make his own peace. Truth is, I did, as well. He said he had made plans to arrive in the area on Sunday and re-affirmed the time for the hearing.

Judgment Day

I arrived at the courthouse before nine—a little more than an hour before the hearing. I would have done so even earlier, but I was waiting for a call from Butch in re Judge McMahon that had yet to come. In anticipation of that possibility, I had scouted out the floor of the courtroom during the week and gave Butch the number of both pay phones at the end of the hall.

A little after nine, with no call from Butch and, more importantly, no Freddy—I began to pace like a wild man. 9:15—nada. 9:30—ditto. What appeared to be an attorney, defined as anyone with a suit that fit and a shirt collar that could button, arrived with a middle-aged Black man with a walker and a portable oxygen tank. Poor schmo.

I felt that they were watching me, but why wouldn't they be? Circa 9:45 the attorney approached me.

"Are you Agent O'Brien?"

I stopped in my tracks—wondering how he knew who I was.

"Please, take a minute. There's someone you need to talk to."

He almost led me by the arm toward the Black man.

CHAPTER 48 — *Just Us* —

"My name is James McGill, I'm Cool Freddy's attorney and, of course, you know Cool Freddy here."

Any semblance of reality just took the train for the coast. I was totally dumbstruck.

"I'm sorry, will you repeat that?"

"This is Cool Freddy and we just need a few minutes before the hearing."

I motioned to the walker and the oxygen tank. "Are those real?"

"Very real. Cool Freddy has been battling stage-four lung cancer and has six to twelve months to live, at most."

You wouldn't expect someone to be happy to hear that, but "Cool Freddy" was beaming from ear to ear. It finally dawned on me.

"Freddy, let me ask you a couple of questions. Do you have a family?"

"A wife, a mother-in-law and eight kids."

"And, how are they going to survive with you gone?"

He smiled, "Let's just say that they're financially secure. I think that's what they call it."

9:50, one of the pay phones rang. I broke away and sprinted to the end of the hall to answer it. It was Butch.

"They had trouble finding Anthony. He's on a golf junket, but he said he would call McMahon and take care of it. How's Freddy?"

I gave him a brief recap of what had happened and he couldn't stop laughing.

"What's so funny? The Judge is gonna know it's not Freddy?"

"That's the beauty of it. He can't admit it without incriminating himself."

9:55. "Gotta run."

I hustled back to the attorney and Cool Freddy so that we weren't late. "It's show time. Let's go."

Judge Wilson's Chambers

When we were ushered into the Judge's chambers, the Judge was seated behind his desk and didn't even look up. Elliot and two assistant D.A.s were off to one side as was a court reporter. When he did look up, he was visibly shocked.

"What's going on here? Will someone tell me?"

Silence.

"Don't everyone speak at once."

I cleared my throat and said, "Your Honor, as agreed to, the defendant Cool Freddy and his attorney, James McGill, are here to discuss some health issues that may have a bearing on his sentence."

The Judge literally jumped up and screamed. "I want everyone except Agent O'Brien to get out. Now!"

Not exit or take your leave. Get out! They scurried like rats to vacate the chambers.

Wilson had his back to me appearing to gaze out the window. When it was just the two of us, he pivoted.

"What the fuck do you think you're doing? I'll tell you this. You won't get away with it. Not in my courtroom."

I did an Academy Award winning act of appearing totally confused. "Your Honor, I've got no idea what you're implying."

"Implying? I'm not implying jack shit. You know that's not Cool Freddy."

I purposefully paused, to let him twist in the wind, before going for the coup de grace. "Question is, how do you know that? You, the issuer of the John Doe warrants?"

There's a reason that you should try to keep your wits about you, particularly in situations such as this. Wilson realized he had been hoisted on his own petard. I almost felt sorry for him. Not just the air went out of him—his spirit vanished as well. He collapsed back into his chair.

"So, Freddy told you I knew who he was?"

"No. I had a hunch and asked him, but he wouldn't answer."

"What do you mean, he wouldn't answer?"

"Just what I said."

"So you don't know for a fact that I do know him?"

"Don't know and don't care."

He seemed to rally a bit. "Let me ask you this. Did Freddy tell you who the redacted member was?"

"Same answer. I asked, but he refused to answer."

"So you don't know that either?"

"Don't know and don't care."

"What's you next move, then?"

"My next move? After the hearing, I pack up my clothes and head east never to return."

"That's it? You're finished here?"

"Your Honor …."

"Bob."

"Bob, I came here to do a job. The goals were twofold. Bring down the murder rate and try to bust the drug suppliers. My job is done."

Wilson reached into a drawer and brought out a bottle of single malt Scotch. "Can I call you Tommy?"

"I'd prefer that."

"Tommy, will you join me? I think I need a nip."

"It's five o'clock somewhere."

Now, both more relaxed, he looked at me. "Tommy, did you plan this?"

"Bob, are we off the record?"

"Totally."

"I was as surprised as you."

"When did you find out?"

"Approx. fifteen minutes before we came into your chambers."

Just then, his phone rang. The receptionist said, "Your Honor, Judge McMahon is on line one. He says it's important."

As he was half way through telling her to say that he would return the call, I got his attention. "You should take this one."

He looked puzzled as he told her to put it through. I excused myself to find the little boy's room.

When I returned, he asked, "How did that happen?"

"From what I understand, it was the return of a significant favor by someone way up the food chain."

"Had to be. Tommy—I still can't connect the dots between you and Freddy."

"Freddy and I grew up in the same neighborhood on the south side of Chicago. I actually saved his ass when we were in high school. We weren't friends—barely acquaintances, but he knew me and knew my reputation."

"Are you saying it was just a coincidence that you both wound up in Gary?"

"Total."

"How did you connect?"

"When I first arrived, I was introduced to the Police Chief, but when I told him I wanted to see his files, he bolted from the room."

"How did you know he kept secret files?"

"I didn't. I was asking for every day files—just to let people know I would be conducting an investigation. After his reaction, I had a hunch that he'd be coming back for his files later that night and had him tailed. He came back with a migrant worker to help him take the files to his house. Later that night, the Police Chief was seen leaving the house with suitcases and departing in the migrant's car. The migrant never left the house. We know the rest of the story."

"So you knew he wasn't dead?"

"I even found out the name of the victim, Serafin Gonzalez, and knew that the ex-Chief was the key to finding the suppliers. Problem was, that's as far as I got—until I received a call from Freddy in the middle of the night."

"I don't get it. What was his game?"

"Freddy's a victim, too. Just like the mystery member might be. He was framed for a crime he didn't commit and did some time."

"I heard about that. I'm just surprised he lived to tell about it."

"It so happened that his father was one of Mayor Daley's precinct captains—for a colored precinct that grew by more than twenty-thousand voters on the night of JFK's election."

"That explains a lot."

"Maybe it was soft time. I don't know—another topic he won't discuss. He got a college degree while in prison and was anxious to get to work when he was released, but there were those thorny issues of race and criminal history."

"He was fucked." Wilson refreshed our glasses. "So—you're saying that Freddy saw this as an opportunity to make a score and get out?"

"Basically what he told me. He knew I'd been seeking the Police Chief and thought he could make a deal."

"Quid pro quo."

"Precisely."

"But, if you didn't know who the mystery member was, why didn't you let me know what you were doing?"

"I hadn't even seen the files. I knew nothing about any mystery member. What bothered me about you were the John Doe warrants. I thought they were a bit much. Plus—at that time I didn't know if Freddy was yanking my chain. I figured that if he delivered, the results would heal a lot of wounds."

"What was your deal with Freddy?"

"Pretty simple. He would deliver the Police Chief on a silver platter and the Chief's files, which would incriminate others and the drug suppliers. The problem with the files was that they basically ended with his faked death. Freddy said that anything that happened after that date was off the table."

"But he implicated the Mayor and the Fire Chief."

"He didn't—the ex-Police Chief did. And, like you said, it would be their word against that of a bad guy—a dead, bad guy."

"Why redact the name?"

"My guess is that Freddy felt the Mayor and Fire Chief would be okay. He must have felt that the mystery member could have been harmed and he wasn't out to hurt anyone. Freddy just wanted out."

"You have any idea where Freddy is?"

"Don't know and don't care."

"So, you think the mystery member should sleep well at night after the hearing?"

"Think about it. Cool Freddy, here, is ready to plead guilty and accept your verdict. Do you seriously think that another Freddy is going to show up someday and claim that he was the real criminal?"

"Final question. Where did this guy come from?"

"Not sure. It turns out he has terminal cancer, less than a year to live, and he's leaving a wife and eight kids. Oh—and a mother-in-law. I asked how they were going to survive without him and he replied that they had been well provided for. He's probably the happiest cancer victim in the world."

"What's his attorney want?"

"Release to home hospice care for his final days. It will actually save the state a lot of money."

Wilson smiled. "So Tommy—it seems that justice has been served."

"In the old neighborhood, Freddy's and mine, we had a saying, 'Justice, is pronounced—just us.'"

Wilson rose and stuck out his hand. "I don't think the hospice request is unreasonable. Do you?"

"Mercy is twice blessed," Wilson joined in unison, "it blesseth him that gives and him that receives."

No one was more befuddled than Elliot to see the Judge and I emerge with smiles on our faces.

When I returned to my house to get my gear together, Otis was waiting for me. He told me that Richie Vecchio wanted to see me before I left town. Had his dealership not been on the way out of town, I might have blown it off. My adrenaline was flowing—the good type. The only other thing on deck for me was a final hello/goodbye to Father Thul and, hopefully, a final blessing. I couldn't wait to tell him what happened. He was spot on. When the time came, Freddy made the right decision.

Someone more jaundiced could feel that they'd been used, but I was returning to D.C. as a conquering hero. That was more than a fair trade. More importantly, I had made a friend and had some great memories to sustain me. I only hoped that we might meet again someday.

When I pulled into the dealership, Richie was waiting for me in the show room, dangling a set of keys. Keys to a new Corvette convertible. "Richie—you know I can't accept that. Besides, my family is soon going to be three. I'm afraid my Vette days are over."

"Tommy, do me a favor. Drive back home in style. Have a last waltz, so to speak. When you get there, donate it to a worthy charity. That way it's a win-win."

It didn't take much for me to rationalize. I just wondered what Father Thul was gonna think.

"Tommy, I regret we didn't get to spend more time together. We've got more in common than that which separates us."

"Richie—I felt that from the start. Maybe we'll meet again someday."

He laughed, "Only if it's for pleasure."

We both laughed.

When I got back home, I gave Butch the keys to the Vette and suggested he auction it off for the Foundation that he and his wife started in their son's name. He later informed me that Carlton Anthony had been the winning bidder with a bid of one-hundred-thousand dollars!

Butch retired a hero. In fact, there was an effort to get him to defer his retirement for a few more years, but he was now happily engaged with the Foundation. He and his wife didn't remarry. What was the point? They were re-united and that's what was important.

Freddy was never far from my mind, but I had no idea where he'd escaped to. I only wished that he knew he would have avoided any prison time. It would have been poetic justice, so to speak. Saved by the system that created his problems in the first place.

I was an instructor at Quantico while Mary Kay was caring for our first child, Joseph. I had told Mary Kay about Marseille and Patrick's family and we both read more about the history of the area and the Natchez Trace, but we agreed that Joey was too young to take a long road trip.

In 1970, we planned an Easter vacation trip to Mississippi. I contacted Patrick to see if we were welcome. He appeared overjoyed and insisted we stay for a few days at minimum. Jenna would show Mary Kay around the area and Aunty Mae was more than happy to baby sit with Joey.

The first night after dinner, Patrick and I adjourned to the Gazebo for cigars and Port, just as before. It had been difficult, but I had not mentioned Freddy's name up to that point and neither had Patrick. I broke that ice.

"Patrick, have you heard anything from Freddy?"

At first, I thought his reply was curious. "Tommy—Freddy, Fat Freddy or Cool Freddy, however you refer to him—is long gone. Doesn't exist anymore."

I was stunned and sat up. "Freddy's dead?"

He smiled, "That's not what I meant. Shakespeare said we're all merely actors on this worldly stage. The actor isn't dead. Just the role he was forced to play. We were always acting in our youth."

"Pirates, as I recall."

"Pirates, indeed."

"Pirates who escaped to an island in the Caribbean."

"You have a good memory. Now that you mentioned the Caribbean—Jenna, little Patrick and I had a great vacation this past winter in the Bahamas. We stayed at a pineapple plantation on the Island of Eleuthera. The plantation has a manor house very similar to Marseille, its own private beach and natural harbor. The host and his family were fantastic. A Mr. Morgan."

"Henry Morgan, by any chance?"

Patrick grinned. "You know, I believe it is Henry. You want to know the best part?"

Now I was smiling, too. "I can't wait."

Patrick reached inside his sport coat and retrieved an envelope. He handed it to me.

"What's this?"

"You aren't going to believe this, but Jenna and I bought a ticket for a local charity before we left Eleuthera and we won. Three first class airplane tickets from New York to Nassau and an Island Hop to Harbour Island. When you arrive, you contact a local Counselor named Dickens—easy enough to remember—and he will arrange to have you escorted to the plantation."

"You're right—I don't believe you."

We both laughed.

"Tommy, you need to go. Mr. Morgan is looking forward to your visit. Maybe, just maybe, if the timing is right, we'll join you. Oh—and he has a beautiful sport fisherman charter. The Captain's name is Louis, pronounced the French way. You'll like him."

Then Patrick started laughing.

"What's so funny?"

"Sorry—it's just—it's just that the First Mate is—shall we say—a little different?"

I had to laugh, as well. "I learned a few French phrases when I was in New Orleans. 'Vive la difference' comes to mind."

"Vive la difference, Tommy. Vive la difference!"

G.D. Flashman's life experience took him from a small farm in central Illinois literally around the world via an international business career.

He is currently at work on a sequel to *Apache Dunes,* his first published novel, and anticipates *Just Us* to be the first in a series of stories based upon the incredible exploits of legendary DEA agent, Tommy O'Brien.

His literary influences include Elmore Leonard, Mark Twain, Robert Crais, and George MacDonald Fraser.

Collectively, those influences taught him to look at humanity through an unfiltered lens. In doing so, Flashman believes that irony will be ever present, and he finds evil, grace and humor in unexpected places. Justice, like beauty, will be in the eye of the beholder, and all too frequently is pronounced, **Just Us**.

He resides in Chicago with his wife, Susanna.

Made in the USA
Las Vegas, NV
14 January 2021